THEY RAISED THEIR HAND

THEY RAISED THEIR HAND

JAMES CARRICK

TATE PUBLISHING
AND ENTERPRISES, LLC

They Raised Their Hand
Copyright © 2014 by James Carrick. All rights reserved.

No part of this publication may be reproduced, stored in a retrieval system or transmitted in any way by any means, electronic, mechanical, photocopy, recording or otherwise without the prior permission of the author except as provided by USA copyright law.

This book is designed to provide accurate and authoritative information with regard to the subject matter covered. This information is given with the understanding that neither the author nor Tate Publishing, LLC is engaged in rendering legal, professional advice. Since the details of your situation are fact dependent, you should additionally seek the services of a competent professional.

The opinions expressed by the author are not necessarily those of Tate Publishing, LLC.

Published by Tate Publishing & Enterprises, LLC
127 E. Trade Center Terrace | Mustang, Oklahoma 73064 USA
1.888.361.9473 | www.tatepublishing.com

Tate Publishing is committed to excellence in the publishing industry. The company reflects the philosophy established by the founders, based on Psalm 68:11,
"*The Lord gave the word and great was the company of those who published it.*"

Book design copyright © 2014 by Tate Publishing, LLC. All rights reserved.
Cover design by Joseph Emnace
Interior design by Jomar Ouano

Published in the United States of America

ISBN: 978-1-63418-131-0
1. Biography & Autobiography / Military
2. History / Military / World War II
14.09.27

ABOUT THE AUTHOR

Jim Carrick and his wife, Kathy, bought a home in Mesquite, Nevada, in 2004 while there on a golf vacation. They moved in as a part-time resident in 2006 once they both retired. Jim retired from PPG Industries as a sales account executive and Kathy from Miller Brewing Company as a research microbiologist. In 2008, they became full-time residents of Mesquite. At that time, Jim responded to an ad where the Mesquite Veterans Center was looking for skilled trade help with the construction of the new Veterans Center. Although not having any of those skills, Jim responded, asking if they could use some laborers. They could, and it began.

Jim is a veteran of the US Army Reserves, 429th Engineering Battalion. He is a member of the American Legion Mesquite Post 24, where he served as chaplain for two years. He is also a member of the Virgin Valley Honor Guard and is on the Mesquite Veterans' center board of directors.

Four individuals were primarily responsible for the center's birth in Mesquite. They were Ed Fizer, retired army command sergeant major; Al Litman, army and Vietnam veteran; Jim

Brown, retired navy corpsman and Vietnam veteran; and Bob Barquist, marine and Vietnam veteran. As president of the veterans' center, Ed asked Jim to sit on the board of directors, which he accepted. After a time, Ed decided to hand over the duties of the center to others. He had started a weekly article called "Veterans' Corner" where he interviewed a veteran, and it was published in the *Desert Valley Times* on Friday. Jim was asked to take over the writing of this article, which he accepted, and the rest is history. The experience of interviewing the veterans and writing "Veterans' Corner" articles has led to the writing of this book.

This book is dedicated to our granddaughter Ashley Marie Hancock (August 17, 1994–July 27, 2012). She wanted to join the United States Air Force.

ACKNOWLEDGMENTS

I would like to thank Tate Publishing for giving me the opportunity to have my dream come true with the publishing of this book about veterans. I'd especially like to thank Shannon Lloyd, acquisitions editor, who was the first person to contact me. She was and continues to be very helpful and professional. The same can be said for the others I have had contact with at Tate Publishing, including Cheryl Moore, graphic designer, and Rachael Sweeden, who is the director of operations. A special thank-you to Maverick Tambiga, project manager, as we worked together regularly.

I would like to thank Mike Donahue, editor and general manager of the *Desert Valley Times*, for publishing each of the interviews. His assistance with editing the articles was invaluable. Mike is also a veteran of the US Marine Corps, who served from 1969 to 1975. Staff writer Theresa Worthington was also involved with the veteran articles. Mike has become a good friend.

Special thanks to Ed Fizer for letting me include some of the interviews he conducted prior to my taking over the duties of writing "Veterans' Corner." He is and will always be a wonderful friend.

To the veterans who trusted me to conduct these interviews, you are all wonderful individuals who have served your country proudly. I am honored to have been able to share your stories and part of your life.

I would like to offer a special thank-you to Kevin Smith. Not only did he let me interview him, but as a published author, he steered me toward Tate Publishing and gave me invaluable advice. In addition, he and his wife, Sue, have become wonderful friends of ours.

I would be amiss if I didn't thank Cal Price, a WWII veteran who is a self-published author, also provided me with some valuable tips and has become a very close friend. He is an amazing individual.

Last but not least, I want to thank my wife, Kathy, who spent many hours reviewing my print for errors in grammar. She has become quite the editor. She has stuck by me through thick and thin throughout our almost forty-seven years of marriage, and after all these years, she remains my very best friend. I love her more than words can say.

I thank the Lord for letting me complete this project, which has been a dream for quite some time.

THE MESQUITE VETERANS CENTER
WHERE IT ALL BEGAN

The dreams of a few have become the realization of many. Yes, the persistence of a few hardworking and determined veterans with a dream developed into our veterans' center. After they got the ball rolling, many others joined in to help develop this significant project into what it is today—a beautiful place that serves the veterans and their families with a plethora of activities.

Ed Fizer was the innovator and motivator with the help of the founding fathers, Tony Hardway, Jim Brown, Mark Buchannon, and Bob Barquist. Significant assistance was provided by Jesse Marsh, Bill Lilleinthal, Art Hammerschmidt, Roger Gessel, Harold Straley, John Nettle, and many others.

Initially, a mortgage was taken out through Nevada State Bank to support the center, but due to the generosity of several individuals who donated a motor home and a boat, the center was able to start a bank account. With the unbelievable help and support of Sun City, the center was able to pay off the mortgage in very short order.

A very sincere thank-you to those who donated, especially Sun City, which continues to support our veterans' center. It has been very gratifying to receive the wonderful support we have from the business community of Mesquite. They have helped in the past and continue to help the veterans' center's projects with support whenever they can. We would be remiss if we didn't give an extra thank-you and show of appreciation to the Eureka Casino for all it has done and continues to do for our center and support of the veterans in general.

Your efforts do not go unnoticed; thank you to the Exchange Club, and thanks for your donations and assistance with the AnySoldier project.

Once we got the center, much remained to be done, and volunteers came to our aid. Veterans with experience as pipe fitters, electricians, carpenters, and general repair came and helped put our center in shape. It took some time and a lot of blood, sweat, and a few tears, but no negative thoughts as we moved forward.

Jesse Marsh and his famous pickup truck moved furniture and anything else we could fit into it to and from various locations. Finally, we had a center with office space, and this was significant. Prior to moving into the center, our service organizations had to scramble to find places to hold meetings. Now the VFW, American Legion, and Vietnam Veterans had its own place to hold meetings and events. Later, the Modern Warfare group joined the service organizations within the center.

With the inside looking good, the outside needed attention, and our own Don Muse took charge along with help from volunteers. Through the work of talented artist Jerry Greenway, we now have a flagpole surrounded by unique insignias of all of the services. Thank you, Jerry. What a great job. Various plants beautify this area, and we now have a victory bridge near the parking lot.

As time moved on and our organization grew, we knew that we would eventually need to expand. A wonderful gentleman stopped by one day and offered to pay for an expansion of our center. He is a veteran, as is his brother, and he said he wanted a worthwhile cause to leave some of his assets. He felt the Mesquite Veterans Center was just the place. We have just completed the 25 percent expansion, and on April 14, 2014, we dedicated the new expansion. It is now the Bob Meibaum Addition, in honor of this gentleman who made it all possible. Much of the expansion was spearheaded by Ken Maynard and Don Muse. We thank them for their hard work and dedication.

The Mesquite Veterans Center is the only center in the United States that houses all four of the service organizations in one building. We are extremely proud of our center and the accomplishments that we have made through the unselfish efforts of our veterans.

THE VETERANS OF WWII
THE GREATEST GENERATION

Carroll Baber, US Army

Born in Iowa more than 93 years ago, Carroll Baber served his country during WWII in combat in both North Africa and Italy. Already serving in the Army, he was scheduled to be discharged just a few days before Pearl Harbor. Of course everything changed and on New Years' Day 1942 he was sent to New Jersey to meet a ship that would take him to his next assignment. On January 12 they set sail with no clue where they were going. Carroll was part of the Army's 34th Infantry Division (Red Bull) and ended up in Northern Ireland after a two week journey and a menu of mainly goat stew.

Carroll remembers plenty of live goats in the hull of the ship waiting for their turn to be supper. From Northern Ireland the unit was involved in the invasion and conquest of North Africa.

The most vivid memories of the war for Carroll were his unit's activity in Italy. The infantry walked everywhere they went and spending time in the mountains of Cassino,

Italy was very difficult. It was cold. Sleeping quarters consisted of the ground or a foxhole with only a raincoat for warmth. Six months without a shower is a long time but probably the furthest thing from the mind of the 34th Infantry Division when they just barely avoided being captured during a battle to take Cassino.

Three other units were wiped out during this engagement and trying to stay alive was foremost on everyone else's mind. Explosions erupted everywhere and one close to Carroll caused a serious concussion and covered him with shrapnel, some of which still remains in his hand today. He was unconscious for two weeks and woke up in a field hospital in Naples. Carroll said he thought he was in heaven. Heaven, however it wasn't. Carroll's dog tags had been blown off during the blast that injured him and no one knew who he was, including himself. He later found out someone had found his tags on the battlefield and they were shipped home to his mother. Of course she thought he was dead, or at least MIA.

When Carroll walked through the door returning home his mom fainted dead away. She had heard nothing more since receiving his dog tags. During his hospital stay, another infantryman from the 34th was in the same hospital and recognized Carroll and that is how they discovered who he was. Carroll spent two months recovering from his wounds in the hospital. While there he learned his unit chaplain had been seriously wounded while helping a wounded German soldier. He crossed into a dangerous area and picked up the wounded German and was carrying him back to be treated when he stepped on a land mine and lost most of his leg.

Carroll said he doesn't think of the war much anymore. The 34th Infantry Division has had several reunions over the years and remained a close knit group as one would imagine with what everyone had been through. A monument funded by members that honors the unit's contribution to the war effort stands in Des Moines, Iowa. The 34th Infantry Division became known as the

Red Bull Division and was part of the 133rd Regiment. Carroll received a Bronze Star, Combat Infantry Badge, two Bronze Stars for the North Africa/Middle Eastern Campaign and a Purple Heart. He continues to have issues because of WWII wounds, but it was all worth it. This country is like no other.

Carroll lost his wife of many years in 1997. He met his current wife Ilene in Mesquite when they were both members of the Mesquite Senior Center. Ilene's first husband was also a WWII veteran who served in the Navy in Guadalcanal and other areas.

Carroll and Ilene moved to Oklahoma for a while to be closer to family, but didn't like the weather so they returned to Mesquite where they live fulltime. After the war Carroll worked most of his civilian life as a postal worker in Ely, Nevada for 28 years. Carroll's been a continuous member of the American Legion for 68 years and was department commander of the 5th District Ely Post 3. He is a member of the VFW and was post commander. He is a lifetime member of the Combat Infantry Association.

Carroll and Ilene became friends before I interviewed him, and that friendship continued afterward. Unfortunately, Carroll passed away the summer of 2013 at the age of ninety-four. My wife and I still see Ilene, and she is doing well. Carroll was a wonderful man and a decorated veteran who dearly loved his country. I will never forget him.

Remember Old Red Bull, the Unsung Heroes of WWII

We were going home. On 27 September, 1945 the division commenced the long but happy trip back to Naples and Bagnoli, a road distance of 800 miles. The 88th Division was to take over our border assignment and many of our latest recruits stayed with the "Blue Devils."

The assembly area near Naples was familiar. It was Collegio Ciano, the same college grounds where so many of our troops had quartered in early October 1943. Then, the unknown and uncertainty lay ahead.

Now eager men knew their destination was home. For them no more long marches, no more mud, mules and mountains; no more worries of Stukas or 88's, night patrols mines or booby traps. No more weary nights on damp cold ground, in snow and caves or pup tents. No more hunting men with M-1's, Tommy and machine guns nor being hunted in return.

It was a proud division that embarked for home; proud in the knowledge that its men had performed in the best American traditions. Proud too, that more days of combat were accredited to the 34th Infantry Division than to any other division in the army.

But there was an air of sad reflection in the minds and faces of the veterans, as in retrospect they contemplated the many scenes that had unfolded during the past four years and nine months of their lives. Comrades had fallen in the snows, on the deserts and in the poppy fields of Tunisia. Wearers of the Red Bull patch lay under rows of gleaming, white crosses along the many purple paths of Italy. In hospitals and homes there were unnumbered comrades whose dreams, hopes and aspirations remained shattered forever.

The price of victory had come high to the 34th. Some 3,737 killed in action, 14,165 wounded and 3,460 missing in action – a total of 21,362 battle casualties. Embarking from Naples on October 22, 1945 the diminished division still under the command of Major General Bolte landed at Newport News, Virginia, and proceeded immediately to Camp Patrick Henry where the troops were mustered out on November 3, 1945.

And so, the 34 Infantry Division covered with glory, had returned to the United States as it had left – totally without pomp and ceremony. No bands, no popular greeting, no public review, no speech making. Public acclaim had been expended on troops who had returned earlier. We had left the shores of America in January, 1942 under the greatest of secrecy. We became at times a "forgotten front." Now we had returned home in almost total obscurity. But in the heart of every man who wore the Red Bull patch will forever glow a pride founded on firm knowledge that the services of his division in WWII ranked second to none and that the name of the 34th infantry will stand high on the scroll of honor among the greatest units that ever carried the stars and stripes into battle. Yes, a pride, too, in the knowledge that the gallant Old Red Bull fought its battles and made its sacrifices to insure Democracy shall ever remain a beacon for all freedom loving peoples of the world.

After interviewing Carroll Babel, I became enthralled with the Red Bull Division and wanted to reprint this article from an unknown author in his honor. May God bless Carroll and the veterans of the Thirty-Fourth Infantry Division. They were one of a kind.

Robert Conwell, US Army

Robert Conwell was born January 24, 1925 in Red Lodge, Montana. He attended Carbon County HS and graduated in 1942 at the age of 17. After graduation he attended a business college for a year in Billings, Montana, but with a war going on decided to enlist in the US Army.

He was sent to Fort Knox, Kentucky for basic training and then to Abilene, Texas for assignment with the 12th Armored division as an infantryman. Upon completion of training, Robert was sent to England for a month where his division organized and moved on into France and then to the front in Germany.

In a battle near the Rhine River in France, Robert was wounded and captured by the Germans and taken to

Germany. He ended up in an area called Bodenbach, in a mineral water resort that was converted into a hospital. The hospital was nothing more than a large room that held 12 POWs. Eleven were American and one was British. Robert said the Germans treated the prisoners humanely and treated his wounded shoulder by stopping the bleeding and constructing a brace to immobilize it. After two months, Robert and the rest were moved further into Germany to a large German hospital. Here many wounded German soldiers were being treated. There was also a section for Russians, Yugoslavians and other nationalities that were sectioned off from the rest of the hospital population. The American and British POWs were kept together. There were now 12 American prisoners and eight British. Seven of the eight British prisoners were captured at the Battle of Dunkirk and had been held since then. Robert was held at this prison camp for four months and again said he and the others were treated humanely.

At the end of four months and the war starting to wind down, an all black unit from Africa under the control of the French came into the prison camp, threw open the gates and freed the POWs without resistance from the Germans. Robert recalled many of the German soldiers changed from their uniforms to civilian clothing and attempted to blend in with the German population to avoid being taken prisoner themselves. They hadn't seen fresh Allied soldiers in quite a while and assumed the worst.

Robert said a big surprise during his captivity was that the prisoners who were able to work were paid in German marks and he had collected two months worth of POW pay. It took five days for the Americans to find these prisoners who were able to fend for themselves quite nicely as the Germans fled the prison camp.

After being discovered, Robert was sent to Paris and then to New York and was given a choice of several posts. He chose Denver because it was as close to Montana as he could get. He was able to contact his mother who had been sent notice that her son was missing in action and had not heard anything until he arrived in New York. Robert spent six months in Fitzsimmons Army Hospital in Denver having his shoulder treated. Although the Germans did some basic first aid while he was captive, much more needed to be done to repair his wounds. He was discharged from the military when he was released from Fitzsimmons Army Hospital after 26 months of distinguished service.

Back in Montana, Robert contacted a friend he had made while attending a business college and ended up working with him in the coal mines in Colstrip, Montana. After a year he enrolled at the University of Montana using the GI Bill. To his credit, Robert finished a pre law curriculum and law school in just five years. Upon graduation in 1950, he went to work with his father who was also an attorney. In 1954 he met his lovely wife Frances. He must have known right away she was the one as they were married six months later and have been together 56 years.

Robert became the county attorney in Carbon County and lived in Red Lodge where he was born. In addition to being the county attorney, Robert also had a private law practice where Frances served as his secretary for 18 years. They were blessed with 6 children who have also been successful and are scattered throughout the country, including Utah, Montana and Alaska.

During his military service, Robert was awarded the Bronze Star, Purple Heart, Combat Infantry Medal and the Prisoner of War Medal. Robert we salute you. Thank you for service to your country.

I only met Robert during the interview. He was not in great health at the time, and his wife was very instrumental in providing information. They are wonderful people who dearly love their country, family, and God. I heard that Robert passed away. May the Lord be with him and his family.

Gene Mansfield, US Army

Gene was born July 25, 1921 in Defiance, Ohio. He was born on the kitchen table by the light of a kerosene lamp in his parents' farm house. He spent 23 years on his father's 2,300 acre farm along with his two brothers. Gene attended Ayersville HS where he was a pitcher for the varsity baseball team for three years. When he graduated in 1939 he went straight to work on his father's farm.

Gene had a friend who drove a convertible and the pair drove into town one day. After arriving Gene noticed, and then winked at a young lady named Beula. She returned the smile and one thing led to another and they began dating. One day Beula told Gene she thought they were getting too serious and should stop seeing one another for a while. "We are just so young," she said. Gene agreed, but a week later told his dad that Beula was the girl he was going to marry. His dad told him if he felt that strongly about it then he needed to do what he felt was right. Gene persuaded Beula to see him again and on the day he turned 19 the couple married in a Methodist Church in Kentucky. The pastor and his wife had dinner for the newlywed couple on their special day. Prior to the trip, Gene's dad gave him the use of his car and $40, a fair sum of money back in the day.

Gene continued to help his dad's farm grow. They had 20 head of cattle and 100 slaughter hogs, a new thrasher and a new tractor, which added up to a full blown operation.

At 23 Gene was drafted into the US Army to fight in WWII. He was sent to Camp Maxey in Texas for basic training. He left Beula and a two year old son behind. After boot camp and a four day leave, Gene was sent to Okinawa to fight the Japanese. He arrived by ship and was immediately moved into the field. Gene's unit was often hit by fierce storms in the jungle that had winds reaching 120 mph. Those storms could drop as much as 20 inches of rain. His unit had few supplies and was often hungry. Gene's foxhole partner was an excellent swimmer and told

Gene he was going to go into the ocean and catch some fish. Well, he did and came back with three. Under cover they built a small fire and ate for the first time in a while.

The following day the platoon sergeant asked for volunteers. After raising his hand, Gene became the new flame thrower for the unit. He was equipped with six grenades and the flame thrower. As the unit traveled into mountainous areas it encountered many caves and it was Gene's job to enter those caves, flame thrower in hand, to make sure there was no enemy waiting to ambush the US troops. Not a pleasant assignment, but one that had to be done, Gene recalled. Gene and his unit were a bit of a mop up crew as much of the outcome of the war had been settled after the atom bombs were dropped. Gene and his unit saw about 60 days of combat. In September, 1946 Gene now an E4 returned to the good old United States.

After getting out of the Army, gene and his lovely wife Beula bought their own 160 acre farm for $18,000. The farm included a house. Gene had saved his money during his stint in the army and he was able to purchase new equipment. The couple farmed for several years. He sold milk containing 5 per cent fat, can you imagine! While Gene was in Okinawa, Beula milked 20 cows a day by hand. Gene and Beula sold the farm in 1955 and Gene purchased a tractor trailer and began hauling truck bodies out of Golian, Ohio. He worked for two trucking companies over the next 25 years and never had an accident or received a traffic violation.

He retired in 1976. However, he wasn't happy without a job so he went to work for his brother-in-law selling powered lifts for the next 12 years. In 1994, at 75 Gene and Beula moved to Las Vegas and Gene continued to busy himself by working for Payless Car Rental for the next 4½ years. Over all Gene worked until he was 80 years old. Tired of the hustle and bustle of Las Vegas, a real estate broker suggested they look at Mesquite. They did and in 2006 bought a home and moved in.

After 72 wonderful years of marriage, Gene lost his beloved wife in February 2013. He was distraught and had no desire to do anything. Eventually he was introduced to a care giver, Melanie, who became his angel according to Gene and he perked up. In 2013 he made the trip to Washington DC to visit the WWII Memorial on the Honor Flight. Melanie went with him as his guardian. Gene was a lonely soldier without his bride of so many years. After meeting him for the interview, we became friends and I visited with him as often as I could. He was a wonderful man with wonderful stories. Gene passed away in early 2014, and is now with his lovely wife of 72 years. May God bless Gene and Beula. Gene, thank you for your service to your country!

Cal Price, US Air Force

Cal was born October 4, 1926, in Geneva, Idaho and grew up in Border, Wyoming, with five brothers and a sister. He attended a school that had only three rooms, no lights and no heat except for a potbelly stove. On a cloudy day it was difficult to even read a book. First and second grades were in one room; third, fourth and fifth were in another and sixth, seventh and eighth occupied another. Cal said the majority of his education came from reading an old set of encyclopedias that were at the school. He read every book in the set from cover to cover. Cal started high school at age 12 and graduated at 16.

After waiting a year, he enlisted in the US air Force and he and one of his brothers signed up to take the test for flight training that included the entire 9th Service Command of the eastern U.S. Cal finished in third place and was accepted into the flight program. His brother did not fare as well, but immediately enlisted into the regular air force.

Cal married his hometown sweetheart and when he returned from basic at Christmas he took his wife Zella, back with him to Keesler AFB in Biloxi, Mississippi, where he was trained. Training lasted a year and Cal was assigned to Ft. Stewart near West Point Air Training Command.

General James Doolittle's son was one of Cal's students. While near West Point, Cal had the opportunity to see army football players Glenn Davis and Doc Blanchard set college gridiron records.

Cal spent his entire enlistment at Ft. Stewart training pilots. While there a Col. Stark would show up with a swagger stick that he would pound into his hand as he reviewed the pilots. One day, a student was trying to land a plane that had lost its brakes. The pilot managed to bring it in, but it went tail up and the student ended up hanging from his harness. The instructors rescued him without further incident, but Stark was on the spot pounding his swagger stick into the palm of his hand in a derogatory way. A few months later the colonel was delivering the first jet to Ft. Stewart from Wright Patterson AFB and, as he was leaving, he forgot to close the canopy, blowing it off along with part of the tail section. He was able to land safely in front of all the students and instructors. Needless to say he never returned to the fort. Cal was discharged from the air force December 8, 1946.

Cal's brother, Lamar, who enlisted in the air force, became a belly gunner in B24's and had more than 30 combat missions. He spent a large portion of his time in Germany. Another brother, Jewel, was an army MP and he also spent most of his enlistment in Germany. A third brother, Doug, was with the army quartermaster and was assigned to the South Pacific, spending a fair amount of time in the Marshall Islands.

After his discharge, Cal enrolled at Utah St. University on the GI Bill. He majored in education with a minor in geology. He taught school for 30 years in California, Utah, Wyoming, Idaho and China.

While in China he taught graduate students English and Spanish. During his stint in Asia he had to sign a document stating he would not bring up religion in any way, shape or form while teaching. Cal was and continues to be a well rounded individual. He owned a 3000 acre ranch, where about 300 head of cattle were raised. In addition, he and his wife had a school of western riding in California. He trained roping horses and although he never entered rodeo competition, he would go and watch his horses perform.

Among other things, Cal cuts stone monuments, using a circular diamond saw. He is commissioned by the Wyoming Historical Society. He also owns a stone quarry. As if that isn't enough, Cal is an accomplished author. He writes for the *Rocky Mountain Rider* and has had two books published; "Reflections" and "My Barney."

A wonderful side light to this incredible man is that he and his wife Zella were married 66 years. After she passed away a lifelong friend Sally lost her husband within two days of Cal losing his wife. Yes, they began to see on another and were married in February 2012. Cal and Zella and Sally and her husband each had two sons and two daughters. They were familiar with Mesquite and lived in Beaver Dam, Arizona for awhile. A real estate agent told them they should look at living in Mesquite, but they said they were not interested. They now own a home in Mesquite and love it here. Sally spends her time with photography and is a rock hound, while Cal makes walking sticks, stone jewel boxes and small furniture items.

Cal has a grandson, Christopher, who is a Navy SEAL who trains other Navy SEALs. He has almost 22 years in the navy. Hats off to Christopher! Cal, thank you for your service to your country!

Cal and Sally became friends after I interviewed him. Cal is one of the most interesting individuals I have ever met. His travels and multiple endeavors are remarkable. I try to get over to his home just to sit and chat whenever I have time.

Harold Hedelnd, US Navy

Harold was born June 8, 1926 in Omaha, Nebraska. He and his family moved to Lincoln where Harold attended Lincoln HS. While there he participated in basketball. Harold left school in June, 1943 and enlisted in the US Navy and left for Farragut, Idaho for basic training. Then it was off to Treasure Island for further schooling. Harold asked that we not discuss his war time experiences, so I'll only say he was trained as an electrician and assigned to a ship and it was off to the South Pacific. It has always been my policy to only discuss what the interviewees are willing to discuss. Harold did admit he still has nightmares about some of his experiences during the war. In late 1945 Harold was discharged from the navy as a seaman 1st class.

He returned to Omaha where he worked repairing motors. He was employed by Northwestern Bell. Harold obtained his GED at Lincoln and took the test at the University of Omaha. In the early 1950's he started college and received his BS in electrical engineering from Los Angeles State College. He accepted an engineering position with Bendix Corp and met his wife Amanda there where she worked as a drafts person. He and Amanda were married in Las Vegas.

After 13 years with Bendix, Harold moved to Las Vegas where he started a business rebuilding alternators, starters, and motors in 1975. Because of all the red tape involved in establishing a business and a technical school, Harold gave up and turned to writing correspondence courses and how-to books on rebuilding starters, generators and small motors. He designed his own procedures and these courses became books, which he sold and still sells to this day.

In the 1950's Harold enjoyed Las Vegas. For $21, you could fly to Las Vegas from Burbank and this excursion included your room and food. He was a student of craps and eventually wrote a book titled *"Over 50 Dice Techniques."* Harold has also written books on micro wave cooking, starting your own business and others. He also was involved in the real estate business in Las Vegas where he co-owned the company.

While living in southern Nevada Amanda passed away and Harold thought of moving. A fire at his home destroyed everything and he decided it was a good time to go elsewhere. He moved to Logandale, Nevada where he bought a small piece of land that had a small home and three RV spots. He continued writing and selling his books and met his second wife. They bought a lot in Scenic, Arizona and built a home. In 2003, after the unfortunate passing of Harold's second wife, he sold his property and purchased his current home in Mesquite, Nevada. Harold continues to write.

In 1968 Harold worked for a sub contractor for Grumman Aircraft. He and his team developed the circuitry for the lunar landing excursion module that landed on the moon. He worked on circuitry for years and was manager for the sub contractor.

A unique note: The picture of Harold in his navy uniform is the only one that exists. He lost all of his memories when the fire struck in Las Vegas. This picture was saved by his parents.

Harold, thank you for your service to your country!

I have not seen Harold since we had our interview.

Edward John Tanner, US Navy

This interview came about in a very unique way. I was attending a function at the Mesquite Veterans Center when I had the pleasure of meeting a lovely woman by the name of Daphne Tanner. During our conversation, she mentioned her husband had recently passed away and that he was a **WWII** veteran. She was gracious enough to grant me a posthumous interview about her beloved husband. So this is a special interview about a special veteran granted by a special lady.

Edward John Tanner was born to Eric and Doris Tanner in Indianapolis, Indiana, July 18, 1925. He attended Caldwell HS in Idaho and graduated at the age of 17. He immediately joined the US Navy serving as a diver. Unfortunately one of his assignments was recovering bodies after the attack at Pearl Harbor.

After a successful enlistment in the navy and the end of the war, Edward attended the University of Southern California where he earned both a bachelor's and graduate degree in engineering. He became a senior engineer with Northrup in Downey, California. Edward held other positions throughout his life including undercover security for the Los Angeles Police Department during the 1984 Olympic Games and later on for the New York Police Department. He was also with the LaPlata County Sheriff's Department; Western Slope Major; Colorado Mounted Rangers Troop D; search and rescue, and he provided security at Vallecito Lake through Animas Investigations.

Edward was CEO of Animas Investigations in Durango. While living there, he was also a llama rancher and loved to show the animals to school children and visitors at Tanner's Llamas of Colorado. He loved to hunt and fish.

Edward was preceded in death by a former wife many years ago. He visited a Parents Without Partners meeting at the Disney Hotel and met Daphne. In addition, he introduced his roommate to Daphne's girlfriend and they hit it off very well also. Both couples ended up getting married.

Edward and Daphne enjoyed 35 wonderful years together. During that time they lived in Lake Havasu where Edward was a member of the Lake Havasu Yacht Club. He had previously been commodore of the San Pedro Yacht Club in California. While in Lake Havasu he worked with the Coast Guard in conjunction with the London Bridge Project. In 2005 Edward and Daphne moved to Mesquite. They had learned about the city after attending a Private Investigators Convention in Las Vegas. One of their most cherished moments was winning a dance contest at the Avalon Ball Room.

A funeral and navy burial of cremated remains was held April 16, 2013 in Veterans Memorial Cemetery in Boulder City, Nevada. Edward, thank you for your service to your country! A special thank you to Daphne for providing me with the information for this article.

James E. Carrick, US Army Air Corp (My Father)

Jim was born February 18, 1924, in Belle Vernon, Pennsylvania to James and Nellie Carrick. His parents immigrated to America from Scotland.

My father attended North Belle Vernon HS where he received all county honors as a two-way 142 pound lineman. He also sang in several high school musicals. He graduated in May, 1942 and immediately went to work for Pittsburgh Steel Company in order to accumulate 90 days of seniority prior to enlisting in the Army Air Corp. You see back in the day if you had 90 days of seniority with the steel mill your time continued while you served in the armed forces.

Dad wanted to be a pilot and took the test. He needed to score a 98% and scored 97.8%. He asked the recruiter how can he keep him from going to flight school for .2%? The recruiter opened a drawer full of folders and said "These are test scores of 97.9%." So dad decided to go to jump school which he completed at Ft. Benning, Georgia. As I grew up I asked my dad a number of times what it was like being involved in a war. I always received the same reply. "We didn't do anything but our job. We did what we had to do and came home and went on with our lives." It was a lost cause. Therefore, the information I was able to gather about my dad came from his younger brother George, who served in the US Navy during the end of WWII and my grandfather.

I do know that dad served with the 46th Troop Carrier Squadron of the 316th Troop Carrier Group. Although he made several jumps, he also served as a truck driver/mechanic and cook. His first overseas assignment was in North Africa and he did tell me about camping in the desert and having to be aware of scorpions among other desert creatures. From North Africa it was off to England, Italy and then France. His unit parachuted into Normandy behind the lines at least four days after the initial US invasion. Dad was fortunate and returned home unscathed in June 1946.

He and mom were married and had been high school sweethearts. I was the first born in 1947, followed by a sister three years later and a brother almost ten years after me. Dad continued his career at Wheeling Pittsburgh Steel. He went to night school and completed his post high school education and moved into management. After 36 years of service he retired at the age of 54. He and mom had divorced years earlier and dad went into the tavern business where he remained until his death at the age of 66.

Like all the other veterans, I thank my father for his service to his country. As I write this book of interviews of all the wonderful men and women who so honorably served, I have to pause just a little when I realize that one of the WWII veterans was my father.

James Miller, US Army

Jim was born June 14, 1919, in Lancaster, Ohio where he attended Lancaster HS. He played the clarinet in the band and orchestra while there. He graduated in 1937 and was an honor student. After graduation, Jim went to work for as a machine repairman at Hocking Glass Plant, now Anchor Hocking. He soon entered a mold maker apprenticeship program learning to make the metal molds in which glassware is made.

In May 1941, Jim married his wife, Jean, and seven months later, right after Pearl Harbor, December 7, 1941, he enlisted in the US Army as an aviation cadet. By the time he finished the written test and physical and everything was processed it was March and there was no place to handle the cadets. Nevertheless, after a seemingly endless wait, Jim finally was sent to San Antonio for training.

Jim's brother Clark had enlisted three months earlier than Jim and by February he had become a pilot and officer, and was eventually involved in combat missions. He flew B24 bombers from South America to Africa and then to Italy. He was involved on oil field raids in Germany.

Jim had another brother Bill, who served in the US Coast Guard during the war.

At San Antonio, training was slow because there weren't enough facilities for all the cadet pilots. Jim spent a lot of time in close order drilling and running the obstacle course. It took eight months to become an officer and a pilot and it was broken down into pre-flight, primary, and advanced training. Jim had pre-flight school in Santa Anna, California, which included weather, code and navigation calculations. Primary training was in Kankin Field California where barnstormers were used as trainers which used fabric covered PT-17 bi-planes.

During a primary training session a spring broke in Jim's plane causing him to go into a spin. Although still a novice pilot, Jim managed to pull the plane out of trouble and land it safely with no damage. Jim then moved on to metal planes where cadets had to learn fuel mixture, flaps, radios and were instructed in cross country flight, navigation and night flight.

Jim had advanced flight training at Luke Field in Phoenix where cadets trained in AT6's, the equivalent to the navy SMJ. Here they became familiar with aerial gunnery and retractable gears. Jim received his wings at Luke field and his wife was there to pin them on.

Jim went on to Randolph Field in San Antonio for one month of flight instructor school where he trained in a BT9.

Then it was off to Sa Pecos, Texas, where he served as a basic flight instructor using BT13's and BT15's. During peace time, instructors usually had two or three students. With WWII underway, more pilots were needed so each instructor had eight students, four in the morning for four hours and four in the afternoon for four hours. To cover all the students, all the instructors worked both shifts. To cover night flying additional hours were necessary. Fatal crashes occasionally resulted from all the work. Officers spent time in the hospital recuperating from exhaustion because they couldn't pass their flight physicals. San Pecos became a twin engine training facility and Jim was sent to Merced Basic Training Base in California where single engine fight was still being taught. Here there were no fatal accidents because the instructors were back to 4 students each. Jim became the flight commander and a member of the Flight Standardization Board. While teaching new instructors coming back from Europe as combat pilots some fatal accidents occurred because these bomber pilots were not accustomed to recovering from a spin.

About the time the war ended in Europe, there were 25,000 pilots with nothing to do. An invasion of Japan was in the process of being planned. Pilots with over 1500 hours were being recruited to become commanders for this operation. This included Jim who had accumulated over 2000 hours, flying multiple engine military aircraft. He had only two engine failures in all that time and attributed that to the excellent maintenance performed by the mechanics. At Roswell the B29's for the mission to Japan were scheduled to make their first training flight on Friday, but VJ Day came on Wednesday. Jim was disappointed because he had always wanted to fly in combat. However, Jim did more than his part by becoming an excellent flight instructor. No matter how many times he volunteered for combat duty as a pilot, he kept getting turned down because the army needed him to continue the great job he was doing as an instructor. Jim was discharged as 1st Lt. in Attlebury, Indiana, October 19, 1945.

Jim returned to Lancaster and Anchor Hocking after his discharge and resumed his job as a machinist. He soon realized weighing only 130 pounds and lifting about 2000 pounds during a normal work days work that his future looked bleak. So Jim who was an honor student in high school enrolled at the Ohio St. University as a Chemistry major. In just 2½ years, he completed his work and received his BS degree in chemistry and graduated summa cum laude.

Employers pursued Jim due to his outstanding academic record and he soon settled on a job with the titanium division of National Lead Co. He and Jean moved to New Jersey. They did not care for New Jersey, so after two years Jim left and went to work for the Battell Memorial Institute. Gordon Battell had organized many pig iron operations into a steel operation that flourished. He was very successful and the institute opened its doors in 1929. It has become a research and development operation for business, industry and the government. They have offices all over the world. Jim stayed there for 33 years and retired as associate division chief and senior scientist. Jim lived in California for 28 years after retiring, but moved to Mesquite two years ago where he has a daughter.

Jim we thank you for your service to your country.

Ray Burgi, US Army

Ray Burgi was born February 14, 1923 in Shoshone, Idaho. He attended Horace Mann Junior High in Salt Lake City, Utah, moving to Tooele, where he went to high school.

His first job was working in a gold mine in Mercer, Utah before he joined the US Army on March 17, 1941. He was sent to the field artillery where he eventually would be training Filipino troops.

Before long, he was assigned to the 739th Tank Battalion at Ft. Lewis, Washington. That is where he met his wife of 45 years. Mildred was an elevator operator he actually ran into on the sidewalk.

Ray transferred to Ft. Knox, Kentucky for additional training before he was sent overseas. While he was shipping over aboard the USS Billy Mitchell, it was involved in a German U-boat attack. He had recently signed up for an Army life insurance policy and thought, "Oh yeah, this is why they made me sign that document."

He served 15 months in Europe fighting Hitler's army. He first landed in Wales and after some time was sent to the front. A few days after D-Day, he landed at Port Le Havre in France. Ray was assigned a tank retriever (13 tons of steel and rubber) and had the job of pulling the tanks off the lines when they were hit. He was part of the famous 70th Tank Battalion that fought in the Battle of the Bulge, the largest battle of WWII. He served at Bastogne, and many other locations in France, Belgium and Germany. His unit won many campaign ribbons and honors.

After the war, he was discharged at Ft. Douglas, Utah. He started his first job washing cars for a local dealership. He worked his way up to parts manager, and then to service manager. He spent time in management with GM dealerships in Utah, Oregon and Arizona, where he lost his wife to cancer. He soon met his new bride, Etheline, at a local golf course. Etheline had recently lost her husband, a 30-year-retired Marine. She and Ray married after a short courtship.

Ray retired and they started RV traveling. They have played golf in many states during their travels. It was on one of these trips that they passed through Mesquite.

They fell in love with our town and made this their winter home for many years. They stayed for a long time at the Oasis RV Park until they moved to Desert Skies, where they now live. While traveling they made some wonderful RV friends and still plan visits to the eastern states for visits and golf.

Ray has outlived his children, but enjoys his three grandchildren and two great grandchildren along with Etheline's two daughters and one son, seven grandchildren and seven great grandchildren.

Ray, your fellow veterans salute you, and the citizens thank you for your military service.

I did not have the privilege of meeting Ray Burgi. The preceding interview was conducted by Ed Fizer, my predecessor of "Veterans Corner." I sincerely thank Ed for allowing me to use this article for my book.

Ed Corpe, US Navy

Ed was born in Alhambra, California in 1927. He attended Victorville HS, where he played the saxophone. Ed said he had a propensity for mathematics. After exhausting all available courses at school, he hooked up with a teacher to study additional advanced math individually.

After graduating in June 1944, Ed enlisted in the navy. He was sent to San Bernardino and trained with 50 Marines. His goal was to become a pilot but he failed an eye test.

He attended various schools while in San Bernardino including a year at the University of Southern California.

His unit performed different jobs on ships that were in port, primarily destroyers. Because the war was winding down, his unit never knew what the future might bring. Nevertheless, he spent his entire two year enlistment in California and was able to amass two years of college credits while in the navy.

Ed went to Logan, Utah, after leaving the navy and passed the U.S. Forest Service test but had to return to school, for one more course. He worked summers in forestry and then went to work full time starting as a patrolman in Big Pines, California where he worked for two years.

His next assignment was the Larimore Forest where he was the fire control marshal for three years. He returned to the Angeles Forest as a fire control officer for another two years. Ed was a GS-7.

Ed eventually became a GS-9 district ranger in the Valerymo District of the Angeles National Forest where he spent three years.

The USFS sent Ed to Vietnam where he worked with three different units as principal U.S. representative to the Vietnam Forest Service. He controlled the operation for 2½ years. He also spent time in Australia and Canada as the principal U.S. representative. He did a lot of work related to the railroad industry.

When Ed returned home, he was promoted to GS-12 and spent the next four years as the forest supervisor at Flathead National Forest in Montana.

His last job with the USFS was running the fire department for all national forests, the equivalent of over half the U.S. He ran all the air operations as well as the fire department. The air operation included 17 planes.

Ed finally retired to Montana with 28 years of service. He lost his wife while living in Montana.

Ed met his present wife, a lovely lady named Loretta, who had also lost her spouse. The couple met at the Mesquite Recreation Center and the rest is history.

They have been married for ten years and have a combined family of six children, two grandchildren and two great grandchildren.

Ed, thank you for your service to your country!

Ed will be making the Honor Flight Trip to Washington, DC, in April, which is how I came to meet him. In my quest to interview as many WWII veterans as possible, I noticed his name on the list of veterans scheduled to make the trip.

Ed Gutierrez, US Navy

Born 13 October 1921, Ed is 93 years young. He always makes me laugh or smile when we meet. He was born in a small copper mining town in New Mexico, but his dad soon moved to LA, California, where he wanted to make sure his kids got a good education. Soon after Ed arrived he had to endure the earthquake of 1933. He remembers just how scary it was standing there and feeling the earth shake. He followed his dad's advice and got his diploma in 1939 from Jordan High, between Compton and Watts California. He married his sweet Josephine in 1940 and they spent 63 wonderful years together before she passed away in 2004. To provide for Josephine he got a job at a gas station, where he was working when Pearl Harbor was bombed.

He decided to take a test for the U.S. Post Office. He passed and started working the night shift sorting bags of mail on January 1, 1943. Then came WWII and Ed got his "Greetings" letter and was drafted into the navy. After boot camp, Ed was about to be sent to a ship when a sergeant asked if anyone knew how to play music. Ed had been a saxophone player since he was in high school and was sent to the Fleet Post Office Orchestra. So Ed played music and sorted mail. Now take a moment and think about the job Ed had. Just how many thousands of GI's serving in the Pacific depended upon Ed for that grateful letter from home or that perfume-soaked love letter. Brings a tear to your eye, did mine.

In April 1946 Mailman 2nd Class Petty Officer Ed was discharged and went right back to his job with the post office, only in San Pedro, California. Ed worked as a clerk selling stamps until he worked his way up to the manager of mail bag depository. Somewhere in there Ed was also able to complete his college degree. Actually Ed became so good at his job he was selected for assignment in Washington D.C. as the chief of distribution and transportation for the nation's mail. He missed California and was transferred back to San Francisco in 1971, where he served as the mail equipment officer until he retired in 1979. He moved to Riverside and played golf, bowled and started his own band that played all the area rest homes and other community events. He also held offices with NRAF (National Retired Federal Employees).

Since moving to Mesquite in 2007 to be with his daughter Diane, he has been very active with the OFG, American Legion and playing his saxophone at the Salvation Army Bell ringing pot. I am proud to call Ed my friend and I salute him.

This interview was conducted and written by Ed Fizer.

Ed Gutierrez is everyone's friend around the veterans' center. A nicer gentleman you will never find. Always wanting and willing to help, even at the age of ninety-three. Ed plays his saxophone at the veterans' center gatherings. He is especially known for his rendition of "Happy Birthday" for all who will admit to having one at an event. I am honored to count Ed as one of my best friends. He is particularly proud of his grandchildren, great-grandchildren, and great-great-grandchildren.

Ed, thank you for your service to your country!

Willis Wilson, US Army

Willis was born February 14, 1921 in Mesquite, Nevada. One of the earlier settlers of this region, Willis grew up with those whose lives consisted of farming and raising live stock, especially cattle.

Willis is the father of Kathy Brown, the wife of our VSO (veterans service officer), Jim Brown. Jim is one of the significant individuals responsible for the Mesquite Veterans Center getting its start.

Willis entered the US Army June 5, 1944 at Ft. MacArthur in California. He became a rifleman with the 413th Infantry Regiment and served in the European, African and Middle Eastern Theaters during WWII.

The 104th Infantry Division was an infantry division of the United States Army. Today, it is known as the 104th Division (Leader Training) and is based at Ft. Lewis, Washington as a training unit of the United States Army Reserve.

The 104th Infantry was first constituted on June 24, 1921 as the 104th Division, before being organized and activated in October of that year in Salt Lake City, Utah. Assigned to the division were the 207th and 208th Infantry brigades, containing the 413th, 414th, 415th and 416th Infantry regiments. As a unit of the Organized Reserves, the division represented assets from the states of Montana, Wyoming, Idaho, Utah and Nevada. In 1924 it received its shoulder sleeve insignia. The division would not see significant action until WWII.

Deployed during WWII, the division saw almost 200 days of fighting in northwestern Europe as it fought through France, Belgium, and western Germany, fighting back several fierce German counterattacks as it advanced through the theater throughout late 1944 and 1945. This was the only combat duty the 104th Infantry Division has served during its history. At the end of the fighting on May 7, 1945 (V-E Day), this division was in central Germany opposite the troops of its allies from the Soviet Army.

The nickname of the 104th Infantry was the "Timberwolf Division," and their motto was "Nothing in hell can stop the Timberwolves." During WWII they were involved in the Battle of Hurtgen Forest and the Battle of the Bulge.

Upon return to the United States July 3, 1945, it continued the process of demobilization until December of that year, when it was inactivated. The division suffered 1,294 killed in action, 5,305 wounded in action, 385 missing in action, and 27 prisoners of war. The division suffered a further 6,396 non-battle casualties, for a total of 13,407 casualties. The division took 51,727 German prisoners during the war, most of whom, surrendered following the armistice.

During WWII, soldiers of the division were awarded two Medals of Honor, 14 Distinguished Service Crosses, one Distinguished Service Medal, 642 Silver Star Medals, 6 Legion of Merit Medals, 20 Soldier's Medals, 2,797 Bronze Stars and 40 Air Medals. The division received 9 Distinguished Unit Citations and three campaign streamers during 200 days of combat.

Willis was honorably discharged April 20, 1946 at Camp Beale, California as a Private First Class after serving almost 27 months. During his service he received the following; WWII Victory Medal, Good Conduct Medal, European African Middle East Campaign Medal, and the Combat Infantry Badge.

Willis passed away, but will be remembered forever by his family for his service to his country and we thank Willis for that.

Samuel Tom Holiday, US Marine Corps

Samuel grew up not knowing about the white man until he was twelve years old. "We were scared of the white man. I guess it would be like being scared of aliens now." His sister said he would hide from the government agents that came to pick up the Navajo kids and put them in boarding schools. He had only seen a white man from a distance when they went to the trading post. One day, while herding sheep, he hurt his knee and was taken to the clinic. While recovering at the hospital he was "caught" and sent to the Tuba City Boarding School. The school enforced English only and if caught speaking Navajo or practicing any traditions they were punished. He would save his cookies, cakes or apples from his meals and give them to the older students to help him learn English.

After five years of boarding school, he went to a vocation school in Provo, Utah. He had previously signed up to join the Marines, while attending school he received his letter to report for duty.

Sam was 18 years old when he arrived in phoenix, Arizona for physical examination. He was then put on a train to San Diego, California where he entered the grueling challenges of Marine Corps boot camp. "Sometimes you could hear the men crying at night because the training was hard" he recalls. Living on the Navajo reservation is a hard way of life, so training was not difficult for him.

He reported for duties at Camp Pendleton in Oceanside, California, where he met other Navajos. "There was a whole bunch of Navajo Marines. The first day, a Navajo instructor told me that the reason I was there was to learn the code that used the Navajo language."

Sam was assigned to the Fourth Marine Division, 25th Regiment, H&S Company from 1943 to 1945. He served duties on the island of Roi Namur, Kwajalien, Tinian, Saipan and Iwo Jima. Phillip Johnston, the son of missionaries on the Navajo reservation grew up with the Navajos and learned the language fluently. He suggested to the Marine Corps to use the Navajo language for to send coded messages.

After raining, they all boarded a ship bound for Hawaii, they met the other soldiers who were coming from the war. One day while going out on a ship they were told they were going to war. The first action Sam saw was on the island on Kwajalien.

Of the islands they were on, the battle on Saipan was the hardest and the most grueling for Sam. As the boat was making its way to the shore it capsized. Sam, underwater, threw of his pack but it caught on his gas mask and it dragged him down onto the water. He was fighting for air, he felt like he was full of water and was choking. By the time he finally made it to shore, he recovered somewhat, but was still very dizzy. During this same battle, there was a bomb that exploded near him and buried him. "I got up and was feeling somehow, kind of numb-like. I was shaking the dirt off; it was black like ashes. It was all over me and in my hair and my ears. I couldn't hear right and there were noises in my head." That explosion permanently damaged Sam's hearing.

Sam was always in danger, not only from enemy forces, but from his own fellow Marines. Japanese soldiers would dress themselves in the uniforms of dead Marines to infiltrate American lines. Twice he was captured by fellow Marines who mistook him as Japanese. A Marine pointed a bayonet in my back, he recalls. "I told him wait, I'm a radioman and I'm a Marine." On another occasion, he was surrounded by five or six angry Marines who believed he was a Japanese soldier who had sneaked into camp. Both tense situations required soldiers from his own company to verify his identity.

Unlike most languages, Navajo was unwritten at the time and practically impossible for an adult to learn. Every syllable carries meaning and sometimes a single word can have four or five meanings depending on intonation. Dialects can vary from region to region even within Navajo clans. In the thick of battle, they would send messages nonstop up to 15–18 hours, passing vital information about enemy fire, troop movement and for medical help. Military historians note that during the first 48 hours of the invasions of Iwo Jima, Navajo radio units sent and received more than 800 messages with 100% accuracy.

When he came back from the Marines, Sam worked up and down the West Coast. When he returned home he became a Navajo Police Officer. Later he worked at the Monument Valley tribal Park for many years then went to work for Peabody Coal Company until he retired.

While he was a police officer he met Lupita Mae Isaac, they were married in 1954. As of mid 2014, they have eight children, 33 grandchildren, 23 great grandchildren and one great-great grandson.

I met Sam this past Saturday, May 3, at the Mesquite Days Parade. I was marching with the Virgin Valley Honor Guard, and he was riding in a vehicle decorated with information on Navajo windtalkers. We did not have a chance to converse, but I was able to gather this information about Sam. What a guy he is! His autobiography was published in 2013.

Sam, thank you for your service to your country!

Joe Klasen, US Navy

This interview was conducted by Ed Fizer, and again I thank him for letting me include it in this book as Joe and his wife are very good friends of ours.

Joe was born November 27, 1926 in Holdingford, Minnesota. The day he turned 17, he joined the U.S. Navy in 1943 to do his part. What a part he played as he served in three wars over the years, WWII, The Korean War and the Vietnam War. Until he became 18 he would sail and train on what was called "Kiddie Cruises."

The main reason Joe chose the Navy was because of what the recruiter told him: "Every day in the U.S. Navy is like Sunday on the farm."

He enlisted in St. Paul and was put on a train to Farragut, Idaho for boot camp. After boot camp, he was sent to Astoria, Oregon where he was assigned to the USS Takanis Bay (CVE-89). During the war, these Casablanca type ships were called Jeep ships, because they ferried planes from the west coast to the big aircraft carriers throughout the Pacific.

Joe's ship had the mission of training pilots for takeoff and landings. His ship trained 2,500 pilots before it was converted to a troop carrier for Operation Magic Carpet bringing troops home from the pacific after WWII. On one trip from Tokyo Bay, he returned POW's back to the USA. He was soon transferred to the USS Major (DE-796) which was on station next to the USS Missouri during the Japanese peace signing. Joe stood on deck watching!

Joe was next assigned to China aboard the USS Prairie (AD-15) and the USS Sierra (AD-18). Officially called destroyer tenders both were maintenance ships that did repairs on larger ships in port. Joe was assigned to sail/canvas duties where he sewed gun covers and other canvas items. It was on the USS Sierra that that Joe spent his time during the Korean War. Joe then received shore duty in the Canal Zone, Atlantic Side. He and Ed spoke about places there that they both visited, Ed years later.

Upon returning to the States, Joe was assigned to the Naval Academy at Annapolis, Maryland where he helped midshipman train on yard patrol and training boats.

Joe's next assignment was to Pascagula, Mississippi, where he boarded one of the two refrigeration ships in the U.S. Navy. Then it was back through the Panama Canal to the west and duty in the Pacific on the USS Vega (AF-59), a ship with a less glamorous yet very important role in the Navy. The Vega transferred food items from shore to ships at sea and was also vital during Vietnam for resupply. When Joe was aboard in 1956, they set a record transferring 218 tons of food per hour.

After all this, Joe applied for radar school and was accepted. He followed that with advanced radar school and was promoted to Chief in 1958. He remained at the school in a staff position.

In 1963, Joe received an opportunity to serve his country during yet another war. On board the USS Ingersoll (DD-652) he was sent to Vietnam, making three different cruises until 1966. He was promoted to the top enlisted rank in the Navy (Master Chief) and returned to a staff position at the radar school for two years.

His last ship was the USS Bonhomme Richard (CVA-31). He was aboard when it was decommissioned and sent to Bremerton, Washington. At that time, Joe decided to retire from active duty, but spent the next two years in the Fleet Reserve so he would have a total of 30 years of service to his country when he retired in 1973.

However, he soon returned to Navy life, this time as a government employee. Back in San Diego, Joe worked with aircraft simulators at Imperial Beach Naval Air Station and at North Island where he worked on the S-3 sub hunter.

In 1991, Joe and his wonderful wife, Carol, sailed off into the sunset onto a 40 acre ranch in Pietro, California where they raised sheep, cattle and pigs. They moved to Mesquite in 2002, where Joe is involved with cowboy poetry, plays the harmonica, is active in the OFG, several veterans organizations and works as a tax preparer part time. Carol is also very active in several organizations and a significant volunteer in the Mesquite Honor Flight Program as well as the Veterans Center.

Joe and Carol have been married 40+ years have six children, 12 grand children and 7 great grandchildren. One of their grandsons has been to Afghanistan four times.

Joe, we thank you for your service to your country!

Joe and Carol have worked on many significant projects within the community and the veterans' center with my wife Kathy and me. We have become wonderful friends.

Anna Murphy, US Army

Born in Schenectady, New York in 1918, Anna lived here until WWII broke out. "I was very patriotic," she says of her enlistment. "I wanted to do my part so I joined the Women's Army Corps and was put in the signal corps where we worked on switchboards, teletype and that sort of thing."

Anna remains a well known nonagenarian, who claims the title as the city of Mesquite's oldest World War II veteran.

During her military career she traveled to Europe where one of the highlights of her three year career was a visit to the bunker where Hitler committed suicide. During her service she was with the first military unit into Germany after the fall of Hitler. Her unit went too far and crossed the Rhine River into East Berlin before they were called back. She had her picture taken with communist soldiers outside of the bunker. This scared her mother when she saw the picture. Anna still has a copy of the newspaper article. She said the bunker had been pretty well ransacked when she got there. It has now been covered and a small sign marks the spot.

After the service, Anna went to dental hygienist school and eventually ended up cleaning teeth in California. She moved to Nevada in 1950 and lived in Las Vegas, Reno, Elko and finally Mesquite in 1989.

"I love it here," she has said. "It's a great place with great people."

Anna is active in Veterans organizations and never misses an event that has to do with veterans or honors veterans. Up until last year, Anna worked at Virgin Valley High School in the teacher's workroom and at the front desk. Anna has made an impact on everyone she has met with her quick wit and bright smile.

The Mesquite Veterans Center has pot luck dinners on a regular schedule and Anna never misses. She loves being with the other veterans and just people in general. One of the veterans, John Nettle developed a racing game that was very unique that we would set up and play after dinner on these evenings. Anna loved the game. We were not able to do it every time we had a dinner, but every time Anna knew there was a dinner her first question would be, "Are we going to do the races?" We loved watching Anna and everyone else enjoy themselves!

Anna we thank you for your service to your country!

Joe "Moose" Martinez, US Navy

Joe was born October 3, 1929, in Tioga, Colorado. In 1945, when Joe was 16 years old he changed the date of his birth certificate and convinced his father to sign the papers showing he was 17 so he could enlist in the U.S. Navy.

Joe went to boot camp in San Diego, California, and afterward was assigned as a gunners mate on the USS Arkansas (BB33), a dreadnaught battleship and the second Wyoming class built by the Navy. Joe said in those days sailors slept in hammocks and it was very crowded.

The Arkansas was one of many ships involved in the first atom bomb tests after the U.S. bombed Hiroshima and Nagasaki, Japan.

Called "Operation Crossroads," the tests consisted of two atomic blasts. The first, "Test Able," was exploded in the atmosphere above the Bikini Atoll lagoon and the second, "Test Baker," was exploded under water in the lagoon.

Joe said Test Able exploded some 200 feet above the water and the sailors were instructed to put their heads between the legs.

"It was the biggest ball of fire you can possibly imagine and the heat from the radiation was just incredible," Joe said.

The test was conducted to see what the bomb would do at sea and after the explosion the USS Arkansas was flushed with an acid-like fluid to reduce the threat of radiation.

Despite the cleaning, however, Geiger counters would still go crazy. Nevertheless, the crew had to go back on board to live, eat and sleep. Joe estimated his ship was only six miles away when the bomb went off.

The USS Arkansas was also in the area when Test Baker was conducted underwater. Other ships near the test site included the USS Saratoga and the USS Nevada.

Before Operation Crossroads, Bikini Atoll islanders were voluntarily resettled on Rongerik Atoll. They were led to believe they would be able to return home within a short time. When it didn't happen, the islanders nearly starved because Rongerik was not able to produce enough food for the population.

The islanders were eventually relocated to Kwajalein Atoll for six months before choosing to live on Kili Island, a small island one-sixth the size of Bikini, their home. Some returned home in 1970 until further testing revealed dangerous levels of radioactive strontium-90, and they were again forced to move.

During Test Baker there were 84 target ships positioned around ground zero. They were all packed with instruments and animals. There were also about 100 non target ships. Test Baker, a shallow water detonation, sent a one million ton column of water and steam shooting 6,000 feet up, and more than 1 mile across, according to "Irradiation Personnel During Crossroads; An Evaluation Based on Official Documents" written by Dr. Arjun Makhijani and David Albright.

This radioactive water rained down on the lagoon, the beaches and the target ships. Everything was severely contaminated. The blast caused immense waves that further contaminated the area. Within a few days the non-target ships were moved back into the lagoon where they were loaded with additional radioactive materials.

Nearly everyone involved in the tests, including Joe and his shipmates, were exposed to considerable doses of radiation. The target ships were so contaminated they became useless and were sunk in deep water.

Joe was discharged from the Navy when he was 18 years old and he went to work in the coal mines of Utah. His father and most of his family were miners.

Joe spent 25 years digging coal in Utah. He also worked in Colorado mines where he became involved with the local union, eventually becoming president.

Joe related a situation to me where he, his father and several other miners were going to lunch when a foreman told them to get back to work. Joe's dad told him they hadn't even opened their lunch pails. "Lunch starts as soon as you put down your tools," the foreman responded.

"First, you don't talk to my father that way and second, lunch starts when we get to the lunch area," Joe told the foreman.

The other miners came to Joe and asked him to be their representative. Joe was involved with the union for more than 50 years.

Unfortunately Joe contacted black lung disease in the mines and still spends much of his time helping other miners with the disease apply for benefits.

Black lung is a terrible disease caused by long exposure to coal dust. It is a common affliction of coal miners and others who work with coal. Inhaled coal dust progressively builds up in the lungs and is unable to be removed by the body, leading to inflammation, fibrosis, and in the worst cases necrosis.

Joe moved to Mesquite because the dry weather and low altitude make him more comfortable. He lost his wife in 2008. He has three daughters, one in Tennessee, one in Colorado and one in California and 21 grandchildren.

Joe has been a member of the Elks for more than 50 years, recently returned from a Southern Nevada Honor Flight trip to Washington D.C. with three other WWII veterans including Cal Price, Ed Corpe and Jim Miller.

Joe, thank you for your service to your country!

A Tribute to the Veterans of World War II

These were and still are a unique group of men and women who came to the defense of their country without hesitation. They answered the call in droves and did whatever they were asked to do to perform dangerous duties as well as support the war effort. In both cases, their dedication has been unmatched.

Many women joined the military and supported the effort in a significant role that varied, depending on branch of service and location. Who can forget the nurses and medical staffs who risked their well-being to save the lives of others? None of it was ever done for the glory of the results, but done because that is what these people felt was their duty.

Although women were not allowed to engage in combat, they did more than their share and survived unthinkable situations because it was country first.

The men, of course, went to war. Facing war on two fronts, they never wavered in their efforts. They faced unthinkable horrors on the German front and in the South Pacific. Many were in combat, but let us not forget those who were in support roles. They too played a significant role in the war.

The most important issue is this: I don't think there was anyone who would have refused an assignment regardless of what it would have involved. I've heard real-life stories of men who cried because they could not enlist for one reason or another, and that says it all when it comes to the spirit of the veterans of WWII.

I can never put into words what I feel for these veterans, nor do I possess the talent to significantly give them their due, but I hope that we all take a moment and realize how blessed we are because of them.

There is a saying that is very appropriate: "All gave some, and some gave all." How true it is for every conflict the United States has been involved with. However, there is an aspect of WWII that is relatively overlooked. When most of our men and many of our women joined the service, there was still much to be done on the home front. Who were to do it? The men who, for whatever reason, could not join the service and the women who were raising families or waiting for husbands and loved ones to return did it! They went to work in the factories to supply our military with ammunition, repair parts for equipment, new equipment, jeeps, planes, ships etc. You name it, and it had to be produced at home.

The people at home also consumed less so the military could have more. Defense bonds, fund-raisers—I could go on and on. Everyone supported the effort. Those at home were heroes as well as those on the front lines, certainly in a different way, but heroes nonetheless.

I know many of us grew up in a different time. Our fathers and grandfathers were probably veterans of WWII, and maybe that is why I, along with many of my friends old and new, am so fond of the WWII veterans. They did their job and asked for little in return. Unfortunately, we are losing them much too quickly, a group that cannot and will not ever be replaced. They did unique things without regard for their own welfare so our country could survive and prosper.

So when you see a WWII veteran, take a moment to thank him or her for the service they gave. You may even want to take a few extra minutes to chat. They will appreciate it, and you will be enriched by the experience.

VETERANS WHO ALSO RAISED THEIR HANDS

After taking over the duties of writing the "Veterans Corner" article for the local paper, this was my first interview. I thought I would play it safe and asked a very good friend, Ken Maynard, if he would agree to be interviewed. He agreed, and I was off and running. You see, my wife and I and Ken and his wife, Deb, were neighbors in the same subdivision and became friends.

Ken was born July 28, 1947 in Neenah, Wisconsin and attended Kimberly HS. When he turned 17, he wanted to see the world and after getting permission from Mom, joined the US Navy. He headed off to the Great Lakes Naval Training Station in Illinois. He received his GED while in the Navy and going through training.

After boot camp, it was off to San Diego and an assignment to the USS Duncan as a ship serviceman/supply. Ken's responsibility included all the store supplies aboard ship. After two tears in this capacity, he and a close friend volunteered for duty in Vietnam. They were assigned to Naval Support Activities in Da Nang and attached to the 3rd Marine Division in Don Ha.

Upon completing his tour of duty in Vietnam, Ken was assigned to the USS Yorktown, again as a supply man, where he had a significant opportunity to participate in American history. The USS Yorktown was designated as the recovery ship to retrieve the astronauts from Apollo 8. There is an autographed picture from this occasion in our Veterans Center that Ken graciously donated.

In addition, Ken had another terrific experience aboard the Yorktown. His ship was used in the filming of the 20th Century Fox movie, "Tora! Tora! Tora!" The USS Yorktown was made up to look like a Japanese aircraft carrier. The movie was filmed in Hawaii. This experience took place prior to the recovery of Apollo 8. After six years of service, Ken was discharged from the Navy, but continued his military career by joining the Wisconsin National Guard. He enjoyed this service as the Guard did a lot of service oriented work, helping people who were victims of natural disasters such as floods and tornados.

After 12 years, ken transferred to the Army Reserves and went to USAR Training School where he was qualified to instruct all MOS's. This is what he did in his final five years of military service. Ken retired in 1991.

When Ken returned from the Navy he went to work for Thilmany Pulp and Paper in Wisconsin as a papermaker. He worked most of his career as a receiving clerk, becoming instrumental in his companies' conversion from manual to computerized systems. After 38 years he retired.

Ken met his lovely wife Deb in May 1980 and they were married in 1983. They have 5 children and 12 grand children. During our interview Ken made it a point to mention that Deb was a significant factor in his military career as she had to make many concessions as he fulfilled his duty requirements. Ken is very involved in our local veteran activities and is always available to lend a helping hand even though he and Deb are in the process of building a new home. Deb is a very active participant at the Veterans Center as well. Ken just completed serving on the Board of Directors as Vice President.

Ken, thank you and Deb for all you do, and Ken for your service to your country.

Tony Hardway, US Air Force

Tony is a veteran who has served his country and the local Veterans community with distinction. Born in Bergoo, West Virginia, October 25, 1931, Tony attended Webster Springs HS until he was 17. At that time with his father's signature, he enlisted in the US Air Force, to start out what turned out to be a long and distinguished career.

In 1950, Tony was assigned to Guam and then to Kadena AFB in Okinawa. Flying on a mission as a gunner on a bomber they were hit by enemy fire during the Korean War. Tony was wounded from shrapnel from the original strike. The co pilot and another crew member bailed out first, followed by a group of four additional crew members. All of the 13 crew members left the plane, Tony being the last one. He landed in water and had to swim to shore, not an easy thing to do with wounds of the arm, legs and back, but he made it. Once on land they were discovered by the Koreans.

Fortunately, they were South Koreans. They aided the crew, moving at night and hiding by day. The men eventually made contact with a British unit that took the crew to a British ship and on to Japan. Tony was treated for his wounds and then sent to Hunter AFB in Georgia.

Later it was back to Kadena. All of the crew survived with the exception of the first two out. They were captured and died in a prisoner-of-war camp. Tony received a Purple Heart and Bronze Star for his service in Korea.

In 1952 Tony went to Duluth, Minnesota for training in air to air missiles and interceptor missiles both basic and advanced. After a year it was off to Goose Bay, Labrador, where he spent two years working with F89J interceptors and supported the missile systems. This included AIM I, II, III and IV. AIM I and II were radio controlled, while

III and IV were infrared controlled (heat seeking). During this assignment, Tony was promoted to E5. In 1960 it was back to Lowry where Tony became an instructor/supervisor teaching the course he initially went through. It only made sense since he had rewritten some of the courses since he had gone through the training. Additionally, he also had maintenance responsibility. From Lowry Tony went to Alaska and an assignment as maintenance supervisor and quality assurance for the nuclear missiles there at Elmendorf AFB. Then in 1963 back to Lowry as an instructor.

In 1966 Tony was assigned to Bitburg, Germany, where he served as the maintenance supervisor as well as part of the missile inspection team. The base primarily serviced the F103 and the F4. In addition, Tony was the NCO in charge. After this tour, Tony was sent to Tactical Air Command at Langley AFB in Virginia. Here, assigned to missile maintenance, he was responsible for making up all the tactical requirements for aircraft that was used for all fighter wings that were anticipated to be used in the next five years. In addition he was assigned to the Maintenance Standardization Team that consisted of 23 enlisted NCO's (E7, E8 and E9) and three officers.

In 1971, Tony received orders for Vietnam and was sent to Blan Hoa. Here he trained the South Vietnamese on all kinds of aircraft including A1's, F5's, gunships, 119's and 130's as well as helicopters. After 10 months it was back to Lowry. Here again, he set up training course for the missile training area for all work stations. By this time Tony has risen in rank to E8. In 1958, Tony had met a lovely lady named Ginger and they were married a year later. While on this assignment, the commanding General had noticed Tony had handed in papers for retirement. Not wanting to lose a good airman, he called Tony into his office and offered him a position on his staff in Hawaii. Tony said that he would have to check with Ginger. He did. Her response was "I hope you and the general enjoy

Hawaii." You see Tony and Ginger had just purchased a home. Tony retired with 26 honorable years of service. He later joined the reserves and ended up with 30 years.

After the Air Force, Tony joined Martin Marietta as a Quality Assurance Engineer in the Electronics Division where he worked until his retirement 13 years later. While at Lowry, Tony met another airman named Jesse Marsh. Jesse is an active veteran (retired Air Force) around the Veterans center as well as the Mesquite Community. The reason I bring it up is both Tony and Jesse left Lowry and went on about their business, but reunited here in Mesquite. Both of them and their wives settled here without knowing about the other and a friendship was renewed.

Tony is a member of the following: VFW, American Legion, Vietnam Veterans of America, Society of The Purple Heart, Board member of Mesquite Veterans Center, past coordinator of the Virgin Valley Honor Guard. Tony and Ginger have a son and a daughter two grand children and two great-grand children.

Tony we thank you for your honorable service to your country and community.

Scott and Barbara Ellestad, US Air Force

This is a very unique interview and story about a married couple that retired from the US Air Force as E9s. As far as I have been able to tell, they are the only couple that has done so with the highest enlisted rank possible.

Barbara was born April 18, 1953, in Cedarville, Ohio, only 20 miles from Wright Patterson AFB. She attended Greenen Vocational HS and graduated after specializing in a secretarial curriculum. She moved into her own apartment and began working for a doctor as a medical secretary, but that didn't last long for a number of reasons.

Over the Labor Day weekend that year, driving around town, Barbara noticed military signs at the US Post Office advertising recruitment opportunities for all of the services. She went in the next day and the first office was the US Air Force, so she engaged the recruiter in a conversation. The Air Force had a quota for women at this time and Barbara was accepted but had to wait four months to begin her enlistment.

It was the fall of 1971 and there was a significant anti war atmosphere in the area. This was due in part to the Kent St. University situation where students were shot in a scuffle with National Guard troops. Therefore, Barbara never told anyone about her decision to join the Air Force. On December 28 of that year it was off to San Antonio, Texas.

Scott was born March 5, 1952 in Minneapolis, Minnesota. He moved around quite a bit as his father was a machinist and traveled around to where the best paying jobs were available. Scott lived in seven states before joining the Air Force. He attended Coronado HS in Scottsdale, Arizona and was active in basketball, football and baseball. After graduating in 1972, he worked for a while and then decided to enlist in the US Air Force. At the time the Air Force made their recruits take a battery of tests to determine where their aptitude would best be used. Scott was placed in Services which consisted of commissary, mortuary, PX, etc and was assigned to a radar station in Bedford, Virginia. Scott worked in this capacity for five years, but had decided that his ambition was to be a loadmaster and continually put in paperwork for cross training. After five years he was granted his wish and he went through training and became a loadmaster.

Barbara on the other hand was assigned to a dental lab tech school which was a six month school. This was not what she was particularly interested in and after nine months, was able to obtain cross training in medical administration. This was where she wanted to be and remained in this field for eight years. From here Barbara again cross trained, this time in computers and was assigned to Personnel, where she spent the rest of her career. This was a significantly responsible position as Barbara had responsibility for much classified information. Her career didn't always keep her in the United States. She spent two years in the Philippines and a year in Iceland. Because of her success Barbara was also moved around within the country as she spent time at Lowry AFB in Colorado, Scott AFB in Illinois, Altus AFB in Oklahoma and Wright Patterson AFB on three different occasions.

Scott's training took place at Altus AFB in Oklahoma, traveling there from Mt. Home Idaho. He was assigned to Uben, Thailand after going through water survival school. Scott spent 12 years at McCloud AFB in Tacoma, Washington in his role as loadmaster. He functioned primarily out of C-141's and there were only five bases where the planes were located. Scott's career continued to blossom and he was assigned to Scott AFB in Illinois and promoted from E7 to E8 and then to E9. He became the Chief Loadmaster of the entire Military Airlift Command. Scott also obtained two associate degrees while serving in the Air Force, one in Transportation and one in Traffic Management. There were more than a few instances where Scott and his crew were involved in secret operations. They backed President Bush during operations in Somalia and Desert Storm, just to name two.

Scott received six Meritorious Service Medals; SE Asia Service Medal, Granada Air Medal, Desert Storm Service Medal, Desert Shield Service Medal, Vietnam Service Medal and Antarctica Service Medal 1983 &1985, just to mention a few. Scott always said 19 was his special number as his first flight was on the 19th of the month as well as his last. He received 19 ribbons and 19 medals.

For someone who was not particularly involved in academics in high school, Barbara outdid herself during her Air Force career obtaining five degrees! Yes, that is five. Two associate degrees, one in management and one in business; a BA in business management; a Master's Degree in management and a Master's Degree in information systems. Quite an accomplishment! Barbara received Meritorious Service with one Oak Leaf Cluster and an Air Force Commendation Medal among others.

When Scott and Barbara were both E8s they were sent to the Senior NCO Academy in Montgomery, Alabama, for a nine week course. This is where they met. They were sitting on the patio one evening discussing golf, which they both played, and the more they talked the more they discovered all that they had in common. After the school ended Barbara and Scott decided to continue to see one another, so they traveled from their respective bases (Barbara in Colorado and Scott in Illinois) and meet in Salina, Kansas. They did this for a while and finally Scott told Barbara that he wasn't going to make the trip anymore, so how about they go to Las Vegas and get married! They did!

Both Barbara and Scott are very positive on how the Air Force bent over backwards to keep married couple together and their situation was no different as they were both assigned to Altus AFB in Oklahoma.

Love sometimes makes it difficult between husband and wife and military duties. Desert Storm had just started. At Altus AFB, Barbara was in charge of personnel and processing troops for deployment. This involved taking the proper steps including shots, paperwork, confirming training, etc. One of the tasks was to check to make certain the individual's insurance was up to date and the beneficiary was correct. At 3 a.m. after working more than 24 straight hours, Barbara told a sergeant to take a break and she would cover the last unit through the line.

As she was reading the beneficiary, which they did for every individual, she asked "and your beneficiary is correct, Barbara Ellestad," she looked up and began to cry. She was processing Scott as the last one through. An officer standing nearby said, "I think you two should kiss goodbye and get your ass back here soon!" Scott and Barbara said it was the most difficult moment they ever had to go through in their married military careers. Much has to be over- looked as the military duty comes first. There were several times when Scott left on a mission and he could only tell Barbara that he was going on a mission, nothing else. But all worked out well.

In 1994, Scott and Barbara Ellestad retired from the Air Force on the same day, at the same rank. They were the first husband and wife to retire on the same day at the same ceremony. Although, the Air Force won't confirm it we believe they are the only E9 husband and wife to retire from the Air Force. When Barbara made E9, there were only 13 females at that rank in the entire Air Force. Quite an accomplishment! Scott didn't do too badly either from a member of the Services Group to Loadmaster Training after five plus years to become Chief Loadmaster Military Airlift Command; not shabby at all.

Scott retired with 24 years and Barbara with 23.

After the Air Force, Scott and Barbara moved to Bozeman, Montana, where Barbara became an instructor at the college level and Scott went into the construction business with his father and brother. After eight years they discovered Mesquite where they bought a home. Scott works in the golf industry at Wolf Creek Golf Course (where he carries a seven handicap) and Barbara is the editor and publisher of the Mesquite Citizen Journal an on-line newspaper.

I can't express what a wonderful experience this interview was. I doubt if I will ever have the opportunity to interview a husband and wife team like the Ellestads. In addition, they have become wonderful friends. Barbara is very involved with projects at the veterans' center.

Thank you, Scott and Barbara, for your service to your country. Sadly, Scott passed away recently. He will be missed!

Mark Fair, US Navy

Mark was born December 3, 1938 in Riverby, Texas, a small town that doesn't even exist today. He moved to Oregon as a youngster and attended Klamuath HS, where he participated in track and field and football. Upon graduation in 1956, he enlisted in the US Navy as part of the Aviators in Training Program as a Naval Cadet. However, a color deficiency in his eyesight resulted in his being bumped from the program. Asked what he would like to do, Mark thought about some alternatives and asked an aerographer was, as this was mentioned as an option. Told that it was weather related, Mark decided to give it a shot. After six months of schooling, he graduated from Aerographer School and was assigned to a weather station in Yakosuta, Japan. It was here that Mark predicted the weather for the entire Pacific for ships that traveled in that area. This was the Navy's largest weather center at that time. Mark spent 3½ years here.

Mark accepted his discharge, but remained a part of the US Navy Reserves. He attended junior college in Redding, California where he took science and math courses, as he wanted to further his education in the technical area of meteorology, but junior college did not offer an Associate degree in meteorology. Mark met his wife Julie while attending school there and they were married 18 months later. He worked at US Plywood while going to school, and then applied to the US Weather Service. He got the job and was assigned to the Arctic (Barter Island) for a one year term. Mark said the coldest it ever got was 40 below, but sometimes the wind was forty mph, which made for wind chills of -100. After six months, Mark returned, married his lovely wife Julie and returned to the Arctic to finish his term.

Julie finished her degree and she and Mark were hired as a team by the Weather Service and sent to Alaska. They settled in McGrath, Alaska located between great mountain ranges. Now here is something you don't hear of happening anymore. It was Julie's birthday and Mark wanted to buy her a ring, so he contacted a jewelry store in Anchorage and told the dealer what he wanted. The man said he had four rings that met the description of what Mark was looking for. The jeweler said, I'll send the four rings to you and you pick out the one you want and return the others with a check for the one you keep." Mark did just that!

On many occasions Mark would call the general store in Anchorage and read off a list of supplies he needed, while the owner put them in a shopping cart. They would then be packaged along with the bill and taken to the airport where they were flown to Mark. Mark would then send a check to the airport for the transport and to the general store for the supplies.

After two years at McGrath, Mark had saved enough money to quit and move to Corvallis, Oregon so he could attend Oregon St. University and pursue his dream of getting his degree in meteorology. However, after two years it was back to McGrath for another year of working with the Weather Service, then a transfer to Ketchican, Alaska where he spent another year. Once again back to Oregon St. and this time Mark graduated with his BS in Meteorology. He was approached by the EPA, received a grant, and 15 months later had his MBA. He stayed at Oregon St. for a year as an associate professor in the Department of Atmospheric Science. Then he was approached by the US General Accounting Office to teach Research Methodology, which he did for a year. To no one's surprise, Mark went back to the National Weather Service in Ft. Worth, Texas and signed up with US Navy Ready Reserves.

In 1990, Mark was activated as an individual during Desert Storm to evaluate what ship selection would work best for the battle group. He was assigned to Pearl Harbor. While there, he developed the annual hurricane exercise for all of Hawaii. Mark worked in Texas, Pennsylvania, California, Utah, Maryland and Nevada. While in Utah, he was the Chief of Meteorology for the eight western states and while in Maryland, was the Science Advisor for the National Weather Service. Mark's last assignment before he retired from the National weather Service was in Las Vegas, where he was Executive Advisor for the Entire National Weather Service. He retired from the weather service in 1995 and from the US Navy as a Lt. Commander in 1999. Even after retirement, Mark has taken on assignments that have been requested of him. He was activated as an individual in 1996 and again in 1997 before retiring. From 1999 to 2004 he was assigned to the Reagan Missile Defense Site as a federal contractor using his expertise as a meteorologist. In 2004, his last assignment involved again working in his field of meteorology for 90 days at Wake Island at a missile site.

Mark and Julie bought a home in Pocatella, Idaho and in 2007 bought one in Mesquite. They continue to be snow birds, but love Mesquite. They have two sons, two grandchildren and one great-grandchild.

What a remarkable career. I find it amazing that so many veterans decided to make Mesquite their retirement home. This has been a bonanza for someone who needed veterans to interview. Mark and Julie have become good friends of Kathy and mine as we belong to an off- road group. They are wonderful people.

Mark thank you for your service to your country.

Art Hammerschmidt, US Army

Art was born April 11, 1940 in Brooklyn New York. He got off to a rough start as he lost his father at age 4 in WWII. His dad was quite a hero as he served in both WWI and WWII. His mom had four children and they all had to pitch in to help pay the bills. Art loved playing baseball and was a huge Willie Mays and New

York Giants fan, which is very dangerous when you lived in Brooklyn. He also enjoyed one-wall handball. While attending Bushwick HS and working, Art found some time to play stick ball, a New York tradition. For those of you who have never seen New York youngsters play this game it is quite a treat.

Art graduated from Bushwick HS in 1957 and enrolled at Brooklyn College as an accounting major. He spent two years there. At about that time his older brother was drafted, and since he made most of the money at home and Art felt he was not the greatest student at the time he decided to enlist in the US Army. Upon completion of basic training at Ft. Hood, Texas and discovering that being a base plate man in a 81mm mortar team was not exactly the career he was looking for, Art applied for OCS at Ft. Sill, Oklahoma. However because of illness, he was unable to complete OCS and went on to Finance School at ft. Benjamin Harrison in Terre Haute, Indiana. From there Art was assigned to Hq & Hq Battery 3rd Gun Battalion, 80th Artillery Bamberg, Germany. Art was promoted to E4 while in Bamberg and to E5 when he was transferred to Wurtzburg. He spent from November 1959 to May 1962 in Germany.

In May of 1962 he returned to the states and was assigned to Nike Hercules 5th Missile Battalion 562 Artillery, Shreveport, Louisiana. At this point in his life Art was considering making the Army a career. However, while on leave he found out that his older brother had become ill with lung cancer, so Art got out of the Army and went back to New York. He lost his brother in August of 1962 at the age of 27. Art enrolled at Hofstra University and finished his degree in accounting. He left New York in 1969 and moved to California to accept a position as comptroller with Hertz Corporation Truck Division in San Jose. He met his lovely wife Ruth in 1973 and they were married in December of 1974. At the time, a friend of Art's was the Audit Manager of a Hawaiian based company called AMFAC and offered Art a position as Northwest Controller in Seattle, Washington. Art and Ruth had visited this area before and loved it so they jumped at the chance to move there. They spent eight years there, until Art was promoted to Division Controller and it was back to San Carlos and Rocklin, California for 14 years. In 1996, Art suffered a major back injury that resulted in major surgery and medical retirement. A friend of Art's had mentioned Mesquite, Nevada as a quaint little town that was a perfect place to retire. Art and Ruth visited and bought a home here in 1998.

Art and Ruth have three children and five grandchildren. Ruth is active in many volunteer organizations and sings in the church choir. As Art says, "She is my right arm, but most importantly she is God's gift to my happiness." Art and Ruth got involved with the Salvation Army Angel Tree Program and took over the Kettle Program in 2000. In 2007 they were awarded the Volunteer of the Year by the Salvation Army. Art is an active contributor at the Veterans Center, past Financial Officer of the American Legion, and Treasurer of the Knights of Columbus.

Art thank you for your service to your country and community.

Lance Barr, US Marine and US Navy

Lance was born September 3, 1947 in Salt Lake City, Utah. He graduated from Skyline HS in 1966 and in August of that year enlisted in the US Marine Corps. San Diego is where he headed for boot camp and then Camp Pendleton for advanced infantry training for three months. An additional two mounts at Pendleton were required for training as an MP.

Lance then received his orders for Vietnam and spent it in the area of Da Nang and north. In combat near Hill 65 Lance was assigned to a battery of LIMA Company 3rd Battalion, 7th Marines and functioned as part of an artillery unit. Many casualties were incurred in the battle for Hill 65, and Lance was reassigned to LIMA Co. Rifle Company. At the time, President Lyndon Johnson's son-in-law Charles Robb, was commanding officer of LIMA Co. Lance's recollection was that he was a good guy and a good commanding officer.

At a listening post at Hill 65, Lance's unit was taking fire and was unable to return fire due to orders, because it was coming from a village in front of them. A river on the other side prevented movement, and they were receiving incoming mortars. Lance and his comrades were able to get to an area where they could call for incoming elimination rounds, and were able to end this particular situation. After 15 months, Lance returned to Camp Pendleton as an E4 and went to NCO School coming out as a sergeant E5. He spent several months working with a training battalion re-orienting Marines returning from Vietnam. From there, he was sent to 29 Palms as part of the 115th Gun Battery until his separation in July 1970.

Using the GI Bill, Lance attended the University of Utah for three years and joined the Utah National Guard. After doing odd jobs until 1970, he went to work as a police officer in Green River, Wyoming for a year. He would have continued there, but he developed a bond with the Sheriff of Sweetwater County, which housed Green River. The Sheriff's son had been a Marine and was killed in action in Vietnam. Lance went to work for him as a deputy for eight years. From here Lance tired of the cold weather, took a job with the St. George, Utah Police Department and then the Washington County Sheriff's Department. In 1999 he accepted a position with the Mesquite Police Department and retired from there.

In 1988, Lance re-enlisted in the US Navy Reserves. He was activated on three different occasions and spent more than three years on active duty. Although, he was never aboard a ship, Lance's law enforcement experience landed him a position as commander of Navy Guard combat units. This was similar to the MP's of the other branches of service. He was assigned to a Seabee regiment and sent back to Camp Pendleton for additional combat training. He served in Iraq as part of the Navy coastal warfare.

At this time he applied for and was accepted into Officer Candidate School. At age 53, he was the oldest ensign ever to graduate from OCS in the Navy. In addition to Iraq, Lance was in Greece when 9/11 occurred. His unit was held there guarding KC150's, the US Air Force's fueling tankers. He also spent time in Kuwait which was a staging area for the war. He was a commander of the only US Navy convoy that ran supplies into Iraq. During his activation, Lance was called to Pasdodula, Mississippi as Chief of Police to provide security for a destroyer squadron while the USS Cole was in for repairs.

While on active duty, Lance met his wife Susan, also a Navy veteran, in 1992. They were married in 1994, while they were both on active duty. Lance has two daughters and five grand children from a previous marriage. Lance and Susan live in Mesquite and have a number of interests.

Lance thank you for your significant service to your country.

Susan Barr, US Navy

This veteran should sound familiar because you just read about her husband. My wife and I had the pleasure of meeting both Lance and Susan when we enrolled in a gun safety course that they conduct and have remained friends.

Susan was born in Springfield, Mass., November 16, 1954. She attended Cathedral High School and graduated in 1972. Susan enrolled at the University of Mass. as Liberal Arts major and attended for a year and a half. At this point of her life, she worked various jobs in the Springfield area. In 1990, she received a marketing letter from the military.

It was an opportunity to put your civilian experience to use in the military. Susan decided to pursue the opportunity and went to the Air Force Base in Chicopee, MA, where she enlisted in the US Navy reserves. On January 6, 1991 Susan was sworn into the Navy. At 5 PM, that same evening while donating blood, exactly four hours after enlisting, Desert Storm started. Because of her administrative experience in civilian life, Susan came into the Navy Reserves as an E3. She was sent to New Orleans for training. This entire program, including the advanced pay grade was part of a program to bring individuals into the service who had experience that related to military openings.

After school, it was back to the home base Reserve center and a promotion to E4 less than a year from her enlistment date. E4 was also Petty Officer 3rd Class or Yeoman (YN3). Her job in administration included: enlistment evaluation, officer fitness reports and a monthly information bulletin about what was happening, including all drill dates, uniform requirements, etc.

During her career, Susan flew and worked in many parts of the world. She spent time in Hawaii, Rota, Spain, Vahinven, Germany; Sauda Bay, Crete as well as the US Embassy in London. Susan also had assignments in San Diego and Coronado, California.

Three years into her enlistment, Susan was in Hawaii and had the only top secret clearance in fleet training. A message came in for the Commanding Officer of Fleet Training and Susan had to retrieve it. A brief case was hand cuffed to her wrist and two Marines escorted her to a building with no windows. The message was put into the case and again hand cuffed to her wrist, and she was escorted back. She gave the message to the CO and never to this day has any idea what the message was about.

In 1991, Susan met her future husband Lance at Nellis AFB on the pistol range, qualifying with the 9mm. By the way, Susan had an expert rating with the 9mm pistol.

They met again in New Orleans while both were on active duty in 1993. In 1994 they were married in Pearl Harbor, again while on active duty. Susan spent 14 years in the US Navy and would have retired from the service, but two foot operations during her last year in the Navy prevented her from being eligible. A successful career was certainly hers however as she left the Navy as an E6 and was awarded the following. Four Navy Achievement Medals; Three Navy Reserve Meritorious Service Medals; 9mm Pistol Expert; National Defense Medal; Navy Defense Overseas Medal.

Susan works for the Department of Motor Vehicles and raises Malti-poos.

Susan, thank you for your service to your country!

Terry Bolen, US Air Force

Terry is a native of Tennessee who was born in Chattanooga, but moved to Oak Ridge at the age of eight. He attended Oak Ridge HS and was a member of the band where he played the clarinet. He was also a member of the student council. Terry graduated in 1952 and attended the University of Tennessee where he majored in mechanical engineering and was a member of the ROTC program. He graduated in 1957 and received a regular commission from the US Air Force as a distinguished graduate. Most ROTC graduates receive reserve commissions.

While attending college, Terry worked for Union Carbide who promised him a job after his three year commitment. However, Terry was offered an opportunity to become a pilot and decided to take it which required a five year military commitment. Bye, bye Union Carbide! After two years at Eglind AFB in Florida as an armament systems officer, he entered pilot training. Pilot training was in Selma, Alabama, at Craig AFB. When he finished the year of training, Terry stayed at Craig as a flight instructor. In 1961 he was promoted to 1st Lt. During his time as an instructor, Terry spent time in the T33, a tandem single-engine aircraft, and the T38, a supersonic twin engine aircraft.

In 1964 Terry was promoted to captain, and after four years at Craig was sent to Wright Patterson AFB to attend the Air Force Institute of Technology. Here he studied Astronautical Engineering and received his master's degree after two years of intense study. In 1968, Terry was promoted to Major.

In 1970, he received his orders for Vietnam. He wondered why, after all the intense education at AFIT, but soon realized there were reasons as he met up with one of his professors from AFIT who was a PhD. In Vietnam, Terry flew A37's, ground attack fighters equipped with bomb racks and nose guns. The nose gun was a 7.62-mm Gatling gun. His unit was based out of Bien Wau and they supported ground missions.

As a pilot of this aircraft he flew, dropped bombs and fired the nose gun in co-ordination with another aircraft as they worked in teams of two. On one occasion they performed a sky spot, a maneuver used over a concentration of enemy. Sixteen planes, four abreast flew behind one another at slightly different altitudes around 15,000 feet and on command dropped their bombs, all at once. The 7th Air Force controlled all flights in South Vietnam. Special missions were conducted in the north and were controlled out of Laos.

In 1973, Terry was promoted to Lt. Colonel and was sent to Vandenberg AFB where he spent the next four years. Then it was on to Wright Patterson again as program director after another promotion to Colonel. Here Terry headed up a program to target identification systems. They were developing a transponder that would operate with all of the NATO countries' aircraft. Then it was back to Vandenberg and involvement in the space shuttle launching. Many of the satellites put into orbit were used and still are used by businesses and communication companies.

In 1984, Colonel Terry Bolen retired from the US Air Force and accepted a position with Lockheed as cargo director. This involved determining the payload for the orbiter of the shuttle program. As weight increased the payload decreased. It was this area that needed to be examined as payload needed to be as large as possible. Terry retired from Lockheed after 10 years, but remained involved, writing proposals as an individual contractor, primarily for Lockheed. In 2007, he retired except for a little part-time work preparing tax returns.

Terry and his lovely wife Betty were high school sweethearts. They both played the clarinet and were members of the band. They also went to the same church. Betty went to the University of Tennessee, a year behind Terry, but after two years left to go to work as she and Terry had married. To her credit she went back to school and graduated from Chatman College with a degree in psychology. Terry and Betty have been married 55 years and have three children and six grandchildren.

Terry, we thank you for your service to your country.

John Nettle, US Navy

John was born October 10, 1941 in Warren Run, Pennsylvania. He graduated from Warren Harding HS in Bridgeport, Connecticut in 1959 at age 17. He decided to enlist in the US Navy so it was off to the Great Lakes Training Station in Illinois for basic training. From here he was sent to Bainbridge, Maryland for a 28 week course to become a radioman. Upon completion, John was assigned to the Naval Radio Station in Sabana Secor, Puerto Rico. This was a relatively small station where John had contact with vessels traveling in and out of the area. He spent 26 months at the assignment and was then separated from the Navy.

John returned home and did various jobs until he enrolled in and completed a five year apprenticeship with the plumbers and pipefitters union in Bridgeport. He worked out of the union hall, but when things slowed down John went to work for the State of Connecticut as a maintenance supervisor for the Department of Corrections. He later transferred to the Department of Education, went to night school for five years to obtain his Vocational Education Certificate, and worked as an instructor for 12 years.

After being separated from the Navy for 11 plus years, John re-enlisted in the Navy Reserves where he served for 17½ years before retiring from the Navy. He retired in 1991. John left the regular Navy as a Radioman 2nd Class and retired as a Petty Officer 1st Class. He also went back to finish a career as a union plumber/pipefitter and retired in December 1997.

John met his lovely wife Carol on a blind date in Maryland in mid 1963 and it worked out well as they were married in December of 1963. They have three children and four grand children.

John flies when there is space available as a retiree on military aircraft and has been to Germany, Spain and virtually all over the U.S. During a trip to Charleston, South Carolina, he came upon a group working in the USS Laffey VD724, which is a museum ship. John became involved and now travels to Charleston every year to work on this ship and belongs to this group who volunteers their time to keep the Laffey in great shape. The ship is located at Patriot's Point in Charleston near the USS Yorktown. John and the crew live on the Yorktown while they do their work.

John has been a mainstay around the Veterans center. He created the OFG Group, where veterans get together for breakfast once a month just to shoot the bull. It has been very successful. He started the group 12 years ago after he and Carol moved to Mesquite. John and I have been good friends for a long time. Together we created a small-stakes poker game that meets once a week for two hours. It is primarily for veterans who can't get around easily, but enjoy playing cards. Not all of the vets have an issue, but we all have a great time. We take money out of each pot and when we get a $100 (over a few months) we vote on what charity we will give it too. In four years we have taken the guys out for a dinner twice and they love it. Just one example of what John does, always thinking about the veterans.

John, thank you for your service to your country!

Jennifer Edmunds, US Marine Corps

This is a unique interview of a special young lady. Based on what I have seen, we are in pretty good shape if Jennifer is an example of our young veterans.

Jennifer was born in Tampa, Florida, March 9, 1983. She attended and graduated from South Side High School in Muncie, Indiana…as her father's career took them to many different places as she grew up. Jennifer competed in track and cross country in high school. Upon graduation she asked her parents to sit down as she had an announcement to make—she was going to enlist in the US Marine Corps. It was quite a shock to her parents, as she had not mentioned a desire to enter the military, but after the initial shock passed they were supportive of her decision.

It was off to Paris Island, South Carolina for basic training, followed by Marine Combat Training at Cherry Point and Devil Dog, North Carolina. Jennifer was then enrolled in Postal School at Ft. Jackson, South Carolina, which was followed by an assignment to Camp Pendleton as a postal clerk. Jennifer spent the rest of her initial enlistment at this assignment until her separation from active duty in 2005. She went to Arkansas and back to Indiana for a short time before enrolling in a program with the Marine Corps. This was a program where you enrolled without knowing your MOS until you got there and there was Iraq. She was sent to 29 Palms for training and then to Falujah as a detainee handler. Her duties included verifying personnel at the front gate and watching internal movement at the prison. They were considered provisional MP's.

On two different occasions her unit was engaged in combat as incoming mortar fire hit inside the detention facility. Jennifer was one of only five women attached to this unit. The fact that Jennifer qualified as an Expert with her rifle, was probably a very good skill to possess in a combat zone. After seven months in Falujah, Jennifer returned to the United States and was honorably discharged from the Marine Corps. She joined the active reserves and finished her career with seven years of service.

Jennifer began studying on-line for her degree and received an Associate Degree in 2008, a BA in Accounting and Finance and her Master's Degree in 2012. During her Marine career she met her parents in Las Vegas and her parents liked Nevada. On a drive through Mesquite they decided that this was a place they might like to retire to. They have! Jennifer and her parents are now Mesquite residents.

Jennifer was active with the Veteran's Center Any Soldier Project, where boxes of goodies are sent to the troops overseas at Christmas. Jennifer helped and was able to ship some boxes to her old unit in Falujah.

Our Veterans center has a wonderful collection of military collectables and Jennifer contributed by donating her Marine Corps uniform including the expert rifle medal.

Jennifer, thank you for your service to your country!

4

SOME UNIQUE STORIES

Jim Lynch, US Air Force

Although every veteran I have interviewed is special, this one is unique. Jim Lynch was one of four brothers who served admirably in the air force. Obviously, a family had to have four boys to have this unique situation take place, but I think it is a tribute to their upbringing and their love of country that contributed significantly to all of them serving their country, particularly in the same branch of service. I will expound upon this later, but first I want to discuss Jim.

> He was born September 9, 1942 in Waucoma, Iowa and attended Waucoma High School. Jim participated in baseball and basketball during high school and graduated in 1960. His class of 13 students was the last graduating class prior to a consolidation of schools in the area. Jim enlisted in the Air Force upon graduation and was off to Lackland AFB in San Antonio, Texas for basic training. After five weeks, he was sent to Biloxi, Mississippi for phase two of his training. Kessler AFB was where Jim was trained as an ACW (aircraft control warning) Radar Technician.

This training took one year to complete. And Jim finished training as an E3. The radar techs repaired heavy ground radar, as well as long range search and height finders.

From here Jim was sent to a radar site at Ft. Fisher in North Carolina at the tip of the Cape Fear Peninsula on the Atlantic Ocean. While stationed here, there were very tense situations existing because of the Cuban missile crisis. U2 spy planes continually watched troop movements from 95 to 100,000 feet. The men who manned the radars were instructed to say that they did not see the U2 spy planes. There were 100 to 200 men who manned this radar site and generally they were not issued weapons, but they were in this crisis with about 50,000 Russian troops on the ground in Cuba, and enough missiles to wipe out the eastern half of the United States. This information came from the U2 aircraft. They were starting to assemble missiles when the U.S.A. finally called their bluff, and the tense situation settled down.

The Navy was in the process of setting up a blockade when the situation finally cooled down. Jim was promoted to E4 while in North Carolina and after 1½ years there he transferred to a Waverly, Iowa site and worked there for 2½ years. After three years in the Air Force, Jim re-enlisted for four years. He was promoted to Staff Sgt. E5. It was then that he was sent to Vietnam as part of the 619th Tactical Control Squadron. Their HQ was in Saigon and this is where they processed in, but as a technician he was responsible for covering seven different radar sites. Vietnam was divided into four Corps 2, 3 and 4. The 620th had responsibility for Corps 1. He traveled in and out of sites, including the height finders in Saigon. The sites outside of Saigon only had radar (scopes) not height finders. 60 and 400 cycle truck mounted generators powered all of the sites as they shared power with the Hawk Missile Sites. There were only 15 or so men at each radar site, and of course in Vietnam they were armed. Jim spent one year in Vietnam. From here he was sent to a radar site in Omaha, Nebraska, where he spent his last remaining eight months in the Air Force.

Jim went to work for the Federal Aviation Administration after being discharged, repairing long range radar systems. He spent most of his 31 years in Des Moines, Iowa. In 1998 Jim retired from the FAA.

Jim met his lovely wife Marty in 1979 and they were married in 1981. In 2003 they moved to Mesquite, where they currently live. They have two sons and a daughter, and six grand children. One of their sons recently retired from the US Army as a Sgt. Major after 29 years of service.

As I mentioned in the beginning, Jim has three brothers who also served in the Air Force. Ray served four years; Don served four years and Dave served five years. Ray was a computer technician in the Air Force and also retired from the FAA. Ray was a Crypto tech (decoder) who retired from the FAA and Dave was a mechanic, and pursued this trade in civilian life. Jim also has a sister who attended the University of Iowa for four years. I can't imagine how proud the parents of these individuals must be.

Jim received the Air Force Accommodation Medal. Jim is very active around the Veterans Center and we have become good friends. I have even had the pleasure of meeting his brother Don on two different occasions when he has come to Mesquite to visit Jim. Like Jim he is a great guy. Jim is a member of The Vietnam Veterans of America and was recently voted in as vice president of the Veterans Center.

Jim, Don, Dave and Ray thank you for your service to your country.

Gerry Toso US Army

Gerry was born January 8, 1948 in Wahpeton, North Dakota. Because Gerry's dad moved around frequently in his job with Western Union, Gerry attended several different elementary schools. He eventually attended Osseo HS near Minneapolis, Minnesota and graduated in

1966. Gerry participated in track and cross country while attending high school.

In November 1966, Gerry enlisted in the US Army and was off to Ft. Leonard Wood, Missouri, for Basic Training, and from there it was AIT, Combat Engineers. During a battery of tests, Gerry had scored well and was told he qualified for officer's candidate school (OCS) if he was interested. He decided he was and it was off to Ft. Belvar, Virginia for six months of rigorous training.

Upon receiving his 2nd Lt. Commission, Gerry was sent back to Ft. Leonard Wood headquarters company, and put in charge of the crane and shovel training course. I found this interesting because in 1967 I went through the crane and shovel course as my AIT assignment at Ft. Leonard Wood. However, I digress! Gerry carried on this assignment for eight months. From here he was assigned temporary duty as a survivor assistant in the northwest corner of Iowa. He operated out of a rented room. He had to notify next of kin when someone lost their life. It was his responsibility to make arrangements, get paperwork filled out, etc. Not a very pleasant task for anyone, much less a 19 year old officer.

I guess this is the price you pay when you are the youngest individual to successfully complete OCS in the US Army. Gerry had received a total of two hours of training for this assignment which lasted four months.

From this temporary duty it was off to Vietnam's Central Highlands. Here Gerry was an S5 (civil affairs) officer assigned to the 4th Infantry Battalion. In this capacity he worked with the Montagard (primitive tribal mountain people). The US military helped the tribes set up defenses, supply villages with medical needs and other support issues. Because the South Vietnamese did not get along with these people, there were many occasions where the military would train the Montagard on how to set up and develop a defense since the South Vietnamese would not supply them with arms.

There were a total of 33 different mountain tribes. The US helped them develop a system of transferring goods using pack animals, but many units would take them to the small towns in trucks. The tribes lived mainly off rice and chickens. They occasionally killed larger game, but it was only eaten for feasts and special rituals. While on this assignment, Gerry was promoted to 1st Lt., but his tour of duty was cut short due to a non-combat shoulder injury that required surgery. It couldn't be performed in Vietnam so after five months it was back to the states and good old Ft. Leonard Wood, but only for a month. Gerry was assigned to Camp McCoy in Wisconsin to evaluate National Guard and Army Reserve units. From here Gerry accepted his discharge at age 20. As a 1st Lt., Gerry gave quite a bit of thought to re-enlisting, but after much consideration decided to enroll at the University of Minnesota.

After attending college Gerry spent a couple of years doing different jobs but then received an opportunity in the trucking business. This organization was primarily responsible for transporting automobiles from assembly plants throughout the country. Gerry spent the next 36 years in this business as loss prevention manager and terminal manager at many different locations that included Minneapolis, Detroit, Newark, Long Beach and Wisconsin.

Going to college and entering the civilian working world turned out to be a good decision for Gerry. Gerry is divorced and has one son and three grand children.

Gerry, thank you for your service to your country!

What makes this interview interesting is when I served, I was with the 429th Engineer Battalion and went to Fort Leonard Wood for basic training and AIT. You guessed it, crane and shovel school. Lt. Gerry Toso was in charge of the school when I went through, but I do not recall meeting him. Maybe that was a good thing, meaning that I wasn't in trouble.

Glen and Arloa Deppey, US Army and National Guard

This story is about Glen and Arloa Deppey, a husband and wife who both served honorably in the US Army and National Guard. Glen was born May 29, 1937 in Wapello, Iowa. In 1948 he moved with his family to Phoenix where he graduated from Phoenix Technical High School in 1955. He obtained 55 college credits through various universities located near or at his military assignments.

Glen enlisted in the National Guard November 21, 1955, and after boot camp served with the Arizona's 3666th Ordnance Co. as private E1 for six years.

In February 1956 he was employed by the Arizona ARNG as a wheel and track mechanic. It didn't take Glen long to realize the national Guard was where he belonged, so after becoming a sergeant in 1959 he attended a nine week National Guard OCS Course at Ft. Benning, Georgia. In January 1960 he was commissioned and became a weapons platoon leader in the 258th Infantry Brigade.

In January 1960 Glen attended fixed wing flight training at Ft. Rucker, Alabama and then the rotary wing qualification course at Ft. Wolters, Texas. After 13 months of active duty for schooling, he returned to the Arizona National Guard in July 1961.

Glen attended the infantry officer basic course in Ft. Benning graduating in March 1962 and then ranger training that May. He returned to Phoenix from May 1962 to March 1964 where he completed several infantry platoon leader assignments in addition to aviation unit assignments. During the same period he was employed as a civilian helicopter pilot.

He entered active duty in March 1964 and assigned to the 11th Air Assault Division at Ft. Benning as a section commander in B Company 229th Assault Helicopter Battalion. In July 1964 went to UH1 instructor pilot training at Ft. Rucker and in August was selected as a member of the 62nd Aviation Company that was deployed to Vietnam in September.

During his first Vietnam tour he served variously as assistant operations officer, intelligence officer, section commander, safety officer, instructor pilot and gunship pilot.

He returned to Ft. Hood for 16 months during which he worked as assistant aviation officer, flight branch chief, airfield commander and safety officer in III Corps G-3.

He returned to Vietnam in January 1967, but first had a temporary assignment (TDY) at the University of Southern California for an aviation safety course and then to Ft. Rucker for CH-47 qualification. He actually arrived in Vietnam in July 1967 where he served with the 228th Aviation Battalion 1st Air Cavalry Division.

The first half of his tour was as HHC commander during the division relocation. He participated in the Tet Offensive.

In July 1968 Glen served at Ft. Sill, Oklahoma with the aviation command as airfield officer and later as S-3 on a newly formed provisional aviation battalion.

Glen joined the presidential support helicopter detachment at Homestead Air Force Base in Florida in November 1969 where he served as aviation safety officer. The detachment was scheduled to relocate to Ft. Belvoir, Virginia in August 1970 but Glen requested and received release from extended active duty.

He returned to the Arizona ARNG he was assigned as operations officer of the 997th Aviation Co. (air ambulance) and participated in its reorganization to an assault helicopter company.

Glen was one of four people selected in 1971 for a 42 day National Guard tour to prepare and teach two-day recruiter training schools at five locations for 11 states. That same year he went back to work for the Arizona ARNG as a flight instructor.

In 1972 he was assigned the drill position of state aviation safety officer after completing the advanced infantry officer course. After being asked by the Nevada National Guard he moved to Nevada in November 1975 where he served as state aviation officer and Army support facility commander where he served for many years. Glen retired after 28 years as a colonel.

Glen and Arloa were married in Phoenix, December 2, 1955 and have shared many years together as members of the National Guard and Reserves. Arloa served for seven years in the military.

Their daughter, Ina-Lee served two years in the National Guard and attended Midland Technical College where she became a licensed practical nurse. Her husband served six years in the regular Army.

They also have a daughter in Lake Tahoe and a son in Reno.

To the Deppey family, thank you for your service to your country!

Thomas Murphy, Eighth US Cavalry, Troop F

A few months ago, an Air Force veteran by the name of Michael Torgerson stopped by the Veterans Center and spoke with Jim Brown, our Veterans Service Officer (VSO). Torgerson was looking for help in obtaining documents and the replacement of the Congressional Medal of Honor earned by his great grandfather Thomas Murphy. Through the efforts of Brown and Torgerson this intriguing story developed. Cpl. Thomas Murphy was a member of the 8th U.S. Cavalry, Troop F and was awarded the Congressional Medal of Honor for his actions under fire at Seneca Mountain, Arizona, August 25, 1869.

Cpl. Murphy and several others were mentioned in a hand written letter that contained the names of the men who deserved credit and merit for their gallantry in several fights with the Indians.

The recommendation for the men to receive medals was signed by 1st Lt. Robert Caucik. It is hard to imagine with most of us thinking about WWI, WWII, Korea, Vietnam Desert Storm, Iraq and Afghanistan that our military engaged in war with Native Americans who were defending their homeland. The Indian Wars lasted from 1832 to 1898. During that time a total of 91 men received the Congressional Medal of Honor. Cpl. Murphy was engaged in battle with the Indians at Seneca Mountain, Arizona, where many other significant encounters took place.

On March 15, 1869, Lt. Colonel Custer captured four chiefs at Medicine Arrows and Little Robe, Cheyenne villages in the Oklahoma Panhandle. Custer demanded the release of two white women or he said he would hang three of the four chiefs. The Sioux later released the women and the Indians subsequently surrendered.

May 16, 1869, Indians attacked a scouting party led by Lt. John B. Babcock, 5th US Cavalry at Spring Creek, Nebraska. June 4, 1869 the Army and Indians engaged in battle at Picacho Mountain, Arizona. On July 3, 1869, the cavalry engaged the Indians at Hell Canyon, Arizona for which Sgt. Sanford Bradbury was awarded the Medal of Honor for bravery. Another soldier, Paul Haupt of the 8th Cavalry was also awarded the Medal of Honor.

On July 8th, 1869 a detachment of three men led by Cpl. John Kyle, Company M, 5th US Cavalry, skirmished with an Indian force of eight men in the vicinity of Republican River. Kansas Sgt. Co-Rux-Te-Ish (Mad Bear) is accidently wounded by his own command after he breaks ranks in an attempt to capture an enemy Indian. Mad Bear also received the Medal of Honor for his heroism during this battle.

July 11. 1869, the US 5th Cavalry along with Indian scouts under the command of Major Eugene Carr engages the "Dog Soldier" Cheyennes at Summit Springs, Colorado. On August 25, 1869, the US 8th Cavalry battled

Indians at Seneca Mountain, Arizona. Thomas Murphy was awarded the Medal of Honor. On Sept. 23, 1869 the US Cavalry clashed with an Indian force at Red Creek, Arizona.

On October 14, 1869, Pvt. David Goodman of the 8th Cavalry was awarded the Medal of Honor for bravery in action against the Indians at Lyry Creek, Arizona. On April 15, 1869, Brig. General George Stoneman assumed command of the Arizona Territory.

This is only a snapshot of what went on during the Indian Wars in 1869 when Thomas Murphy earned the Medal of Honor. I had the opportunity to read the synopsis of the entire Indian Wars and it is amazing what took place. It is well worth one's time to read up on the time.

At the end of the Civil War the ranks of the regular cavalry regiments were thin, as were other regular regiments. Of the authorized 448 companies of cavalry, infantry and artillery, 153 were not organized and few if any were at full strength. By July 1866 this shortage had eased since many of the members of the disbanded volunteer outfits had enlisted as regulars. By that time however, it became apparent in Washington that the Army even at full strength was not large enough to perform all its duties.

Consequently, on July 28, 1866, Congress authorized four additional cavalry regiments and enough infantry companies to reorganize the existing—then under two different internal organizations—into 45 regiments with 10 companies each. After this increase there were 10 regiments of cavalry, five of artillery and 45 of infantry.

Today the 8th Cavalry is made up of:

The 1st Battalion, organized as a Combined Arms Battalion, is assigned to the 1st Brigade of the 1st Cavalry Division stationed at Ft. Hood, Texas.

The 2nd Battalion, organized as a Combined Arms Battalion, is assigned to the 1st Brigade of the 1st Cavalry Division stationed at Ft. Hood, Texas.

The 3rd Battalion organized as a Combined Arms Battalion, is assigned to the 3rd Brigade of the 1st Cavalry Division stationed at Ft. Hood, Texas.

The 6th Squadron, organized as an Armed Reconnaissance Squadron, is assigned to the 4th Brigade, 3rd Infantry Division, station at Ft, Stewart, Georgia.

Cpl. Thomas Murphy through his great grandson Michael Torgerson, is the most historic veteran with a direct association to the Mesquite Veterans Center. Torgerson and our VSO Jim Brown were able to confirm Cpl. Murphy's military record and achievements. A special thank you to these gentlemen!

Thank you, Michael Torgerson and your great grandfather, Thomas Murphy, for your service to your country.

Ed Jaworski and Leo McGinty, US Air Force

You will read more about these two veterans later in the book, but this is a unique story about the two of them that is stranger than fiction. You always hear of unusual stories but never expect to experience one. Two of our Mesquite veterans experienced one of the strangest.

Ed and Leo, both Air Force veterans during the Cold War, had an occasion to become closer friends than they already were. They were casual acquaintances via the Mesquite Veterans Center. Both had served in the Air Force about the same time. Ed was a radar technician while Leo was a communications technician. They had occasionally discussed their experiences in the service. Leo is an active participant at the center, while Ed spends a great deal of time traveling the country visiting with veterans that he served with at radar sites where he was stationed.

Several months ago, Ed posted an e-mail to a group he belongs to (USAF Radar Site Veterans) to see if any of them knew Leo. This group has more than 5,000 members from all over the world. While online he received an e-mail from an individual named Ron who was looking for a guy named Leo.

Ron's from Bullhead City, Arizona and published his phone number. Ed gave him a call. Sure enough Ron was looking for a Leo McGinty and Ed assured him he knew an individual by that name. He told Ron he would try and get in touch with Leo and pass on his phone number so they could make contact. Ed called me and I supplied him with Leo's number.

Ed called Leo and explained what had transpired. He said Ron was from Bullhead City and that perked Leo up because he had lived there previously for about 10 years. Eventually Leo called Ron. Before the call went very long however, Ron asked if he could ask Leo some questions. "Of course," Leo Said. What is your service number and what religion are you? What is your blood type? Just as Leo was about to say, "Okay enough of this," Ron said, "I have your dog tags." "What?" said Leo. I haven't seen them for a long time and have no idea what happened to them.

Ron said he and his wife and another couple frequented garage sales in the Bullhead City area and came upon one where a gentleman had a set of dog tags he was selling for $1. Interested in military items, Ron purchased them and then started a crusade to find the owner. He originally posted the name "Leo" on the internet along with U.S. Air Force, but the list was way too long to provide any assistance. However, because Ed Jaworski had supplied an e-mail to the members of the organization he belongs to, his e-mail appeared and the chain began.

Leo lived in Bullhead City from 1994 to 2004, just before coming to Mesquite. He doesn't remember where or how he lost his dog tags but obviously it was in Bullhead City.

Ron eventually returned the tags to Leo and the men have periodic conversations and plan to get together and meet face to face. Leo is currently searching for just the right chain to wear with those tags, so they don't turn up missing again. There were also some pictures that have a reference to Leo, but that's another story for another day. Thanks to Ed and Leo for bringing this to my attention. What a great story!

Dennis (Archie) Widener, US Army

Archie was born in Pendleton, Oregon where he attended Athena HS. He participated in baseball, basketball and football and graduated in 1962. After graduation Archie worked on some local farms before going to work for Phillips Petroleum in Idaho Falls, Idaho, at their Atomic Energy Site outside of Arco. After starting out in the employee kitchen Archie moved on to maintenance, where he was involved with a crew responsible for removing radioactive material from rail cars and truck beds. There were material test reactors above and below ground. The ones below ground were 20 feet under water, and gave off a spectacular blue color. The Russians came to visit but were not permitted to observe the control panels for the reactors. They were covered with plywood during the visit. Archie worked here for a year and a half and then returned to Oregon and attended Blue Mountain Community College. While back home he enlisted in the Oregon National Guard. He stayed with his grandfather and worked at several different service stations while going to school.

He was sent to Ft. Polk for basic training and AIT. Prior to AIT he spent two weeks at PLDT (training for squad leaders) as he had been charged with being a squad leader in AIT. He was trained as an 81 MM mortar gunner. Archie continued to work at the service stations and other jobs for the next three years.

In 1969 his unit went to Boise, Idaho for summer camp, and he and a buddy decided they liked Boise and moved there. While there, he saw a recruitment sign for Warrant Officers School to become helicopter pilots for the US Army. Archie decided to inquire. He took the test, did very well and was accepted into the program. However, he was still in the National Guard but the Army told him they would contact his unit and tell them of his acceptance into the Warrant Officers Program. They gave him a date to report, so he had time to go back to Oregon and spend some time with his mother before going to the helicopter program. While at home he received a registered letter, which read, "Since you have neglected to attend scheduled drills, you have been ordered to report to Ft. Lewis, Washington, to serve 16 months and 5 days to fulfill your commitment. In addition your rank of E5 has been reduced to E2." Shocked by this, Archie contacted his unit, the Warrant Officers School and the Presidio where all orders originated all to no avail.

He had to report to Ft. Lewis. The Army had screwed up.

Archie was assigned to a replacement company and re-issued his gear. He was sent to Germany, assigned to B Co., 3rd Battalion, 35th Armor, 4th Armor Division. As he sat with his new 1st. Sgt., he was asked what his plans were based on all that he had been through. His response; "I want to be a career soldier." Archie completed tank communications school, and was made an E4 and acting E5 in Vilseck, Germany.

In November of 1970 he went before the E5 board, made E5 and re-enlisted for four more years.

Archie met a friend in Germany, whose wife was back in Birmingham, Alabama. She had a friend. Archie's friend, Kelly encouraged him to write to her, which he did. As a matter of fact, he took thirty days leave and went to Alabama to meet her. In 1971 he and Shirley were married. In 1972 they had a son and in 1974 a daughter.

Archie was assigned to Bamberg, Germany and spent two years there. In 1973 he was sent to Ft. Hood, Texas and assigned to the 1st Battalion, 81st Armor, 1st Cavalry

Division where he became the training NCO. At Ft. Hood, Archie was twice selected as the Brigade soldier of the quarter and promoted to E6. He was sent to Ft. Knox, Ky. for BNCOC training for eight weeks. He was given the physical training award. He returned to Ft. Hood and was assigned to Range central.

Archie re-enlisted for six more years. His commitment to becoming a career soldier was becoming a reality. Again he was sent off to training for ANCOC School.

In 1975, Archie was sent to Aschaffenberg, Germany and assigned to Alpha Co., 4th Battalion, 64th Armor, 3rd Infantry. He spent 39 months with this unit. While there he was selected to go to M60A3 Master Gunner Course. Guess where? Yep, Ft. Knox. He completed the course with flying colors and then went back to Germany. After completing this assignment he was shipped to Ft. Polk as a Senior Instructor for 19 Echo BNCOC, 5th Infantry. While there, Archie was the NCOIC (non commissioned officer in charge) of the NCO Academy. In addition, he was given responsibility of the 5th Infantry Color Guard. During this assignment Archie was awarded the Meritorious Service Award.

In 1981, it was back to Germany again, this time with A Co., 4th Battalion, 64 Armor, 8th Infantry Division. He spent two years as a platoon sergeant. When the 1st Sgt. left the unit, Archie was made the acting 1st sergeant. In 1983 he took the course and after completion was promoted to E8.

He left Germany in 1984 and went back to Ft. Polk as the 5th Infantry Division 1st sergeant. He spent two more years here, and was promoted to Master Sergeant. Then to Ft. Knox as a Team leader with armor branch NCOIC. This was part of the Readiness Group Knox under the 2nd Army headquartered in Atlanta, Georgia. They were part of the Supply Army Infantry that was responsible for all of the National Guard troops in the state of Kentucky. Archie spent two years in this role.

In 1988, the regimental officer of Bad Kissinger, Germany, 2nd Squadron 11th Army Cavalry Regiment S3

Operations, requested Archie, and he didn't know why. They knew who Archie was and the job he had done. Archie was a Sergeant Major in Fulda, Germany in RS3 Operations.

In 1990 Archie went to Ft. Benning, Ga. HHC 3rd Brigade, 24th Infantry Division where he operated as sergeant major. In 1991 he was sent to Saudi Arabia (100 day war) as a Sergeant Major and then returned in March of 1991.

August 1, 1991, Dennis (Archie) Widener retired from the US Army, fulfilling what he said he was going to do that first day he was assigned to Germany from a replacement unit out of Ft. Lewis Washington. Who would have guessed that a young man would complete the career he said he wanted? Not only did he complete it, but he also retired as a sergeant major. This is no small accomplishment—26 years (21 active and 5 reserves).

A Special Note:

An individual searched for Archie on Google. During this search, retired General Anthony M. Taguba's name also appeared. The General said that there were two men that were extremely important in his advancement and his career.

One of those men was Dennis Widener. You see Archie knew him and worked for him, long before he became a two star general and retired. General Taguba was Archie's company commander. Archie thought very highly of the General as well.

After retiring from the Army, Archie went to driver's school through JB Hunt and eventually became an owner operator. After retiring from driving, Archie settled in Mesquite, where he lives full time. Archie is active at the Mesquite veterans Center, Sergeant-at-Arms of the American Legion among other activities. He enjoys, golf, bowling and softball.

Archie and I became friends initially via the American Legion. He is a great guy and never speaks about his significant accomplishments in the Army. A practical jokester, you have to be heads up when Archie is around!

Archie thank you for your service to your country!

Patrick Anderson, US Navy, US Marine Corps, and US Army

Talk about unique stories, Patrick Anderson honorably served in three of the armed services during his military career. Born in Burlingame, California, March 13, 1956 Patrick moved relatively early in life to Westminster, Colorado. He attended Westminster High School where he played football and was a member of the Air Force ROTC program.

With a grandfather who was a Navy commander in both WWI and WWII and a father who served in WWII as a member of the US Coast Guard, Patrick decided to join the US Navy at 17. It was off to San Diego for basic training and radioman schools A and C which took 10 months. Patrick remained in San Diego and decided the Navy was not what he expected, so he accepted his discharge after two years.

Patrick worked in the automobile industry for a while and then decided to join the Marine Corps Reserves on December 31, 1980. He was attached to Alpha Battery, 14 Battalion, 4th Marine Division in Spokane, Washington. He became an infantryman and Cannoneer operating a 105 howitzer. His second weapon was the .50 caliber machine gun. After three years, Patrick got out of the Corps and joined the Army Reserves.

He was part of the 385th Combat Support Hospital Unit in Spokane. He was assigned as a medic because of previous training as an EMT in civilian life. He accepted a grade reduction in rank to PFC. He then went to Ft. Sam

Houston for additional training as a surgical technician. This training lasted seven months. His sergeant major told Patrick of an opening for a company clerk in Walla Walla, Wash., as part of AGR (active guard reserves). He wanted Patrick to accept this position, which he did. Again, off to another school, this time at Ft. Benjamin Harrison in Indiana for three months. He served on active duty in this capacity for the next three years. He switched to a Civil Service Unit as an administrator, where he worked for the Army as a civilian. Then it was back to being a surgical tech because that unit was being activated and Patrick wanted to go with them. There was a rule, however, that prevented civil service workers from volunteering for active duty. Patrick said he would quit his civil service job so he could volunteer. The rule was changed however, and Patrick was off with the 45th Station Hospital Unit and deployed to Heidelberg, Germany as part of the 130th Station Hospital. He spent the next five months there.

Then it was back to work at his civil service job. But things changed quickly as he was selected for the 6th Army National Victory Parade in Washington, DC. There were many dignitaries present, including George H. Bush, Dick Cheney, Colin Powell, General Schwartzkopf. Patrick became a member of the 6th Army Rifle Team where he fired the M16. His team retired the traveling trophy twice. In 1993, his unit was shut down and Patrick transferred to the 104th training division where he became the Operations NCO. He was now a Staff Sgt. Two years later the unit was deactivated and Patrick took a transfer back to Walla Walla where he joined the Washington National Guard in 1995. He became a tank repairman which required only on- the-job training. In 1997, he became part of the 396th Combat Support Hospital Unit after leaving the Guard and volunteered for active duty.

Only 69 out of more than 400 members were granted active status and Patrick was one of them. They were off to Bosnia. He was stationed in Tuzla as senior personnel

NCO. He also worked in the operating room when time permitted. These volunteers spent one year in Bosnia. After returning home he stayed with the 396th and ran a pre-administration clinic at St. Mary's Medical Center, a civilian job.

In 1998, it was back on active duty in Salt Lake City with the 96th Support Command. Patrick managed the data base that allowed recruiters to put recruits into the Reserves. He was now an E7, Sgt. 1st Class. Patrick did this assignment until May 2003. At that time he was transferred to Army HQ in Atlanta, Georgia, as data base managers were reduced from 44 to 6 and the six were transferred to Atlanta. All six were hand-picked based on their performance. Patrick spent the next three years there.

In November, 2004 he was shipped out to Iraq and based in Kuwait. He was assigned to the 3rd Army and was the Army Reserve Affairs NCO. This assignment included trouble shooting for the area. He conducted town hall meetings, gave advice and was involved in insurance issues for members of the military and their families. He spent much of his time flying around Iraq and Kuwait observing the situation. One year later, he returned to Salt Lake City. Here Patrick was given the task of starting a new unit, a medical training brigade, where he is currently the senior human resources NCO. Patrick retired in October of 2012 with a grand total of over 37 years service, twenty two years, 4 months of active duty and 15 years of reserve duty.

Patrick is a life member of the VFW, a member of the Elks, K of C and NRA. He is also an active participant around the Mesquite Veterans Center. He and his lovely wife Jill live in Mesquite.

Patrick thank you for your service to your country!

Patrick is another great individual who has become a good friend. It is difficult not to become friends with these veterans and their spouses when they are active and are terrific people.

Jon Amundson, US Army

Jon was born June 25, 1946 in Barnesville, Minnesota and lived with his grandparents in Rothsay. Rothsay had a population of about 150 residents. In 1949 Jon moved to Southern California with his mom. She had been doing defense work there and then went to work as a roller skating car hop, earning more money than she did working in her defense job.

While on this job she met and worked with several "Roller derby Queens" who were on the roller circuit.

In 1960 Jon moved to Las Vegas and attended Western High School and then Las Vegas High School, prior to enlisting in the U.S. Army as soon as he turned 18.

It was off to Ft. Polk, Louisiana for basic training and AIT. Jon was then sent to Schofield Barracks in Hawaii where he attended language school. He was then assigned to the 25th Infantry, 2nd Battalion as a rifleman. Language school was taught at the facility in Hawaii by instructors from the Presidio and he was chosen for this school based on his performance on a battery of tests given when he arrived in Hawaii.

In December 1965, Jon and his unit left Hickam Air Base for Vietnam. They were stationed in the north near Pleiku, for a 13 month tour. They were deployed in the bush as well as many other places, but were constantly in the field. The field deployment lasted for six months at a time.

Because of his language skills, Amundson did interrogation of prisoners in the area. He was one of only three Americans who could speak Vietnamese and had clearance to do so. There were also South Vietnamese attached to the unit who could question prisoners, but there was always some doubt to their trustworthiness.

During card games with some Vietnamese participants it was discovered that they had a fear of the ace of spades. It was while laying a card game called cat te' that this came to light. Jon was part of the group playing cards and discovered this phenomenon. At the time they were part of the 35th Infantry, 2nd battalion, 3rd platoon—their platoon became the "Ace of Spades Platoon."

Jon went back to the states in January 1967 to an assignment at ft. Leavenworth as part of the honor guard. They served at funerals for those killed in action. He did this for the next six months. In the summer of 1967 he received his discharge, bought a car and drove to Las Vegas to pick up his sister and then went on to San Francisco.

He attended the City College of San Francisco for awhile and then moved to Northern California where he enrolled at Shasta Community College and earned an associate's degree in communications. From here it was on to California State at Chico, where Jon completed the work for a bachelor's in psychology and social science.

From the time of his discharge he became involved in supporting programs for veterans and worked diligently as a volunteer in many organizations. He moved north to Portland, Oregon, and became involved in research work with post-traumatic stress disorder (PTSD) while working as a pressman apprentice for a printing company.

Realizing this was not what he wanted to do with his life he moved on, this time to North Carolina, where he went to work for a management search firm and did very well. He accumulated some money and went back to school and obtained two masters degrees; one in communications and the other in counseling.

Amundson worked in school systems, hospitals and for the Veterans Administration, before deciding to open his own counseling practice. He obtained his license and was on his way. He concentrated on PTSD, adolescence counseling and trauma counseling. He was also a screening agent for the police department.

The only thing he would not do was work with Vietnam veterans with PTSD, because it brought back his own difficulties. Jon developed a program called guided imagery that was very successful. He dealt with cognizant behavioral therapy, stress reduction and addiction.

One of the best things that ever happened to Amundson, according to him, was meeting his wife Dawn. They met after he moved to North Carolina and were married in 1990. Dawn has three masters degrees; library science, counseling and English Literature.

Jon retired in 2008 and he and Dawn came through Mesquite on a motorcycle trip and loved it here. They bought a home in Sun City in 2013. Dawn still teaches in North Carolina as she has less than two years to retirement, but spends as much time as possible in Mesquite.

Jon, we thank you for your service to your country!

Jon is a member of our group that gets together on Friday and plays cards. He has brought a new face and new laughs to the gang! He also has been given the nickname of Patches. You see, Jon wore his Vietnam veteran's vest to play cards one day, and his vest was loaded with patches from everywhere. It also had a wide range of patches. One of the guys said, "Hey, Patches, it's your deal." It has stuck ever since! Jon is a great guy and has become a good friend.

Cliff Holliday, US Army

Cliff was born April 12, 1928 and raised in Minneapolis, Minnesota where he graduated from Franklin Junior HS. He left school a few years later to go to work as a delivery truck driver for Wolk Transfer Company, in Minneapolis.

He just missed the draft near the end of WWII, but the government remembered good ol' Cliff and he was drafted at age 22 for the Korean War. On November 25, 1950, Cliff left for basic training at Ft. Riley, Kansas. After boot camp he stayed at Ft. Riley another eight weeks for heavy weapons training. Then he went directly to Korea with the 25th Infantry Division, 1st Battalion, 35th Regiment, Company C.

Cliff said his unit saw almost constant combat as part of the CCP spring offensive, the summer/fall offensive and the second Korean winter of the war. War is terrible and young soldiers quickly learn to just do their jobs and react the best way they can to situations as they arise. Cliff Holliday did more than that!

As his unit advanced up a hill the soldier next to Cliff was shot and went down. Cliff picked him up and continued up and over the hill coming to safety on the other side. "You just have to react and keep going," Cliff said.

Cliff was awarded the Bronze Star for this valiant effort. Anyone would be proud and honored to receive even one Bronze Star. Cliff, however, later was awarded two more during his tour of duty in Korea. He said he honestly can't recall the specifics of his actions that merited the other two medals since it was so long ago. The modest Cliff said he was, "Just a soldier doing his job."

Nonetheless, it's easy to imagine the young Cliff Holliday as a man who was very aware of everything happening around him and doing his level-headed best to complete his mission. There is no doubt members of the 25th Infantry were glad Cliff was part of their team.

In addition to three Bronze Stars, Cliff was awarded the Korean Service Medal, National Defense Service Medal, and Good Conduct Medal.

"Like WWII veterans, we just did our job and moved on with the rest of our lives," Cliff said.

Before he was discharged from active duty, Cliff was offered a field promotion to 2nd Lt. if he would re-enlist. "With all due respect sir," Cliff said, "you can put that where the sun don't shine. I'm going home." The officer smiled and responded, "That's what I thought you'd say."

Cliff was discharged August 28, 1952. He spent the next five years in the inactive reserves. Back in Minneapolis, Cliff resumed truck driving but not without a small battle.

After being out of the Army for just two weeks he sought work with his former employer. The boss told Cliff he wasn't hiring. After several attempts to explain he just got out of the service brought no results, Cliff visited the Teamsters Union Hall and explained the situation. One call and 15 minutes later, Cliff had his job back.

After a few years Cliff took advantage of an opportunity with the Minneapolis Park Board. A job he held for 12 years. Cliff's son had an ear problem the doctor said would lead to deafness if he didn't get out of the cold weather, so Cliff moved to Fallbrook, California, near Camp Pendleton where he began a new career as a heavy equipment operator.

Cliff met a lovely lady named Ellie in California via square dancing. Cliff had gone through a divorce and this lovely lady had lost two husbands. Their mutual love of square dancing eventually led to the altar and Cliff and Ellie have been married for 27 years. Cliff has two sons and a daughter and Ellie has a son and a daughter.

After 23 years in California Cliff and Ellie retired to Mesquite where they are active in several organizations including the Elks Club where they volunteer often. Cliff is a lifetime member.

He is also a lifetime member of the VFW; the Mesquite American Legion Post 24; and a former member of the Virgin Valley Honor Guard. Ellie was a member of the American Legion Ladies Auxiliary for 46 years.

Cliff thank you for your service to your country!

Cliff and Ellie are wonderful people that we see at a number of functions at the veterans' center. They are always willing to lend a hand. I have to relay a story that I'm not certain many people are aware of. Cliff is a very modest man, and not many of the veterans are aware of his accomplishments in the service (three Bronze Stars). A mutual friend, John Nettle, whose interview was in the book previous to this one, felt that Cliff should be honored but would not like the attention. So John went to Nellis AFB in Las Vegas and purchased duplicates of all the medals Cliff had received and a shadow box. He put the medals in the box, and when he came upon Cliff at the veterans' center, he asked him to come outside for a moment. Cliff did, and John presented the shadow box with the medals to Cliff. He was really touched. This is just a sample of the camaraderie that exists among veterans throughout the country.

Ron Rigatti, US Army

One of 11 children, Ron was born in Staten Island, New York, November 18, 1948. He attended New Dorp High School and participated in football and bowling. Upon his graduation in 1966, Ron went to work on Wall Street as a stock clerk for Gruntal & Co. On April 23, 1968, Ron was drafted into the US army and sent to Ft. Jackson, South Carolina for basic training. From there it was off to Ft. Gordon, Georgia, for AIT.

While there, Ron played touch football and was a pretty good player. The quarterback was a colonel from Notre Dame and he and Ron became friends. The colonel was a commander and assigned Ron to HQ Company. His MOS changed from infantry to R&R Specialist.

In November 1968, Ron received his orders for Vietnam. His brother was in Vietnam from 1967 to 1968, so Ron couldn't go until his brother returned. At that time a family could only have one member in a combat zone at a time.

Ron was stationed at Vung Tau, located near the Me Cong Delta on the southern peninsula of Vietnam. R&R Specialists provided entertainment for the combat troops who were on R&R and couldn't leave the country. This included fishing trips, pig roasts, water skiing, crafts etc. Ron was responsible for operating the craft shop for a while. The Australian troops loved it. They could purchase models to build for about one third the cost at home.

R&R specialists were required to ride along when they went to get supplies in deuce and-a-halves. There were times when they were fired upon during the supply convoys. Ron went from E1 to E5 in his first eight months in the Army. Ron did this job for eight months.

A new commander came into Vung Tau and didn't like the setup for whatever reason and things changed significantly for Ron. He received orders that changed his rank from a Specialist E5 to Sergeant E5. There had been battles in the area and quite a few guys had been severely wounded or killed. Replacements were needed as crew chiefs. Ron was assigned as a crew chief on flights that ferried people from one camp to another as well as providing support for USO shows. They also flew helicopters to retooling areas located on the South China Sea, where the machine guns from the helicopters were retooled. Ron's flights were occasionally called on to drop Green Beret troops into the mountains for special assignments. Ron continued in this capacity for the balance of his tour in Vietnam.

On January 5, 1970, Ron returned to the states via California and then Ft. Dix, New Jersey. His rank had changed back to Specialist E5 as soon as he left Vietnam. Although Ron still had a little less than five months left remaining in his obligation, he was discharged because the Army didn't believe there was enough time to train him in another MOS.

Ron returned to New York and went back to work at Gruntal & Co. and began networking and meeting people within the Stock Exchange Business. He worked as a relief clerk on the floor of the exchange and eventually went to work for Kaufmann & Co., a brokerage firm with a floor presence. While working for Kaufmann, he had a tremendous opportunity to meet significant traders and learn the language and ropes of the stock exchange business. Ron felt he learned from the best on Wall Street.

As he got involved with independent brokers, Ron opened up his own brokerage firm in 1988. It was involved in institutional trading on the floor of the exchange. Ron's organization had between four and six people with independent contractors as accountants and legal advisors. Ron eventually attended Richmond College (now Staten Island College) and received an Associates' Degree while working on Wall Street. He then went to Bernard Baruch College to get his BA in management in 1980.

Ron met his wife in 1975 who was also from Staten Island and worked for Merril Lynch. They were married in 1982. Ron moved to Mesquite in 1982, although he goes back east fairly often to visit his large family and three sons – Anthony, Ron Jr., and Michael as well as his three grandsons and granddaughter.

Ron thank you for your service to your country!

Michael Rigatti, US Navy (Son of Ron)

Michael is the son of Ron Rigatti, the veteran you just finished reading about. Michael was born June 13, 1984 in New York City, New York. When he was four, his family moved to Chester, New Jersey, where Michael attended Mendham HS and graduated in 2002. At Mendham, he participated in hockey and baseball, which was his real talent. He participated in a summer traveling program that included players from 15 to 18. Called the "Baseball Factory," the boys traveled from Maryland to California and Hawaii. At 15 Michael was chosen as the captain of this squad. He played 2nd and 3rd base.

After high school, Michael attended Fredrick Community College in Maryland. During his second year he became ill and had to withdraw from school and move back to New Jersey, where he enrolled at Morristown Community College. Just short of graduation, Michael decided to enlist in the US Navy, July 2006. It was off to Great Lakes Naval Station in Illinois for basic training.

From here it was off to Coronado, California, and BUDS where Michael was accepted into the Navy Seal training program. After two months, however he had to withdraw due to some unforeseen circumstances. Then it was back to Great Lakes for 13 weeks of corpsman school.

He signed up for basic reconnaissance with the Marine Corps and received orders for additional medical training at Camp Pendleton, California. This was an additional eight week program. His orders for Marine Recon medical training at Camp Pendleton resulted in his being rolled out of the class and was chosen for medical lab tech training at the Naval Medical Center in San Diego for a 13 month program. This class had the distinct honor of being the first where every student passed the program. Michael graduated as the valedictorian. Quite an honor!

He was assigned to National Naval Medical center in Bethesda, Maryland. He was part of a department known as transfusion services. He was assigned to the presidential unit. This meant doing the lab testing for the president and his family as well as other VIP's in the US government. This was an honor bestowed upon very few Navy technicians.

Getting this assignment was no easy task. Michael had to go through two stringent interviews with Navy Commanders. However, graduating as valedictorian from the 13 month program in San Diego gave Michael the opportunity to negotiate his own orders. In addition, Michael attended the University of Maryland while serving his country and obtained his degree in Kinesiology with a 3.3 GPA. Not too bad for an individual with the responsibility he had in his position at the national Naval Med center. Michael did a great job until his discharge in February 2012.

After serving six years, Michael went to work for the Henry M. Jackson Foundation, where he is involved in cancer research.

He is also very much involved with the Wounded Warriors Project, participating with wounded veterans in a team river-running, etc. This is quite a background for a young man who has served his country for six years.

Michael, thank you for your service to your country!

Mike Olson, US Navy

Mike was born in Pendleton, Oregon, December 21, 1946. He graduated from Hudson Bay HS in Washington State in 1965. Mike was active in track, football and baseball while in school. After graduation, Mike enrolled at Clark College and attended for a year and a half. In his second year, his credit load fell below 15 credit hours and he lost his deferment. When Mike received his draft notice, his father, a WWII Navy veteran, suggested Mike join the Navy and he did.

Off to San Diego for basic training in 1967 and then to Great Lakes Naval Station for a promised vocational school. Mike was enrolled into Basic Propulsion and Engineering school at Great Lakes and graduated in the top three of his class as an E3 fireman. All of the graduates were assigned to a ship except the top three. They were given orders for Saigon. For this assignment Mike was required to attend Vietnamese language school and basic Navy Seal training at Coronado Beach, California. This did not mean Mike and the other top graduates were going to become Seals, but just participate in part of the training the Seals go through. After three months, training continued with small boat training, small arms and automatic weapons training, and emergency medical training. This took place in Woughby, Washington and added two additional weeks. From here it was on to Vietnam.

Arriving in Saigon, they were escorted to Annapolis, the name given to the billets where new arrivals were given their shots, M-14's, green uniforms, etc. It was quite a shock as there were no toilet facilities. It was a place to get your basic gear, get assigned and sent off.

Mike was assigned to River Division 535 which along with River Division 534 patrolled the rivers of South Vietnam. On the way to My Tho from Saigon by helicopter Mike and his buddies kept hearing noises coming from the bottom of the copter and asked the pilot what they were. The pilot replied, "Oh, by the way you might want to sit on your flak jackets. We're being shot at—happens all the time."

The patrol boats were 31 feet long and their purpose was to control contraband that would be beneficial to the enemy. They worked for the 9th Infantry Division and patrolled from My Tho to Dong Tam. While Mike was there, Palmolive and Colgate would send items such as soaps, toothpaste, toothbrushes, shampoos, etc that the Navy would take into the villages to help the people with personal hygiene and disease. It was one of the good things that took place in the area, according to Mike.

In September, 1968 a woman in a sampan was in the river. She was a decoy for the enemy and as she was being watched, a bale of hay was thrown into the water at the rear of the patrol boat. The jet propulsion engine sucked the hay into the pumps and left the boat dead in the water. The enemy came from the surrounding area, throwing grenades aboard the boat. Several landed in areas on board where they rattled around, but were picked up and were able to be thrown into the water. Fifty mm fire from the boat scattered the enemy and fortunately there were no casualties. This was not an uncommon occurrence.

Orders came to move to Tan Am at the mouth of the Saigon River where the USS Garrett, a barracks ship was moored. Mike's unit established a base camp at Moc Hoa and every five days returned to the barracks ship for one day.

One December 22, they were on night patrol during what was being observed as a Christmas truce. Their boat went up the Vam Co Pay River, cut the engines and tied off on the beach. It was extremely dark and Mike noticed a bad odor. They used a starlight search scope to observe in the dark and Mike was using it this night. The bad odor persisted and many movements and reflex actions were the result of signs including smells. As Mike looked down the river his scope greened out indicating some kind of activity and he fired his 12 gauge shotgun as his buddy emptied 18 rounds from his M16 into the area. The commotion woke up the ship personnel and they went down to investigate. Much to their surprise, their kill was a seven foot monitor lizard. You tend to get jumpy in the dark on the back rivers of Vietnam. During Mike's duty, 23 of the 37 men assigned to his boat were wounded and 21 of those came back to finish their hitch in Vietnam.

Seal Team 2 was assigned to River Divisions 534 and 535 as they continued to patrol for several more months during Mike's assignment there.

After Vietnam, Mike went back to Great Lakes to attend C school. This was training for mechanics for very large engines for ships and planes. From here he was sent to Little Creek, Virginia, home of Seal Team 6 and assigned to the USS Suffolk County. This ship made several cruises in the Caribbean, conducted joint operations with the British Navy in Nova Scotia during a North Atlantic Cruise, conducted operations in Veagas off the coast of Cuba, and took 650 Marines to the Island of Crete to quiet a disturbance there.

Mike's enlistment was extended three months to help prepare for the pre-decommissioning of the USS Suffolk County and its eventual moth balling. He was finally discharged in June, 1971.

Mike became a union sprinkler fitter and went to Alaska where he lived for 33 years. He lived in Fairbanks which was a hub for the business Mike was involved in. Later he moved to Juneau. He met a wonderful lady there named Denise in 1991 and they married in 1997. Denise was an Alaska native and Mike moved to Ketchican to open a new office so he could be close to Denise. Mike has a son and a daughter from a previous marriage and his son still lives and works in Alaska.

Mike's parents were snowbirds in Mesquite from Vancouver, Washington for 22 years and Mike and Denise would come to Mesquite to visit. It is no surprise that they are now full time residents of Mesquite.

Mike, thank you for your service to your country!

Chuck Thompson, US Air Force

This is not only about Chuck Thompson, but a family that has served its country admirably for well over a hundred years. Chuck's grandfather fought in the Spanish American War with the 115th Cavalry. Afterward he was sent to the Philippine Insurrection to train Filipinos and was killed in action. He was a corporal. Chuck's father served in the US Navy in both WWI and WWII. He saw action in France in WWI and was a Seabee during WWII in the Aleutian Islands. Chuck had three older brothers who also served. Lee Jay was in the Army and was in the Pacific Theater during WWII. He was discharged at the end of his enlistment as an E5. Robert was in the Army and served with General George Patton during WWII. After the war he re-enlisted in the Air Force and served in the Korean War. Then there was Leonard who joined the Air Force and became a medic. He served in China. After his enlistment was up he returned home and joined the National Guard. During the Korean War, his unit was activated and sent to Korea. While involved in combat in Korea as a medic, Leonard earned two Bronze Stars and a Silver Star. He went on to retire from the Army as a Master Sergeant.

So it was no surprise to anyone when Chuck enlisted in the Air Force at the age of 17. But let's start at the beginning. Born in Wyoming in 1939, it was almost Chuck's destiny to become a military man. Carrying out his desire to follow his families' tradition, he was concerned that he might have some difficulty passing the physical as he had contracted polio as a child. Although he had recovered he thought in the back of his mind that something could keep him from being able to enlist. When he took his physical they said they couldn't find his heart! Therefore, he had to go to the hospital for an electrocardiogram.

It worked out okay so he went back to the indoctrination center to get some additional meal tickets and several people with cameras were there. The gal at the desk said she couldn't give them to Charles Thompson because he was dead! What? That morning a flight had been chartered out to take recruits to basic training. Chuck missed the plane because of the medical tests he had. That charter flight crashed in the Cheyenne Mountains killing everyone on board. Chuck was later shipped to Parks AFB in California for basic training.

After completing basic, Chuck was sent to Lowry AFB in Colorado for additional training. Here he attended school for six months to become an aircraft weapons specialist. After completing his training he was off to Keflavick AFB in Iceland. Here he was assigned to the Security police and small arms, which was somewhat confusing after finishing six months of schooling as an aircraft weapons specialist. However, Chuck managed to serve well in this capacity and moved on to Geiger AFB in Spokane, Washington, and was part of the load crew for the F86, 102 and 106.

After some relatively short assignments at various Air Force Bases, Chuck was assigned to Nellis for training on the F105. From here it was off to Kadena AFB in Okinawa. He was assigned to Kadena on four different occasions and spent 10 years of his career in Okinawa. It was here that Chuck met Sayo. After a year they decided to marry. Not as easy as one might expect. Chuck had to hire a detective just to get through the paperwork and Sayo had to go through a complete physical, while her entire family had to go through an investigation that lasted six months. But they were finally able to marry...twice—once on base and once in Okinawa.

Chuck was then assigned to McConnell AFB in Kansas. After less than six months he received orders for Vietnam. He and Sayo had not even received all of their belongings from Okinawa at this time.

However, because of a regulation that stated if a spouse did not have a driver's license or was fluent in English, the military would send her back to her home country while her spouse was in a war zone. Fortunately, this worked out well for the Thompson's. Chuck was stationed in Blen Hoa while in Vietnam. After his tour of duty in Nam, Chuck was assigned back to Kadena in Okinawa where he spent the next five years. He was now an E6 Tech Sgt. From here Chuck and Sayo were sent to Grand Forks AFB in North Dakota. Just a bit too chilly for his taste and being the AFB with the highest rate of retirement in the USA, Chuck decided it was time to make the move. After a little over twenty years of honorable service, Chuck Thompson retired from the US Air Force.

He and Sayo moved to Salt Lake City as Chuck searched for employment. Times were tough and finding work was not easy. After holding down a number of jobs, he heard that the US Postal Service was accepting applications. Chuck applied, was hired and spent 16 years working for the Post Office. One of Chuck's brothers lived in Caliente, NV and he and his wife and Chuck and Sayo used to get together in Mesquite. So when it came time to retire Chuck knew where it was going to be. In 1997, he and Sayo bought a home here and have been here ever since.

It's no secret how active Chuck has been in Mesquite. He has been the Commander of the local VFW, active in the American Legion, instrumental in the formation of the Virgin Valley Honor Guard as well as the development of the Mesquite Veterans Center. In addition to being an active member of the community and member of the Board of trustees with the Elks, he continues to help wherever he can. From serving his country, his fellow veterans and his community, Chuck Thompson has always been at the head of his class.

Thank you Chuck for your service to your country!

115th Wyoming Cavalry

Chuck Thompson's grandfather served with this military organization.

On February 14, 1941, the 115th Cavalry of Wyoming National Guard unit was ordered to active duty, although all other National Guard units had been activated six months earlier on September 16. The Wyoming Regiment, 115th Cavalry numbered 1,051 men who were all sent to Ft. Lewis, Washington.

Because the Wyoming National Guard has been reorganized and renamed a little history is in order.

Troop B had its origin in Old Company G of the Third Wyoming Infantry and as such served in the Mexican Border campaign of 1916. Next it was organized into Battery E, 148th Field Artillery; then became known as Troop H, First Wyoming Cavalry. Next it was organized into Troop B of the 115th and then the 300th Armored Field Artillery. Now it is in the headquarters Battalion of the 49th Field Artillery.

Capt. George Pearson was a Sheridan man who started and ended a long military career with the National Guard. He was commander of Troop B as it went off to war. Pearson was later to command a regiment of the 11th Airborne through the South Pacific. It made the first drop into Japan to end what is affectionately called "The Big War."

Pearson then took over Landenberg and Berlin, Germany commands in Europe and finally returned to the Wyoming National Guard retiring as its adjutant general.

Forward Observer, a publication of the Wyoming National Guard, had this comment on what National Guardsman found in 1941: Winter was at hand and many of the training camps didn't have permanent quarters. Tents and winter coats were in short supply and confusion seemed to be the order of the day. Conditions in most of the mobilization camps were poor. Many of the WWII camps had been dismantled. Others were almost uninhabitable due to lack of upkeep in the 20 years since they had been active camps."

The history of the 49th Field Artillery says the 115th served for a while as a roving patrol on the Washington-Oregon coast until fear of a Japanese invasion subsided. The craving for real action was too much for most of the men and transfers to the Airborne, Air Corps and other branches filled the desire in assault landings in the Pacific air drops into Japan, bombing raids in Europe and service in all theaters.

History reveals that more than "a third of the men became officers." The 115th became a cavalry group headquarters and received streamers for the Northern France and Central Europe campaigns.

What also was unique about the 115th Cavalry is that the unit still had horses when called up in 1941—a true cavalry of days gone by. At pre-mobilization training at Ft. McKenzie in October 1940, the men trained on horseback as any true cavalry unit would.

This unit has a record excelled by few anywhere, with origins going back to 1890. It saw its colors rise over Manila in the Spanish American War and was in the nation to respond full strength for Mexican Border call up. Its guns were the first American heavy artillery moved to the front during WWI. One of its officers was the first decorated for bravery in that war and its insignia, a bucking horse; the first use of this now famous Wyoming symbol.

What else makes this story so interesting? It was taken from articles published from newspapers written over 50 years ago. In addition, Chuck Thompson, one of our own, who I interviewed is from Sheridan and has significant ties to the 115th Cavalry.

His brother Lee Thompson was a member of the 115th when horses were very much a part of its operation. A special thank you to Chuck for providing this information!

5

THE MEN WHO HAD A DREAM

As was mentioned earlier in this book, four men were primarily responsible for blazing the trail for our veterans' center. Although many others were involved and did yeoman's work, Ed Fizer, Jim Brown, Bob Barquist, and Al Litman showed the way. These are their stories.

Ed Fizer, US Army

Ed was born July 3, 1943 in Slater, Missouri. He was raised here and attended Marshall HS where he participated in track and football. Ed graduated in 1961 and enlisted in the US Army. His desire was to be a heavy equipment operator and was therefore assigned to Ft. Leonard Wood, Missouri. He finished basic training and started AIT, then decided to volunteer for the airborne. His training immediately ceased and he was transferred to Ft. Benning, Georgia. This all took place within a week of his decision. At Benning, he went through Infantry Training and then on to Airborne School which lasted four weeks. Five solo jumps had to be made in order to claim your wings. While training he noticed some individuals who were in tip top shape and were able to do back flips from a standing position. He inquired as to who these men were and was told they were Special Forces. Ed, of course, volunteered for Special Forces. He was assigned to the 7th Special Forces Unit and remembers that the members of this outfit were hard core. They became like a father figure to Ed. He and another young soldier were welcomed into the unit by these men. It was a unique experience.

Ed was transferred to Ft. Bragg and was present when President Kennedy came to Bragg to give the 7th Special Forces the Green Beret. The 7th was a reactivation of a WWII unit and this is the unit that took Ed under its wing. Ed was transferred to the 3rd Special Forces Unit and the to the 5th when he was sent to Vietnam. The 5tht was the only Special Forces Unit that went to Vietnam. After a six month tour Ed returned to Ft. Bragg. In 1965 he would return to Vietnam with the 5th Special Forces Unit as a Specialist E5.

In 1966, Ed was assigned to Indianapolis, Indiana as a trainer of High School ROTC students. He did this for the next three years. In 1969, he was assigned to the 8th Special Forces Unit in Panama, where he became a trainer at "Jungle School." Every 2nd Lt. from every branch of the service had to go through this training. Officers from other countries were also trained at this school. It was a four week course. It was basically a course in how to survive in the jungle and have the officers become familiar with the animals and environment. To graduate the students were dropped off in the jungle and had to return to base camp without being captured by the instructors.

In 1970, Ed now an E7 was back in Vietnam with the 5th Special Forces. This was a very unique experience as Ed's unit was placed in the mountains with the people who were natives of the area. This was the Montagards. Only eleven men made up this Special Forces Unit and they lived with the people of the region. They trained them as well as lived with them. The people spoke their own language and communication was not easy. There were frequent drops of cattle and pigs that were alive as well as chickens and other fowl that were already prepared for cooking. The three things that the natives loved most were, "Sweet Tarts," tennis shoes and Ivory Soap. Prior to this they were bare foot and their only weapons were cross bows and spears. This was an experience that very few individuals will ever live. These people were hated by both the north and south in Vietnam.

In 1971, it was back to the United States and recruiting school in Indianapolis. Upon completion, Ed was sent to Florida and after a year he was promoted to E8 and was responsible for all the other recruiters in Florida. During this time he was sent to Atlanta where he became a recruiter of nurses. He and his team went to Nursing Schools in the area and Puerto Rico. They also attended state and national Nursing Conventions. Army Nurse at that time needed to have a BS Degree.

Ed was selected to attend the Sergeant Major Academy in 1980 in El Paso, Texas. Many instructors were from the Command General Staff College. This course was six months in duration. The highlight was meeting General Bradley. Upon completion, now a Sergeant Major, Ed was sent to Salt Lake City where he was in charge of all recruiters in a five state area. In 1983, Ed retired from the US Army.

While in the service, Ed continued his education where ever he was stationed and received his Degree in History from Columbia University and taught school for nine years. He also delivered mail for seven years after teaching. Being familiar with this part of the country, Ed and his wonderful wife Patty decided to retire in Mesquite in 2002.

All of the veterans in Mesquite (and there are a bunch!) are aware that Ed was a significant player in our Veterans Center becoming a reality.

Ed was Commander of the Mesquite American Legion, Founder of the Mesquite Chapter of Vietnam Veterans Chapter 993, and a Lifetime member of the VFW.

He and Patty were married in 1987. There are four children and 12 grandchildren.

Ed, thank you for your service to your country and all you have done in the community and continue to do!

Al Litman, US Army

Born in Duluth, Minnesota, December 22, 1942 Al attended Duluth Central HS. He played hockey when he wasn't working to support his avid interest in cars. He graduated in 1960 and enrolled at the University of Minnesota as an Education/History major. He was awarded a bachelor's degree four years later and immediately moved to California to escape the cold weather.

While in high school he dated a lovely young lady, Phyllis, who moved to California a year after high school. They hooked up again and were married July 25, 1965.

On July 27, 1965, Al received his draft notice from Duluth. He hadn't even registered in California but did so upon receipt of the notice. While the transfer was taking place, his draft was delayed until January, 1966, when he was shipped to Ft. Carson, Colorado for basic training. Ft. Carson had only recently opened to accommodate the huge draft call up.

After boot camp Al, like every other soldier, went to AIT. He was handed an 81 mm mortar plate and told he would be trained as a mortar gunner. Believing he could do better because he had a college degree he mentioned to his captain his desire to do something else. The captain disagreed with Al's assessment and refused his request to see the adjutant general. Not to be deterred, Al went to the general on his own and managed to get in to see him. He explained his thoughts, the general agreed. Al was re-assigned to HQ.

His captain was furious but had no choice but to drive Al to his new unit where he was assigned to training. Part of Al's duties were to feed the 1st Sergeant's mule.

He was fortunate to train with a warrant officer helicopter pilot who was wounded in Vietnam. The pilot became quite a mentor. Al spent the next year at Ft. Carson as part of the 5th Infantry Division. He and his wife Phyllis had been living in a small apartment in Colorado Springs, but this quickly changed when Al received orders for Vietnam as a replacement and his wife went back to San Francisco.

Records in hand, Al flew commercial to Vietnam where the buses that took men to their destination had heavy weapon screen mesh on every window. He arrived in Bein Hoa on December 23, 1966, as a SP4 and was immediately put in charge of a group of guys, digging ditches.

He was then put on a helicopter and flown into the jungle where it was pouring rain. He was staged in a tent and went a day and a half before he was finally fed. The first of the year, a jeep driven by a 1st sergeant came for Al.

A reservist, the man was a very pleasant individual who was experiencing his first active duty. He took Al to his unit where he was assigned to a tent that had a cot and blankets; no air mattress, no sleeping bag, nothing but a cot and blankets.

Al took off his boots, lay on the cot and fell asleep and woke up in the morning with no boots. It had continued to rain hard during the night and his boots had just floated away.

He was given a .45 caliber pistol. The New Year was coming and all weapons were taken and locked up in Conex Containers so there would be no injuries as the men celebrated. The weapons were later returned.

Soon after arriving, incoming mortar got everyone's attention. Al was given a shotgun and a box of shells to help defend a golf course where all the helicopters were located. After the initial chaos, Al settled in at HQ battery, division artillery. He was the designated personnel clerk even though he was an artillery intelligence specialist. He and a trained personnel clerk Vern Johnson shared duties.

By the way, at this time our own Ed Fizer was only 50 yards away across the road. Of course Al didn't know Ed at the time.

As part of his duties, Al took secret documents to forward observers in brief cases attached by handcuffs to his wrists. He would fly by chopper and deliver the documents when it landed. After two months, the messengers received flak vests. The chopper pilots told them to take off the vests and sit on them since the enemy liked to shoot through the bottom of the helicopter. This all took place in the highlands of Vietnam. One advantage was it was cool at night, which made it easier to sleep.

On one occasion, two helicopters took men into the area where information was to be delivered. Weather was bad but the assignment was accomplished. Later that evening back at base camp, several of the men were having some refreshment and asked if they had seen one of the young soldiers who was with them on the day's assignment. No one from either chopper had. "Are you sure we brought him back?" Al asked. No one could answer for certain.

Al went to the flight pad, found there was a chopper available as well as a pilot and a gunner. They assembled and went back to where they had carried out the day's mission, Walking through the bush, Al was cutting the bush as quietly as he could when he heard the distinct sound of a rifle action. His party froze expecting enemy gunfire.

"Identify yourself or I'll fire," said a voice from the jungle. "It's us," Al said. "point that rifle away!"

The young soldier had had contact with the enemy earlier in the evening, but was glad to see his buddies. They all returned safely to base. For this rescue and realization that a member of the team hadn't returned, Al received the Bronze Star. FO's the men and women to whom Al's unit delivered messages and documents were often killed in action.

Things started to slow down and men were being sent out of camp a little at a time. The area started closing down, including mess halls.

There were fewer people left to defend the camp and no one really knew what was happening. The word came out they were preparing for the Tet Offensive.

As things wound down, Al was assigned to grave diggers registration, which meant identifying bodies. He hated this duty. It included writing letters to the families of those killed. He had nightmares about the duty.

Although, close to the action, Al's unit experienced very few casualties during the year he was there. After that year, it was back to Ft. Lewis, Washington, to be discharged. On December 7, 1967, Al Litman, was again a civilian.

He began teaching in the Los Angeles School District where he stayed for two years. While teaching, he attended Pepperdine University and earned a masters degree. He also began working at Simi Valley School District and headed up the handicapped children's program.

He stayed there for the next 15 years. He received a PhD from Pepperdine in 1978 where he taught psychology part time. In 1984, because of his continued love of cars, Al started an auto service business that he built from scratch.

He later sold it, retired and moved to Hawaii. After becoming a bit bored, Al went into psycho-therapy work. He also worked for the Hawaiian mental health services as an independent contractor. He worked with families of autistic children as well.

In 2003, Al and Phyllis toured the southwest and discovered Mesquite. They liked it and settled here in 2004.

Al is involved in a number of activities in the community in addition to being a Mesquite city councilman. Al is also president of the Mesquite Veterans Center.

In addition to the Bronze Star, Al was also awarded the Air Medal and the Army Commendation Medal.

Al, thank you for your service to your country and community!

Jim Brown, US Navy

Jim was born August 11, 1946 in Ontario, Canada. At a young age he moved to Houston, Texas. At age 52, he discovered that he had been adopted when he was applying for a concealed carry permit. The application process uncovered the fact that he was a naturalized citizen and had to go through some additional paperwork to get his permit. Coming as a surprise, Jim began to investigate his background and discovered that he had two brothers and two sisters.

He met three of the four and continues to maintain a relationship to this day. His younger brother was an Air Force veteran but unfortunately passed away before Jim had a chance to meet him.

Jim moved from Houston to Whittier, California and then to Pico Rivera, California where he attended El Rancho HS. Jim participated in cross country and track and field, and football. He also enjoyed photography and performing in the school choir show.

At 17, Jim enlisted in the Naval Reserves with the hope of becoming a pilot. His Boy Scout Master was a retired Navy chief who served in WWII and had started an interest for Jim in the Navy and flying.

After attending college for a semester as a pre-dental major, Jim realized he just couldn't settle in on the studies. He was attending reserve drills and had attended basic during Christmas for two weeks. The Navy noticed he was a pre-dental major and transferred him to sick bay operations.

Jim went to active duty as an E4 in San Diego at the Naval Training Station to become a Corpsman. Since he had already gone through some schooling as a reservist, he ran the shot lines for the new recruits. While driving the huge Pontiac Bonneville ambulance one day responding to a call that a recruit was down, Jim ran over a railroad tie that was mostly buried in the concrete drive at the barracks, splitting the ambulance in two up to the drivers seat.

The Navy, having no sense of humor, transferred Jim out. He then went to camp Pendleton to train with the 5th Marine Division.

Doctors, dentists, clergy, corpsman, etc. all trained together in this program regardless of rank. They were to learn the tactical operations of the Marine Corps. All were assigned to the 5th Marine Division in Los Pogus. The corpsman were assigned to rifle companies.

While in training, an older gunnery sergeant was running his unit without a corpsman. Near the top of the hill the gunny suffered a heart attack. Jim was the closest to the hill and ran up and began working on him and continued to do so for 3½ hours. By the time they got the gunny out to a hospital he passed away. Jim called it his first casualty.

Since the 5th marine Division was being re=established everything had to be ordered. Jim was put in charge of all things medical. This meant establishing spots on the ship for transport as well as receiving and checking that everything was received. Three separate battalions were getting ready to ship out.

After 2½ years in the Navy, Jim headed to Vietnam. The corpsman were assigned to scout for sniper teams and were issued M14's not 45's. He was assigned to the division surgeons where he worked unless needed to replace a corpsman in the field.

When the 5th Marines hit HQ in Dong Ha they became the 3rd Marine Division. Dong Ha was right on the de-militarized zone. Later in Phu Bi, Jim was assigned to medical civil affairs. Marine units were sent into villages where medical teams would hold sick call.

Time was also spent at the 5th Medical Battalion, which was the main medical hospital. This is where major issues were handled. Gunshot wounds, chest wounds, major surgery were all performed here for allies as well as US troops.

Jim went from Phu Bi to Khe Shan, which was up in the mountains. Some of the worst trauma of the Vietnam War took place in Khe Shan. The medical staff was hounded by the need for body bags and the need to get wounded out of the area. Jim re-enlisted while in Vietnam and became an E5. After 15 months he returned to the states. It was off to another school, Medical Administration School that was 52 weeks long. This was a pre-requisite for Medical Officers School.

Jim came out of this school as an E6. In1967, he met his wonderful wife Kathy. Although they went to the same school in California he didn't know her while attending school. In 1968 they were married just before Jim started Medical Administration School.

After school, Jim was assigned to the USS Midway as a medical administration tech, and it was back to Vietnam to the Gulf of Tonkin. Here they observed the Russians taking pictures of the US operations directed at Hanoi. Jim was not thrilled with his assignment on the Midway and ran into a friend who was able to make him aware of other openings within the fleet.

Jim accepted a position with the Armed Forces Police in Guam. He and Kathy spent three years there and Jim received his bachelor's degree from the University of Guam in Public Administration.

From this point in his career—now an E7—Jim transferred into the reserves and took a job with the L.A. County Sheriff's department. While working there he received his masters degree in education and was certified to instruct police and fire science. Among other endeavors, Jim and Kathy started a very successful company that provided security for trucking companies.

In 1990 they moved to Mesquite and became involved in a number of operations both volunteer and for pay. Becoming involved with a local church, Jim attended Lake Charles Bible College and received his doctorate in theology in 2004. He also worked for the Mesquite Fire

Department as a volunteer and as an instructor for the Navy Fire Fighter School.

After 27 years of service, Jim retired from the Navy. He and his wife Kathy have two sons, one of which is also a Navy veteran and one grandson.

Jim serves as the Veterans Service Officer for the Mesquite Veterans Center. This is a huge job and he is assisted by his wife Kathy. He has been doing this since 2008.

Jim thank you for your service to your country and community!

Bob Barquist, US Navy

Born in Boulder City June 4, 1947, Bob was raised in Henderson, Nevada and attended Basic High School. He was a member of the photography club and it was his job to take year book pictures of the of the school's varsity lettermen. He had a hard time getting the group to hold still but managed to get three shots. Bob was relieved until he realized he left the lens cap on and they had to be redone. He sent someone else to do it with the excuse the photos had been ruined as he was developing the film.

Bob graduated in 1965 and enrolled at Dixie State College in Utah for one year. He transferred to Southern Nevada University (now UNLV) where he completed a second year of college. Believing the draft was imminent, Bob enlisted in the US Navy. He wanted to be a pilot but was color blind so that was out.

He went to boot camp in San Diego and then to Hospital Corpsman School to become a hospital apprentice. After graduation he was assigned to Naval Hospital in Oakland, California. He later returned to San Diego for hospital lab school. After lab school, he was assigned to Moffett Federal Airfield in Sunnyvale, California. All in all, Bob spent more than three years training.

He returned to the Naval Hospital in Oakland and went through advanced training at the field medical school. He was then assigned to the 3rd Marines Amphibious Assault Force. After a 24 hour layover, in Okinawa, he landed in Vietnam, December 24, 1970.

Bob trained with the 2nd Combined Action Group that lived with the Vietnamese and trained them how to defend their villages. There were four Combined Action Groups in Vietnam.

Bob was part of the MEDCAPS whose job it was to inoculate the villages against disease. CAPs platoons consisted of 13 Marines and one Navy corpsman responsible for one square kilometer to train and defend.

At night they broke up into alpha and bravo ambush sites where they would dig in and wait for the Viet Cong. This cut down on smuggling. Bob's outfit only engaged with the North Vietnamese Army on one occasion.

He said CAP's were one of the most successful US operations. Villagers felt safer and were able to do their chores and farm. However, villagers who worked with US troops were made examples of by the Communist guerillas.

During one combat operation, a Marine in Bob's platoon was badly wounded from an enemy antipersonnel device that had been concealed in waist high elephant grass. Although aware the area was probably mined, Bob pushed through to reach the side of the wounded Marine. He stayed in this dangerous position until he had stopped the bleeding and provided the intensive first aid needed to enable the Marine to be medivacked. For his heroic action Bob Barquist was awarded the Bronze Star.

Villagers loved the Marines that lived with them. The troops were invited to Buddha Feast, which was quite an honor. The MEDCAP units disbanded in April 1971.

Bob was assigned to the 1st Marine Division, but had gall bladder problems and ended up having surgery to remove it. After recovering, the brass discovered Bob hadn't ever been to sea. So with less than a year to go on his enlistment, Bob was assigned to the USS Morton (DD948) a Forest Sherman Destroyer.

The USS Morton received permission from Morton Salt Co. to use the Companies logo on its flag. Then it was back to Vietnam and the Philippines Port of Subic Bay. The medical compliment for destroyer was three people including a chief, corpsman and a striker. Bob was part of that three man team.

After returning from his first and only navy cruise, bob was discharged after serving 4 years 10 months and 6 days, but who is counting?

It was back to UNLV to continue his education. He changed his major to anthropology and he received a bachelor of arts degree. He spent the next two years doing research in Guatemala through a Cultural Field Research program. Going to school full time and working full time became a little too much and Bob decided that anthropology was not going to provide much of an income. So he decided to do what he knew best and in what field he'd been thoroughly trained, the medical field.

He received his medical tech certification at a number of different labs and hospitals in various capacities, most of which were supervisory. Bob eventually ended up working part time at Mesa View Hospital in Mesquite, but in a very short time he was asked to become the lab manager. He retired as the Laboratory Administrative Director in 2012.

About 27 years ago while working in Laughlin, Bob met a lovely nurse named Coleen. They were married and today live in Mesquite.

In addition to the Bronze Star, Bob received a meritorious service citation for operations against hostile forces as part of the Combined Action Force, 3rd Marine Amphibious Force., 3rd The Combat Action Ribbon and a citation of service with the Combined Action Program.

Bob is a charter member of the Vietnam Veterans Chapter 993, Member of the VFW, and former

Commander of the VFW Posts in Mesquite, Pahrump, and California.

He is the state VFW surgeon in Nevada. This position delivers medical information to all VFW posts in the state.

Bob thank you for your service to your country!

VETERANS OF THE US MARINE CORPS

Fred Toval

Well known for his involvement in the community for various projects, Fred was born in New Orleans in 1936. He graduated from St. Augustine HS in 1955 and enlisted in the US Marine Corps after graduation.

Fred spent 23 years in the Corps, a unique career that saw him enter as an enlisted man and retire as a Field Grade Officer.

His career began with boot camp training at Paris Island, South Carolina, and advanced Infantry Training at Camp Pendleton, California. Further schooling provided him with occupational training as an electronics technician.

In 1964 Fred, a sergeant at the time, applied for and was accepted into the Marine Corps Warrant Officers Program. This was only the fifth class conducted by the Marine Corps at that time. Upon receiving the rank of warrant officer, Fred was assigned to Marine Attack Squadron VMA 211, where he was the Squadron Electronics Officer. VMA 211 was a unit with approximately 250 enlisted men and 30 officers. VMA 211 operated the Douglas Sky

Hawk attack aircraft, the A4E. This squadron deployed to the Philippine Islands on the USS Kitty Hawk for combat theater training and then to Chu Lai, South Vietnam, where an expeditionary air field was being completed. The squadron operated on Marston matting laced over sand and used JATO (jet assisted take off) to make up for short runways. They also had to use tail hooks on runways to land planes just like aircraft carriers. Fred was assigned to this squadron, known as the Wake Island Avengers, from October 1965 to July 1966

From August 1967 to November 1967, Fred was involved in the transporting of six two seat versions of the A4E, the TA4E. Fred flew aboard a command C130 that followed the aircraft. The course was Yuma, Arizona, California, Hawaii, Midway, Wake Island, Guam, Philippines and finally Vietnam.

In 1966, Fred was promoted to from W3 to 2nd Lt. through a program where senior enlisted men and warrant officers were given the opportunity to accept a commission. Fred's commission came while he was serving in Vietnam. In 1968 he was selected to attend the Navy Technical Training Institute in Memphis as a full time student, where he earned his degree in electrical engineering. While in school he was promoted to captain.

In 1969 and 1970 there was a military reduction in force, and senior men who had accepted commissions were asked to return to their previous ranks. More than 8,000 men had accepted promotions, and only 500 were able to keep them. Fred was among the 500.

Transferred to Beaufort, South Carolina, as the base electronics officer in late 1968, Fred attended and graduated from Air Defense (traffic control) School. This was preparation for a command.

In 1972 Fred was ordered back to Marble Mountain, Vietnam, to take his command of H&HS-18. This was late 1971 and early 1972 and the war was winding down.

Fred took control of the rear unit and brought it to Iwakuni, Japan.

In 1973 Fred enrolled in the college degree program while stationed at El Toro, California and attended Chatman College in Orange, California. He graduated magna cum laude with a degree in Economics. Later in 1974 he was assigned to Wing Equipment Repair Unit (WERS-37) as executive officer and promoted to major in 1975. In 1977, he was transferred back to Iwakuni, Japan, where he was assigned to the duty of wing avionics officer of the 3rd Marine Air Wing at El Toro.

Later in 1978, Fred declined orders to Command and Staff College in Washington D.C. because of the terminal illness of a family member. He decided to retire from the Marine Corps in June of 1979 after 23 years of service, a period of time where he served his country with honor.

Fred's decorations include: the Navy Achievement Award w/ combat "V' for valor, the Marine Corps Expeditionary Award for service during the Cuba missile crisis, the National Defense Ribbon, Good Conduct Award, Combat Action Award for battle at Chu Lai S Vietnam, Navy Unit Citation, Vietnam Service Award and the Vietnam Campaign Award. After his much cherished career in the Marine Corps, he went to work for Sperry Univac (now L-3 Communications) as an industrial engineering manager and configuration manager.

Fred was married to Charlotte Johnson and they had three daughters, Renee, Chrystal and Patricia and one grandson. Charlotte passed away in 1986. Fred married Gracie Siniscalco in 1990. They reside in Mesquite where they are both involved in their various civic interests.

One thing I took away from this interview is that Fred is extremely proud of his grandson, Corporal Andrew Toval DeBoer who is a Marine, who served his country in Afghanistan.

Thank you Fred for your honorable service to your country!

Fred and I became friends and see one another at church and around Mesquite. He is a proud marine veteran and should be. He served his country well!

Jack Castro, US Marine Corps

Born in Pamona, California, October 25, 1956 Jack's family moved when he was very young to Azusa, California where he was raised. As a youngster, Jack participated in Pop Warner Football for six years. He attended Azusa HS where he played varsity soccer. He graduated in 1974.

Prior to graduation, Jack enlisted in the U.S. Marine Corps via the delayed entry program and reported to basic training in San Diego, July 8, 1974. After graduation he was put on graduation hold because of a severe foot infection.

Jack was eventually assigned to the Marine Corps Air Station El Toro near Irvine, California where he was part of the motor transport group. He spent the next year at El Toro. Jack was later assigned to the 3rd Reconnaissance Battalion and was sent to Okinawa where he spent the next 13 months.

After Okinawa, Jack was stationed at Camp Pendleton with the Marine Infantry Motor Transport Group. Jack was promoted to sergeant E5. He considered re-enlisting but decided instead to return home.

Back in Azusa, Jack married a girl from his high school and accepted a job with Hydro Conduit. The couple moved to Baldwin Park, California so Jack could go to work for U.S. Pipe. He was then transferred to Aurora, Colorado, where he worked for the next five years. Because of an industrial decline, Jack was laid off and accepted a job with Coors Brewing as a casual worker. As a casual worker his hours were limited so after three years Jack left Coors and went to work at Denver's Stapleton International Airport.

When an opportunity arose with a California disposal company, Jack took advantage of it so he could move back to the Golden State. The company was purchased by Safety Kleen and Jack spent the next 12 years working for them. In 2001 Jack divorced and went to work for deRosa Foods in Ontario, California where he met his wonderful wife Janie. They were married in 2006.

Janie had always wanted to live in a Del Webb community and Jack was familiar with Mesquite. When he heard Del Webb was building a community in Mesquite, he and Janie went to check it out. They purchased their home in 2008.

They love Mesquite and the residents of the community. Janie is a retired insurance adjuster and Jack works for Auto Zone. They are active in several community organizations and are always willing to help others.

Jack was a chaperone with his kid's high school ROTC program and cross country team. One of his sons served 13 months in Iraq. They have a family of 4 children and 4 grandchildren.

Thank you, Jack for your service to your country!

Cliff Jenkins, US Marine Corps

Cliff Jenkins served as president of the Mesquite Veterans center for three years. He was not only a close friend of mine, but of every veteran or individual that stepped foot into the center. He was truly loved by all because of his concern for everyone with whom he came into contact with. He and his wife Susan had a significant presence at their church and at the center.

Cliff was born April 5, 1939 in South bend, Indiana. At age five he moved to Milwaukee, Wisconsin due to a split between his parents. He was placed into a Children's Home in Wauwatosa, Wisconsin. At the age of 11, he moved in with an aunt in Waukegan, Illinois and worked with a cousin doing cement work. Pretty tough for an eleven year old, so he moved to Texas to be with his dad. Unfortunately after only six weeks in Houston, Cliff's father was killed in an automobile accident and it was back to Illinois to live with his brother.

Cliff attended Zion Benton HS and played football and baseball. He graduated in 1957. While a junior, however, Cliff enlisted in the U.S. Marine Corps Reserves. During his junior and senior years he was also involved in a program where he went to school for a half day and worked a half day at Abbott Laboratories. He went to summer camp with the Corps his junior and senior years, the first one in Philadelphia and the second in Coronado beach, California. After graduation, Cliff was off to fulfill his obligation of basic training and ITR. Basic was in San Diego and ITR Camp Pendleton in California. During this time, Cliff decided to enlist in the Marine Corps. He wanted to be a boatman aboard ship but very few were granted that desire and Cliff was assigned to the infantry and sent to the Philippines.

Once there he put in for five openings that were available for the motor pool and was granted one of the openings. Cliff developed a reputation for keeping his vehicles in tip-top shape. He remembers going on liberty in open air Toyota-truck-type vehicles. From the Philippines Cliff was sent to Okinawa. General David Shoop came to the unit for an inspection and was so impressed with the shape of Cliff's vehicles that he offered him a job as his jeep driver.

Of course, Cliff accepted. He was promoted to corporal and drove for the general for the next 18 months. A short time later Shoop was made Commandant of the Marine Corps and asked Cliff to go to Washington D.C. with him to continue to be his driver. This meant a six year re-enlistment and Cliff asked for a few days to consider. Since Cliff was a short timer he declined the offer and was sent to Oakland, California to finish out his enlistment.

A sergeant in Oakland told Cliff about all the benefits of retiring from the Marine Corps and Cliff agreed they were great, but replied "If I was going to re-enlist for six years don't you think I would have stayed with General Shoop!" After being released from the service, it was back to Zion, Illinois and Abbott Labs. After two more years, Cliff moved to Denver and became involved in the bowling business. He worked as an assistant manager and did such a great job was promoted to manager.

A bowling alley competitor came to visit Cliff and asked him if he thought he could do the same for his establishment. He said yes. That answer got him a new managers job and a share of the business.

Unfortunately, the majority owners sold the business and Cliff moved on to the trucking business. After building a successful trucking operation, Cliff was offered a management position with Coors and sold his business.

He was transferred to Kansas City to open that transportation department. Cliff again became the victim of a company decision as Coors decided to eliminate its transportation group. With all his experience, Cliff had no problem finding work; first with Novak Truck lines and then with Cisco Foods as fleet manager.

After 10 years with Cisco, Cliff decided to retire in 2002. When he moved to Denver he met and married his lovely wife Susan. During their marriage they had visited Las Vegas often. During one of those visits they found Mesquite. They stopped and looked at a new housing development and Susan told Cliff that this is where she wanted to live and this is where they settled.

Cliff and Susan have five children and nine grandchildren and one great grandchild. Both are very involved in various activities within the Mesquite community. In addition to being president of the Veterans Center, Cliff is commander of the American Legion Post 24 Mesquite and a member of the Elks.

Thank you Cliff for your service to your country, community and to the veterans!

At the age of seventy-four, Cliff lost his battle with leukemia in December 2013. Despite his valiant effort, he lost the battle at home, surrounded by his family. His passing left a huge hole in the veterans' center as Cliff took his presidency very seriously. During the time when we knew the end was not far away, an extreme effort was made to finish the veterans' center expansion as this was a dream of Cliff's. Through the efforts of several veterans, especially Ken Maynard, the interior was completed, and Cliff was able to see it. About ten days later he passed away, but he was thrilled that he was able to see the completion of the expansion.

Cliff was instrumental in fostering positive relationships throughout the community that helped the center with successful fund-raisers. He is missed by all and will never be forgotten.

Ron Bird, US Marine Corps

Ron was born March 7, 1984 in Reedsburg, Wisconsin. When he was young his family moved from Wisconsin to Lake Havasu, Arizona. The move was from a very cold climate to a very warm one.

Ron's dad started an insurance and investment business in Lake Havasu and later transferred to Mesquite, Nevada, where Ron graduated from Virgin Valley HS in 2002. While in high school, Ron was a member of the band as a trumpet player. Prior to graduation, Ron enlisted in the U.S. Marine Corps on a deferred enlistment, and left for basic training in September 2002.

It was off to San Diego and then Camp Pendleton and infantry training regiment (ITR). After 16 weeks, Ron was assigned in his MOS school of administration that took him to Camp Lejune, North Carolina, for a seven week course. While in school he met a lovely young lady who was also a Marine and enrolled in the same course.

They hit it off and began to date. At the completion of school Ron and his lady Caroline took a 10 day leave and went to New Jersey so Ron could meet Caroline's father.

Then off to Mesquite so she could meet Ron's parents. From here they flew to Camp Pendleton where they had both been assigned permanent duty stations.

Ron was assigned to the 3rd Amphibious Assault Battalion, 1st Marine Division. He spent his entire enlistment at this assignment and was discharged a Sergeant.

After he and Caroline returned to their duty stations from visiting their respective parents, they continued to date and became engaged in April and were married in October in Mesquite.

They had their reception at the Oasis Club House. A wonderful experience but both still had about three years left of their enlistment and returned to Camp Pendleton to complete their obligation. During this time Ron and Caroline had two lovely daughters. They lived in off-base housing and moved to Mesquite when they were discharged from the Corps.

During his enlistment, Ron attended American Intercontinental University and received an associated degree in business administration. When Ron left the service he joined his dad in the insurance and investment business in Mesquite.

Ron has three brothers, one of whom served six years in the Navy. Ron is active in the Mesquite Veterans Center and is President of the Veterans of Modern Warfare. He is also the bugler for the Virgin Valley Honor Guard.

Ron, thank you for your service to your country!

Caroline Mathews Bird, US Marine Corps

You have just read about Ron Bird; now it is time to hear about his wife's military enlistment. It is really unusual to have the opportunity to interview both husband and wife about their experience in the service. This is where they met, developed a relationship, and started a life together as well as a family.

Caroline was born July 9, 1982 in Riverside, California. She graduated from Bellevue High School in Bellevue, Nebraska in 2000. Caroline didn't participate in many high school activities, although as a Marshall Arts student she was very busy. Moving from place to place was a common event for Caroline and her family as her father was career Air Force. He retired from the Air Force after 23 years of service as a master sergeant.

From Nebraska it was on to Atlantic City, New Jersey, where Caroline's father settled after retiring from the Air Force. Caroline was interested in pursuing fulltime employment with a future, but that was difficult in Atlantic City as all the promising careers were with the casino industry and you needed to be 21 years old.

After finding employment with a local bank, Caroline worked there for two years and decided it was time for a change. Quite a change! She enlisted in the Marine Corps and it was off to Paris Island for basic training, then Camp Lejune for ITR and finally Personnel School.

While at Lejune she met another marine who was attending personnel school and they began dating. (I think you may have heard of this before!) Dating was complicated since you never knew where you and the individual you were dating would be assigned, but Caroline and her date ended up both receiving orders for Camp Pendleton. Both were assigned to very similar posts.

Therefore, prior to leaving for Camp Pendleton Caroline and (you guessed it) Ron Bird took leave to meet each other's parents. Six months after being assigned to Camp Pendleton they were married. They set up housekeeping in off-base housing and went on with their lives. They had two beautiful daughters while they were still in the service. Caroline was discharged in 2006 and she and Ron moved to Mesquite.

Caroline initially worked at Financial Concepts when they first came to Mesquite. She took some time off and then went back to work as an Administrative Assistant for

Ernest Luke after their daughters started school. Recently Caroline became involved with marketing and sales with Discover Mesquite Magazine.

Caroline thank you for your service to your country!

Donald Tobin, US Navy and US Marine Corps

Born in April, 1927 in New York City, Don was raised in a Boys Home in Brooklyn. Not having a father at home, he left school at 16 and went to work doing various jobs for a year before enlisting in the Navy.

He went to Sampson, New York for basic and advanced training as a storekeeper. From there Don was assigned to the Brooklyn Navy Yard. After making 3rd Class, Don was transferred to the Panama Canal where he spent time until he was assigned to a ship that was headed to Guadalcanal where he and others were involved in the Okinawa Landing. This group of ships was attacked by the Japanese kamikaze pilots and was forced to retreat. Crews from the lead ships pulled back and onto the ships in the rear. Several ships were lost and many casualties occurred.

From here Don and his crew transported the casualties to Saipan then it was back to the states and then to China where his ship transported marines to Guam. While doing so, they ran into a huge typhoon which added 5 days to their journey, but they survived without too much damage.

Don was assigned to the USS Iwo Jima, which took him back to the U.S. Don decided to get out of the Navy and go to college on the GI Bill, as he had earned his GED during his enlistment.

After several years, no degree and out of money, Don decided to re-enlist in the Navy. However, they wouldn't re-instate him at his old rank, so he enlisted in the Marine Corps, which meant back to basic.

So Don was off to basic training at Paris Island and a new beginning. After boot camp and additional schooling, Don was assigned to Pearl Harbor as an MP.

After a year at Pearl Harbor he was transferred to Guam and spent the next three years working security. When his three year enlistment was up, he went into the reserves to decide what he was going to do with regard to a military career.

He didn't have long to think about it. He was activated due to the Korean War and he was assigned to the 7th Marine regiment, and became part of an Artillery Group.

He was sent to Korea. Although combat was no picnic, Don said the terribly cold weather was more difficult to handle than the actual combat. During his 11 months in combat, he spent 21 days at a listening post where he was supposed to have been relieved after one day. Don was promoted to Corporal when he returned. After a three week leave he was promoted to sergeant E5.

He returned to Korea for another six months in 1952. After experiencing combat in Korea, Don took an opportunity to attend Recruitment School. After completion he recruited in Kansas for four years and in Racine, Wisconsin for three years.

Don developed an attachment with the people he recruited and it affected him when some of those recruits ended up wounded or killed.

He was tired of attending KIA and WIA Programs and decided it was only right to volunteer to where his recruits were being sent.

So in 1968 Don requested and was granted his wish and was ordered to Vietnam during the Tet Offensive. His unit was the blocking force used to prevent Da Nang from being overrun. Don was now a gunnery Sergeant E7 and he and a Major were the two highest ranking men of this unit. Don and his squad of 12 to 14 men were used to suppress fire, and therefore were liable to take enemy fire at any time. Don was part of the 5th Marines.

It was estimated the unit lost 200 men and had 300 to 400 wounded. After 13 months Don returned to the U.S. and Camp Pendleton. He was assigned another recruiting position in Waterloo, Iowa. Don Tobin decided after three wars and 26½ years of active military service with 30 years of total service that it was time to retire.

After leaving the Marine Corps as a gunnery sergeant E7 Don worked in various sales jobs until he retired at 62. Although Don is not currently married, he has three children, nine grandchildren, and one great grandchild. One of Don's granddaughter's will be retiring from the Air Force this year.

During his honorable career Don received the following honors: WWII Okinawa Combat one star, Korea two tours Inchon, Chosin Resevoir Combat five stars, Vietnam Tet Combat five stars, Presidential Unit Citation for Combat, four stars, Meritorious Unit Citation for Combat two stars, Good Conduct Medal six stars and Korean Presidential Unit Citation 2nd Award with leaf.

What a career! I interviewed Don at his home and he is a very proud Marine, but I have not seen much of him lately.

Don, thank you for your incredible service to your country!

7

VETERANS OF THE US ARMY

Jesse Samuels, US Army

Born in Brooklyn, New York, January 8, 1944, Jesse's parents moved to Manhattan when he was a year old. When he was eight the family moved to Paramus, New Jersey, where he grew up and graduated from Paramus HS in 1961.

Jesse was seriously overweight and was relentlessly ridiculed in school. As an incentive to lose weight and get classmates off his back, he joined the wrestling team. He continued with it and lost almost 200 pounds.

After graduation, Jesse enrolled at Teterboro School of Aeronautics at Teterboro Airport. His parents were disappointed Jesse hadn't enrolled at a traditional college but he explained that he wanted a hands-on career.

He received his airframe mechanics license after a year and transferred to Spartan University of Aeronautics and Technology in Tulsa, Oklahoma, where he went to classes day and night year around. He earned a power plant mechanics license; airborne maintenance technician certification; multi-engine certificate and a Bachelor's in Airport Management.

Jesse passed the test for a federal aviation license for aircraft maintenance and inspection authorization for light and heavy aircraft. He was also a licensed engineer representative.

After graduating in 1964 Jesse was drafted. Because he wanted to pick his military occupation specialty (MOS) he beat the draft and enlisted in the Army, which guaranteed an MOS of single engine fixed wing aircraft maintenance.

After boot camp at Ft. Dix in New Jersey, it was off to Ft. Eustis, Virginia, for training. Now the fun began. Jesse said he was appalled at how ineffective the training program was.

A sergeant major jumped on his case and asked if he thought he could do better. "Yes," he replied.

So he was escorted to the Company Commanders office and given an opportunity to explain. A full bird colonel was present and wanted to hear what Jesse had to say. "I'm a Spartan graduate and your program is all theory," Jesse told him. "You need to go to the bone yard and bring back what is there and do work on engines and planes."

"You can do this?" the colonel asked. "I can," Jesse said. "Then go at it," the colonel replied.

So Jesse started the Advanced Avionics training program at Ft. Eustis. He was an E2 teaching the officers. Jesse stayed at Ft. Eustis his entire enlistment. He said he was offered the chance to go to Officers Candidate School (OCS) but didn't want to make the Army a career. He was discharged in 1967 as an E5.

Jesse had no problem finding a job in the aerospace industry. He was hands-on and eventually fulfilled his dream of working on a wide variety of aircraft. During his career he was responsible for several different teams, some with up to 30 members.

He was eventually promoted to chief aircraft inspector. His career took him all over the U.S. and Europe. In 1996 Jesse retired from aerospace, but soon became bored, so he went into business marketing mining supplies and metal detectors.

Jesse had married in 1988 and became a full time care giver to his wife, who became ill several years ago. She died in 2013.

He was fortunate to meet a lovely lady named Mariam who also hailed from the east. She also lost her spouse, so Jesse and Mariam married are now settling in Mesquite.

Jesse, thank you for your service to your country!

Robert Meibaum, US Army

Bob was born in St. Louis, March 9, 1930, where he attended Roosevelt High School and was a drummer in the school's marching band. Bob graduated in 1946 at 16 and worked for a blueprint company where he received some photographic training in which he had developed an interest. After a year Bob enrolled at Rochester Institute of Technology in New York and earned a degree in photographic science.

After graduating Bob went to work for EG&G a company formed by Harold Edgerton, Kenneth Germeshausen and Herbert Grier. Edgerton, a professor of electrical engineering at the Massachusetts Institute of Technology, developed the electronic flash that is used on all cameras.

The company handled all types of energy and eventually developed aerial photography used on atomic test sites.

After graduating from college at 21, Bob enlisted in the U.S. Army. After basic training he was assigned to train new recruits, which he did for two years. He was later assigned to the signal corps where he was able to use his photography skills. He spent his entire enlistment in Hawaii.

Bob's older brother, Walter served as a bomber pilot in the U.S. Army Air Corps during WWII, flying over 24 missions. Walter spent his working career with General Electric, in management.

After the Army, Bob worked for EG&G for 44 years. After retiring, he spent much of his time traveling and enjoying the country. There are few places that Bob hasn't visited. Twelve years ago Bob found Mesquite. He liked it here, bought a place and never left. Walter lived with Bob for a while but recently moved to Texas.

Bob is a frequent visitor to the vet center and enjoys a cup of coffee and discussions with the other veterans. When Cliff Jenkins was president of the center he and Bob often had discussions about what Bob might do to enhance the facility.

Cliff told him was beginning to outgrow its current space and an expansion would probably be necessary.

"If you want to do that, I'll take care of the cost," Bob said.

Several veterans worked long and hard and the expansion was recently completed inside and out. Although Cliff died before it was finished, he did get to see much of the interior work and loved it.

A dedication dinner was held Monday in Bob's honor to thank him for the generous gift. A plaque will be hung over the doorway to the entrance to the new expansion.

From all the veterans and their families, Bob we sincerely thank you for your generosity and service to your country.

I had the distinct honor of meeting Bob recently, and he is a special individual, not because of his generosity, but because he loves his country and the veterans who served. He is a brilliant man evidenced by his academic credentials.

Herb Cleary, US Army

Herb Cleary, was born in New Scotland, Nova Scotia, February 22, 1944. He attended Stellarton High School and was an outstanding athlete. He participated in football, hockey, rugby and baseball and did well in all four sports, but just a little better in baseball. When he graduated in 1962 he received a baseball scholarship to BYU.

After 2½ years at BYU, Herb needed to get a job, so he left school and found one in Montpelier, Idaho. Herb's girlfriend and future wife was from Idaho and her dad worked for Monsanto Chemical Co. in Montpelier and was able to get Herb hired.

After a very short time Herb was promoted to supervisor in the manufacturing area. He and his lovely wife Sheila were married September 30, 1965. While living in Idaho, herb and Sheila moved to Deer Lake where Herb also became employed with the Deer lake Police Dept. as an officer, so he was holding down two jobs. Life changed in December, 1965 when Herb received his draft notice and was inducted into the U.S. Army and sent to Ft. Ord, California for basic training, and from there to Ft. Gordon for AIT and Military Police School. Herb did well and his unit received orders to go to Germany.

All set to leave, Heb was informed he couldn't go to Germany because he wasn't a U.S. citizen. Confused by this, he went to the commanding officer to seek an answer as to how he could get drafted and then not be allowed to travel with his unit. He never got a satisfactory answer. Herb received orders to report to Camp Roberts in California.

He landed in Los Angeles and had no idea where Camp Roberts was located. Asking around yielded no significant help, so he started hitching on highway 101 toward Ft. Ord where he had taken basic. He was in uniform and after a while a lady in a Cadillac stopped and picked him up.

"Where are you headed," she asked. "To Camp Roberts, but no one seems to know where that is," Herb replied, "Really? My husband happens to be the commander at Camp Roberts," responded the lady. So on his way to his designated assignment went Herb. The commanders' wife said she would inform her husband of his presence in the morning and that there was a barracks where Herb could bunk for the night. Herb found the barracks and threw his duffle bag on the bunk and someone hollered, "Who in the heck is making that racket?" "I am!" shouted Herb. "I'm trying to get settled after a long BS day, so I don't need any bull from you." "Is that you, Herb?" the voice responded.

Sure enough, a buddy from Nova Scotia who Herb played hockey with was in the same barracks. Herb was getting settled in as his new wife made it back to Idaho from Georgia and he was anxious to find out about his future in the Army.

The commander of Camp Roberts met with Herb the next morning and although the installation was virtually closed except for a small artillery company, they had decided to form a small MP unit at the camp and Herb was put in charge. Again things changed! Herb was assigned to the 227th Military Police and in March 1966 the unit received orders for Vietnam. Now, how does an individual get turned down from traveling to Germany with his unit because he was not a U.S. citizen, but gets sent to Vietnam? By the way this my question, not Herb's, although he did say it crossed his mind!

In Vietnam the 227th was put out in combat situations with the 1st and 7th Cavalry. Being assigned to infantry units was not unusual for MP units. On one particular occasion while on Jeep patrol, Herb and two other MP's ran over a claymore mine that blew up the vehicle. The three MP's, including Herb, were blown free and none was injured. Herb's only comment was, "Someone special must have been riding along with us that day!"

On a more pleasant note, Herb was assigned to Protective Services and had duty when Bob Hope, Barbara McNair, Raquel Welch and Miss World were in to entertain the troops. Not bad duty! After 13 months in Vietnam, Herb returned to the U.S. and Ft. Manmouth, New Jersey. At Ft. Manmouth, Herb played on the base baseball team. He pitched and played first base and the team was the 1st Army Champion.

With his enlistment about to expire, he was asked what his intentions were with regard to the military. Herb told a general he would re-enlist for six years but heard his unit was scheduled to go back to Vietnam. He was willing to go anywhere else at the time but didn't want to go to a combat zone because his wife was pregnant. The general said he would look into it, but his response was a no go for Herb.

So Herb went back to Deer Lake, Idaho and his job with Monsanto and the police department. Soon after getting settled back home, Herb went to Pocatello to see a judge about becoming a U.S. citizen, something he had wanted for a long time. Herb took the test, which he aced and became a citizen. Herb retired from Monsanto and continued to work off and on with the Deer Lake police as needed.

He and Sheila did some traveling and visited Mesquite while staying in Logandale in their RV. They liked it here and in 2001 bought a home. They continue to remain busy. Herb worked as a security guard at the Virgin River for eight years. He is now employed at the Eureka in the same capacity. He enjoys people and his job. He and Sheila have three children, six grandchildren and one great grandchild.

Herb, thank you for your service to your country!

Gary Krull, US Army

Born in Green Bay, Wisconsin, March 22, 1949, Gary graduated from West DePere High School in June, 1968. While attending West DePere, Gary played basketball and spent a lot of time in wood shop. As a matter of fact, he made furniture for several teachers while waiting to leave for the US Army. Gary had enlisted in January on a late entry program and didn't have to depart until June 15. Therefore, he had some time to do some productive work making furniture.

But depart he did, and it was to Ft. Campbell, Kentucky, home of the 101st Airborne for eight weeks of basic training. From here he went to Ft. Leonard Wood, Missouri for eight weeks of Wheeled Vehicle Mechanics School. This included learning how to repair anything with wheels on it from class I to class IV maintenance, minor maintenance to rebuilding an engine.

Gary then went on to Ft. Knox, Kentucky for Track Maintenance School. Now that he had learned how to maintain vehicles with wheels, he had to learn how to repair vehicles that ran on tracks, like APC's (armored personnel carriers), tanks, self propelled artillery, etc. This was also an eight week program and after 16 weeks of school Gary went from an E1 to an E4.

Gary was assigned to the Service battery 3rd Artillery Ft. Knox. While meeting with his First Sergeant, he was asked if he could type. He said about 18 words per minute. "Great," said the 1st sergeant, "You are my new company clerk!"

After getting a security clearance, Gary served as the company clerk for eleven months, after going through 16 weeks of mechanics training with flying colors.

Things changed from his company clerk job as Gary was sent to Korea. He landed at Kimpo and was assigned to the 1st Battalion 32nd Infantry at Camp Matta at the DMZ. He was sent for a week's training and then assigned to the Ground Surveillance Radar Team. They were at a guard post at the DMZ where 60 caliber machine guns were installed at every outpost. North Korea would play propaganda every night. The radar team would use ground surveillance and scan for N. Koreans, and take proper action if found. Gary volunteered to go on patrol into the DMZ as 2nd in command looking for the enemy. Both the N. Korean and the U.S. troops wandered through the DMZ infiltrating this area looking for information on the other's operation. This was an extremely dangerous area and took an exceptional kind of soldier to carry out the mission. Gary was that kind of soldier. After six months, Gary's unit rotated off the DMZ to Camp Kaiser.

He was assigned to the motor pool and put in charge of all the log books, since he hadn't turned a wrench for a while but had done a lot of paper work. He was responsible for the motor pool records and after two months was promoted to E5. He did well with inspections and redid the entire motor pool records system. Gary left Korea on Thanksgiving Day, 1970. He processed at Ft. Lewis, Washington and was sent to SeaTac airport to go on leave when an unfortunate incident occurred. Anti-war demonstrators were around when Gary and other military personnel were boarding and they were spit upon. Not taking kindly to this disgusting act, they responded and were delayed. However, things worked out and they went on their way.

Gary went to Frankfort, Germany and was assigned to the 3rd Armor Division Command Maintenance Inspection Team. Their job was to inspect all maintenance records, vehicles and anything to do with their operations. They wanted to inspect a unit right out of the field for readiness, so they did. An E6 was inspecting the turret of an M60 A1 tank and put a card in the turret to check for an electrical charge to see if it would fire. Unfortunately a 105 howitzer was loaded and exploded taking out the officer's club. Fortunately no one was in the club. After six months Gary was added to the Annual General Inspection Team. They were due to inspect the Administration Company. The night before the inspection they noticed the company was loading deuce and a half with things from their building that they didn't want inspected. So during the inspection they were told to unload the trucks they had loaded the night before. Needless to say they failed the inspection.

Gary left for Ft. Dix to process out of the Army. When he got there he was told they did not have his records and could not process him. Gary said this was the only reason he was there. It took 10 days to get his records sent to

Ft. Dix so Gary could process out and with those records came a note from the administration company that had failed their annual inspection. Payback is a _ _ _ _ _!!! Instead of three years and eight months, Gary spent three years eight months and 10 days in the Army.

After the Army, Gary worked as a mechanic for Firestone Tire and Rubber and drove a semi until 1986. Then he built a truck stop in the Green Bay area. That worked out so well that he built two more and bought out his partners in 2004. Gary met his lovely wife Diane in 1972 and they were married in 1976. They have two very successful daughters. Gary's wife had a bout of illness in 2006, so he sold his business and they bought a home in Mesquite in 2007. He and Diane are doing fine. Gary received the Army Commendation Medal.

Gary thank you for your service to your country!

Having come to Mesquite from Wisconsin myself, Gary and I have shared a lot of Wisconsin stories, most of which we agree on. However, there is one thing we will never agree on. He is a huge Packers fan, and I originally hail from Pittsburgh and will always be a Steelers fan.

Larry Morton, US Army

On June 19, 1938 in Rock Springs, Wyoming Larry Morton was born. When he was four years old his family moved to American Fork, Utah. His mother was from American Fork originally and her brother needed assistance due to poor health. At this young age, Larry and a friend were exploring the hills and mountains and discovered what appeared to be some kind of military camp. Suddenly they were approached by what appeared to be a couple of MP's (military police). WWII was going on and the boys had run into an American Prisoner of War (POW) camp for captured Germans.

The MP's treated the boys kindly and invited them for lunch. They accepted, but nothing was ever said about the place being a POW camp. Not there, nor at home!

Larry attended American Fork HS and graduated in 1956. While there he played football, basketball and ran track. In 1955, with his parents' permission, he enlisted in the Utah National Guard.

Enlistees went to Camp Williams for four days for summer camp in his first year. After four days they went to bivouac at American Fork Canyon.

On a 24-hour pass, prior to the move to American Fork Canyon, Larry and a few buddies stayed out a little late returning to camp just an hour or two prior to the move to the canyon. As a jeep driver for the company commander, Larry was instructed to block a road at a crossroads after delivering him to his position.

Larry did as instructed. A little later (actually a lot later) Larry was rousted by the 1st sergeant. He had fallen asleep and a long line of cars was backed up. This was not so bad except the convoy that he was blocking the road for had passed a long time ago. Fortunately the 1st sergeant gave Larry a break and all ended well.

After graduating from high school Larry decided to enlist in the regular Army. He had injured a knee during his first summer camp and showed up limping for his physical. He had already had a physical when he joined the National Guard, but the regular Army insisted on another. When asked about his limp, he just said he twisted his knee.

After two days of exams, the Army said his knee disqualified him from active duty. Disappointed he reported back to his guard unit and told them what happened. Their response was if the regular Army can't take you then we can't let you continue to be a member of the National Guard. Larry was given an Honorable Discharge after two years of service.

Not sure what to do now, Larry worked several jobs and then hooked up with General Refractions Inc. This company made bricks. He started in maintenance and ended up as superintendent. Larry married during this time and he and his wife had five children.

After 32 years, he retired from general Refractions. Larry's working life was not over, however. He started two businesses, one of which he sold to his son-in-law. That business continues to flourish in American Fork as well as another in which he is still involved. During this time Larry started a pheasant hunting business in South Dakota, but after spending two winters there decided this wasn't for him. He sold it!

So Larry went back to Utah. He decided to visit Mesquite and stayed a week and talked to some local residents. He liked what he heard and for the next six months he rented a condo here. In 2010, Larry decided to buy a home and is now a fulltime resident. Larry is involved in a number of activities in the community.

Larry, thank you for your service to your country!

Larry is a member of our card group, so I see him virtually every Friday. He is a great guy and a pretty good joke teller. We have become good friends.

Francis "Buzz" Rakow, US Army

Francis Rakow, or "Buzz" as he is known to his friend and fellow veterans, was born April 27, 1940 in Ponca, Nebraska. He attended Ponca High School where he participated in football, baseball, and track and played the trumpet in the marching band. Buzz graduated in 1958 and attended Augustana University for a year before going to work for his father who owned a candy and tobacco business. In October 1963, Buzz was drafted and sent to Ft. Leonard Wood, Missouri for basic training.

While waiting to fill up a basic training unit, Buzz and the rest of the recruits were assigned work duty consisting of raking leaves and KP. This set them back in their basic training so Christmas came around and his unit was forced to take two weeks leave over the Christmas holidays.

This was pretty unusual for soldiers who barely had two months in the Army. After basic, Buzz was sent to artillery school at Ft. Sill, Oklahoma where he trained as an artillery surveyor, both as a positioned and target area surveyor. After eight weeks of training Buzz was sent to Ft. Dix, where he sat for a week before being shipped out to his assignment in Augsberg, Germany. It was a rough trip as they crossed the Atlantic in the middle of winter and many became seasick.

Augsberg, located in Southern Bavaria, was Buzz's home as part of the 1st Battalion 13th Artillery, 24th Infantry Division. He spent 19 months at this assignment, which was his entire tour of duty. Fifty per cent of the unit's time was spent in field training. During the revolt in Cypress there was a serious alert.

The unit spent two full days at an airport waiting to be deployed to Cypress before it was finally called off. Buzz was sent home and discharged after his tour here.

He worked at a packing plant for about six months after being discharged and then enrolled at Chadron St. University where he graduated with a degree in Earth Science in 1971. It took an extra year to finish college due to the death of Buzz's father.

Upon graduation, Buzz took a job with Susquehanna Western as a geologist. After two years, he returned to school at the University of North Dakota to seek his Masters Degree. He worked part time as a teacher and during the summer months while attending school, but decided to go back to work full time just 54 credits shy of his degree. Then it was on to Casper, Wyoming, where Buzz worked as a geologist for Casper Mineral Corp in 1977.

He was sent to Cannon City, Colorado, but after eight months was laid off. So he moved on to Riverton, Wyoming and Pathfinder Mines, but another layoff put Buzz out of work again.

So he went to work for the BLM on a part time basis which would play a significant role in his future. In 1986, Buzz took a full time position with IDS a division of Ameriprise, but after a relatively short period of time the BLM offered Buzz another part time position and he accepted. The job later became full time as a geologist.

This was in Hanksville, Utah and it worked out so well that Buzz stayed with the BLM for the next 23 years until he retired.

In November, 2010, Buzz bought a home in Mesquite and has become very active in the community, including his church, the Mesquite Veterans Center and The Mesquite American Legion Post 24.

Buzz, we thank you for your service to your country and the community!

Buzz has become a great friend. He is always willing to help out anyone who has a need.

Bill Losh, US Army

Born in 1947 in St. Benedict, Pennsylvania Bill's family moved to Cleveland when he was very young. Bill attended Benediction High School in Cleveland and then transferred to Max Hayes Technical High School to study metal pattern making. He graduated in 1966. He was hired as a machinist in a job shop where he worked until Uncle Sam drafted him six months later.

In October 1966 it was off to Ft. Knox, Kentucky for basic training and then to Ft. Campbell, without any MOS school or training along with others from his basic unit. They were told they would get on the job training for a supply MOS. Bill and the others were attached to the 101st Airborne because the transportation company they were in to be sent or had already been released and sent to Vietnam.

Since Bill and this group of GI's had no real training at this point, they spent a lot of time pulling KP duty. Bill however, being a pretty good athlete, went out for the company basketball team, made it and the team went on to win the Post Championship. Each of the players received quite a trophy, one that Bill remains proud of.

When the 101st was sent to Vietnam, Bill and all the others who were attached to the 101st could not go as they were not paratroopers and were transferred to the 3rd Army. Here they were finally assigned to supply.

Bill spent his entire hitch at Ft. Campbell and was discharged as a sergeant in October 1968.

Upon his return to civilian life Bill went to work for Dove Die as an apprentice tool and die maker, where he worked for the next four years. He became a journeyman tool and die maker in three. He left Dove and worked at several jobs in the same capacity over the next several years.

Bill met his lovely wife Mary Jane in 1972 and they married in 1982. They always loved the west and had been through Mesquite several times. Unfortunately, Mary Jane passed in 2009, but Bill continued on with their dream and bought a place here in 2012. They had two sons who are very successful. One is a mechanical engineer in California and the other a teacher in Ohio.

Bill has become a welcome addition to the Mesquite Center, where he gets involved in many projects as a volunteer. He also volunteers at the senior center and loves the outdoors. He is a golfer, loves to ride his bicycle, is involved in Gold Butte and just recently became involved with the local off-road group.

Bill we thank you for your service to your country!

Joe deGanahl, US Army

On May 25, 1948 Joe deGanahl was born in Eugene, Oregon. His family moved early in his life and he was raised in Yampa, Colorado. He attended high school where he was a wrestler on the varsity wrestling team. After graduating he attended the University of Colorado and majored in History. He became a member of the ROTC program at the university.

Joe left school before he graduated and was drafted into the US Army. Because of his ROTC background, Joe became involved in a special program with the Army and after AIT was sent to Ft. Benning to a unique NCO program.

Joe had been trained as a mortar man prior to his assignment to Ft. Benning and had been a member of a special group called the Persian Rifles. Joe spent six months in the program and graduated 2nd in his class. He went into the program as an E1 and emerged as an E6. Quite an accomplishment in anybody's book!

Joe was assigned as a mortar section sergeant for an 81mm mortar team that consisted of 32 men. That team was part of the 2nd Battalion 501st Infantry, 101st Airborne. They were sent to Vietnam and assigned to the north where Viet Cong consistently attempted to infiltrate the major cities of the south. Their job was to keep them out, or at least limit their success as this was a major logistics route of the Viet Cong.

During combat situations Joe's responsibility was to evaluate incoming information and adjust the mortars using direction, elevation and amount of charge prior to launching. All of their calculations were based on a military grid reference.

There were three teams attached to the unit, each with three mortars. Although this was combat, Joe and his men felt reasonably secure as the mortar teams typically had a rifle company in front of them consisting of two hundred riflemen when they were at capacity.

The tricky part was making certain how far out in front of the mortar teams the riflemen were, so the mortar fire could be adjusted so they wouldn't endanger their rifle teams. Although this unit was part of the 101st Airborne they had been relieved of their parachutes and operated more like the Air Cavalry.

Here is an interesting note that came from Joe's experience. Joe Luer, now a retired Brigadier General, was commander of the unit when he was in Vietnam and Joe got to know him. Years after both had left the military they were talking on the phone one day when General Luer mentioned he was going to Ft. Benning for something or other. Joe mentioned his nephew was graduating and getting his wings that week and Genera Luer offered to pin the wings on Joe's nephew, and he did! What an honor that must have been!

During another bit of combat action Joe and his unit were waiting to be moved out. They were told helicopters would be there to take them away in five minutes. Thirty minutes passed and still no choppers.

The men learned later the helicopters had been converted to medivac units so those alive and without injury has to wait.

The helicopters finally came and moved to Joe's unit. As they arrived at the combat zone, a 2nd Lt. Joe Hooper met Joe and told him he had bunkers all ready for Joe's team.

The unique story about this was Joe Hooper had been an enlisted man who was highly decorated and had been given a field commission and had been awarded the Medal of Honor. The next day Hooper's actions led to his being awarded the Silver Cross.

Joe Hooper was the most decorated soldier in Vietnam. Joe saw him again when he appeared with Bob Hope at a show in Vietnam. When Audie Murphy died in a small plane crash, Joe Hooper was asked (and accepted) to be a pall bearer at his funeral.

Joe served in Vietnam until August 1971. He left the Army that year as well. However, he didn't leave his fellow veterans.

We all know what the Vietnam Veterans put up with when they returned home. Joe became involved with veterans organizations that lobbied state and federal legislators for issues that directly affected the Vietnam veterans, including labor issues.

Joe did this for three years and went back to the University of Colorado in addition to his veteran work. Joe obtained hid degree in History and became involved in the ranching business that his family had started in 1954.

Joe met his lovely wife Carol in 1980 and they married in 1981. Carol also became involved in the ranching business and kept the books. Carol had come to Colorado via her transfer with her job at Motorola.

The ranching business grew with facilities in Colorado, Nebraska and Arizona, but with four brothers and a sister who was a veterinarian the family had lots of help. Because Joe had made trips to this area for auctions and putting calves together at feed lots, he and Carol decided to buy a home in Mesquite. In 1996 they purchased a home and have been residents ever since.

Joe officially retired in February 2012. He and Carol enjoy canoeing, fishing, etc. and have a place to do that as well as being involved in activities in Mesquite.

Joe, we thank you for your service to your country!

Joe and Carol have become wonderful friends of my wife and me. Carol and my wife share membership to some common organizations in Mesquite, and Joe and I see each other at various functions. They are wonderful people, and we are honored to have them as friends.

Mike Scott, US Army

Mike was a 4th of July baby in 1945 in Los Angeles, California, where he lived until he was five. His family was in the restaurant business and they moved frequently. Mike lived in California, New Mexico and Michigan, and then back to California. He attended Santa Maria High School where he played football and was on the varsity swimming team. He graduated in 1963 and moved to Sacramento and worked at various jobs for the next five years.

In September 1968, Mike enlisted in the US Army, as his two older brothers were Army veterans. The oldest was in the Army Air Corps at the end of WWII.

Mike went to boot camp in Ft. Lewis, Washington, and then to Ft. Gordon, Georgia for military police (MP) school. After completing the MP training, Mike decided he wasn't cut out to be an MP and requested additional schooling.

After his request was granted, he went to Ft. Jackson, South Carolina for training as a heavy truck mechanic and then to Ft. Benning for training on track vehicles. He was assigned to Ft. Carson, Colorado as part of the 5th Army and spent the next 10 months there.

Mike got orders for Vietnam where he was part of a platoon attached to the 101st Airborne Division in Hue and Quang Tri. The installation was Camp Evans and his platoon's responsibility was to maintain all of the division's vehicles in good operating condition.

The platoon also supplied fire bases, hauled troops and whatever else was required to keep the unit in tip-top condition. There were times the unit had to go out on convoys with the 101st.

After a year, Mike was sent back to Ft. Lewis where he was discharged in 1971.

Mike enrolled at Colorado St. University and worked part time jobs while attending class. In Colorado he met a lovely lady named Annie who was also attending Colorado St. Mike left school and moved on to San Diego, where Annie joined him. They were married in San Diego in 1984. Their wedding took place on a 161 foot schooner that included dinner and 300 guests for $160. How would you like to find that deal today!

Mike and Annie stayed in San Diego for three years, Mike worked as a painter and the couple enjoyed the beach and a carefree way of life. From San Diego it was up to Olympia, Washington, where Mike developed a relationship with his mother and older brothers. Mike continued to paint and started driving a truck.

After three years they moved to Rhinelander, Wisconsin, where Annie was originally from. In Wisconsin Mike became a long haul trucker and Annie worked as an executive assistant and legal secretary.

Mike had stopped in Mesquite while driving his truck and in 2004 he and Annie moved here. Although Annie still works as a medical secretary they have settled in Mesquite as retirees.

Mike is an avid metal detector enthusiast and a member of the Gold Prospectors of America (GPA). He still swims 1½ miles a day and loves to grill.

Mike feels Americans should always defend the Constitution as he has some concerns about the country.

Mike, thank you for your service to your country!

Terry Zorn, US Army

Terry was born in Price, Utah, July 16, 1949. He was raised there and attended Carbon High School where he played football. Terry graduated in 1968 and enlisted in the US Army in June.

He left for basic training at Ft. Bliss, Texas and then went to Ft. Polk, La. for advanced infantry training. After AIT, Terry received orders for Vietnam and was assigned to Long Bihn as a staff car driver.

He spent 13 months in this capacity and then came home for Christmas. After his Christmas leave he went back to Vietnam for an additional five months in the same capacity. While in Vietnam, Terry's brother Clyde, two tears his senior, was in Saigon completing a 12 month tour of duty while Terry put 15 months in Vietnam.

Getting his assignment is an intriguing story. When Terry was in basic, the troops were told to count off, which they did. Every fourth man was told to step forward and informed that they had just volunteered for M16 training. This was pretty much a guarantee that they would be headed off to an infantry company and to Vietnam. They were off to Ft. Polk but had one stop prior to their flight. The small plane Terry was to board to complete his trip to Ft. Polk had some mechanical problems and he was delayed.

He finally arrived at Polk at 2 AM the following Saturday morning and was met at the airport by one individual. "Where are your orders?" asked the GI. "Right here," Terry replied. "You're infantry!" the GI said. "Oh my goodness, we don't have room for you. We had a whole boatload of infantry come in over the last few days and the infantry barracks are so full we even have guys sleeping on cots in the hallways. There is no way we can get you in there. So here are your new choices. You can go to cook school or truck driver's school."

"You can do that right here?" Terry asked "I can," the soldier replied. "Then I'd like to be a truck driver," Terry said "Done'" and his new found friend and Terry ended up with a truck driver MOS.

Terry's unit received orders for Vietnam and just as it was ready to leave, the men were told there had been a change in plans. Their departure would be delayed for two weeks.

Terry took leave and went home for two weeks. When he returned his unit left for Vietnam. When they arrived at Long Bihn, an officer asked him where he had been. You were supposed to be here two weeks ago. The guys responded they were told there was a change in plans and their departure was delayed for two weeks.

"Well, that is a problem" the officer said. "We've had several units of truck drivers come in the last several weeks and we have no more room for any more. So you guys now have a new decision to make. You can either become cooks, clerks or staff car drivers."

Needless to say, Terry became a staff car driver. Can you believe it? Two exact situations happening to the same guy from Price, Utah.

On his return to the states, Terry was assigned to Dugway Proving Grounds in Utah and was part of a Military Funeral Unit. This group attended funerals in Idaho, Wyoming and Utah. Terry mentioned he had no training in this area and the officer said no problem. "We have a funeral in Utah that you can attend as an observer," the officer said.

Terry went, but when they got there it was discovered the deceased soldier's parents were divorced and a flag had to be given to both parents. Terry was no longer an observer. He had to participate and did very well.

During his only other funeral duty in Salt Lake City, a father blamed the Army for his son's death. He had been putting up quite a fuss prior to the service. The Military Funeral Unit had to have a police escort to the cemetery, but no incidents. All worked out well.

Terry was discharged in 1971 and took a job with Utah Power and Light as a grounds man. He obtained an apprenticeship and went on to become a journeyman linesman. From there, he moved into supervision and ran his own crews. After 34 years of faithful service, Terry retired.

In 1972 Terry met a lovely young lady named Sheila who was out with her friends in Salt Lake City celebrating her 21st birthday. In all the excitement, he must have made a good impression as they were married in 1974. They have two sons. One lives in Salt Lake and one in Rock Springs, Wyoming. They are the proud grandparents of four granddaughters and a grandson.

They enjoy traveling and especially visiting their grand kids. Terry remains active in the Mesquite Veterans Center and the Vietnam Veterans of America Chapter 993.

Terry, we thank you for your service to your country.

Jim Sheldon, US Army

Jim was born in Hartley, Iowa on October 14, 1937. He attended Central HS in Sioux City, Iowa, where he graduated in 1955. He then attended Iowa St. University where he played football and obtained his degree as a Doctor of Veterinary Medicine. While attending Iowa St., a Brigadier General of the U.S. Army came to the university to recruit veterinarians for the Army. Sheldon accepted their offer, which meant the army would pay for the remainder of his education in return for a four year commitment.

He worked as a veterinarian between his junior and senior years at Ft. Knox, Kentucky. Upon graduation from Iowa St, he entered the Army as 1st Lt., assigned to the U.S. Army Veterinary Corps and sent to Ft. Sam Houston for training.

It was excellent training—a program where you were assigned to a medical doctor pathologist for training.

Jim was then assigned to Walter Reed Army Medical Unit, but was stationed at Ft. Detrick, Maryland in the pathology division. His work involved biological warfare and pathological support for infectious disease research. This work included using an impinger. Samples of air were sucked into a tube-like tool (impinger) and samples were analyzed for disease-causing bacteria such as anthrax, sleeping sickness, etc. Some of Jim's training included a trip to Puerto Rico and he was required five to seven showers a day to prevent the spreading of disease.

Jim was promoted to Captain during his service with the Army and after being released from active duty, remained a member of the active reserves. Due to his specialty MOS Jim accumulated 1½ years of active service due to reserve call ups.

Jim entered private practice dealing with large animals prior to entering the Army, and moved into a mixed practice after fulfilling his obligation.

He was also a student research assistant at the Department of Veterinary Pathology at Iowa State University. He was an associate animal pathologist from 1964 to 1966 at the University of Arizona specializing in animal and poultry disease diagnosis and pathology support to NIH projects dealing with the pathogenesis of deep mycotic infections.

He was also as Associate Professor at the University of Arizona then went on to become a professor at the University of Missouri, Department Veterinary Medicine.

Probably the interesting accomplishment to this writer is Jim's development of cattle feed yards and laboratories throughout the southwest and parts of the world. At one time he had four labs just in the southwest. The labs were used for pathology and diagnostic work. The organization was called Central Arizona Veterinary Laboratories. (CAVL)

Jim married his lovely wife Carolyn 21 years ago—he knew her well as she had worked for him running the labs. Carolyn is a Microbiologist. Together they have continued to keep the operation going—although not as big as it once was. They still have labs and cattle feed yards in the southwest.

Jim met some wonderful people in his business life. One of them was John Wayne. Jim had a feed yard in Arizona on a ranch that Mr. Wayne had some interest in. They became friends, and Jim said John was a great guy and a true gentleman. John Wayne also partnered with James Arness owning some cattle together.

At an event at their ranch, the 20 Bar Hereford Ranch, they castrated some bull calves for a get-together (I assume you all know what Rocky Mountain Oysters are). John Wayne, who was an excellent gin rummy player, and some of the guys were playing cards and eating those oysters when a woman came up and asked Mr. Wayne for an autograph. He obliged, as he never turned around anyone down.

As he was signing his name the woman helped herself to an oyster. Mr. Wayne asked her if she liked it, and she told him it was delicious.

"Do you know what it is?" "No," she said. That is when he told her it was a calf testicle! She immediately became ill. True story!

Jim established operations in Mexico and New Zealand at his peak, and set up treatment and protocol as well as diagnostic work.

Since 1973, he has become a Veterinary Medical Consultant and acts as laboratory diagnostic support to the feedlot industry in the Southwestern United States because of his extensive experience and work. He also is a consultant and product evaluator for several of the major chemical and pharmaceutical manufacturers.

Jim is president of Sheldon Agri-Business and Partner, JC Agri-Business.

He is a member of a number of professional organizations including the American College of Veterinary Pathologists, Academy of Veterinary Consultants, American Veterinary Medicam Assoc. and many more. Jim also authored scientific articles.

Jim is certainly a unique individual who has not only served his country well, but also his community and profession.

He and his wife Carolyn live in Mesquite, but their continued involvement in their business keeps them on the go. Jim has one daughter and four grandchildren.

Thank you for your service!

Jay Young, US Army

Jay was born in Salt Lake City, September 18, 1944. He was raised in Linden, Utah and attended Pleasant Grove HS where he participated in football and baseball. He graduated in 1962. Upon graduation, Jay enrolled in a technical college in Salt Lake City with an emphasis on electronics. After a year, he and two buddies went to California to work for the summer. While there they decided to enlist in the military. One buddy enlisted in the Navy and Jay enlisted in the Army.

Off to ft. Ord, California and then Ft. Benning, Georgia for radio school. After school Jay received orders for Thailand.

He was assigned to the 809th Engineering Battalion whose HQ was in Karat, Thailand. Jay's MOS was changed from communications to truck driver after arriving at his new assignment.

Instead of regular orders, each of the men in his outfit received passports that read "assigned on official assignment for the US Government." They were not allowed to wear uniforms or carry weapons.

They dressed in T-shirts and fatigue pants. Their job was to build roads and highways in Thailand that were to be used to transport supplies to Saigon. Jay and his unit were to be used to transport supplies to Saigon. Jay and his unit were told prior to leaving the states that some of them would not return; so prepare yourself.

Much of the work was in deep jungle, filled with snakes, including cobras and pythons. Jay saw what he considered very strange caged fights between ferrets and cobras. The locals bet on the outcome of these fights. They were very similar to cock fights.

After serving in Thailand for a year, Jay was sent home on a 30 day leave. Even though he wanted to stay on this assignment, he was informed that no one could be there longer than one year. He had found the assignment a little strange, but extremely interesting.

After completing his leave, Jay was assigned to the 619th Ordinance Company Special Weapons Depot in Kraigsville, Germany. This was a NATO Base that housed nuclear weapons. It was called North Point. Jay was again re-classified back to his original communications MOS, but had to receive a Top Secret Clearance due to his use of teletype equipment where he conversed with other installations throughout the world.

While in Germany, Jay developed a friendship with a man from Holland who was serving with the US Army. His parents had a place in Ireland and they invited Jay to stay on as his enlistment was getting short. His friend and family were very nice people and Jay gave it considerable thought, but in the end decided to return home. Back in the U.S., after having served three years, Jay received his discharge in October 1966. He spent three years in the Inactive Reserves and then joined the National Guard for a year, but with his job that didn't work out very well.

Jay met his lovely wife Kathy through a mutual friend in April 1967. Jay went to work for Geneva Pipe, a manufacturer of concrete pipe and man holes.

He started out as a laborer where he learned everything about the business. He spent 20 years in sales and then moved up into dispatch and quality control.

After 42½ years Jay was laid off and basically decided to retire. He and Kathy live in Mesquite. They have three children and 14 grandchildren.

Jay, we thank you for your service to your country!

Ovid Pinckert, US Army

On July 3, 1946 in Dimmitt, Texas Ovid Pinckert was born. At age five he moved to Colorado, where he attended Durango HS. While there he participated in football, baseball and basketball. He obviously participated well as he went on to Northern Colorado University on a combination football/baseball scholarship. After a year Ovid transferred to Ft. Lewis College and finished his second year there.

In the fall of 1966, he enlisted in the US Army and it was off to Ft. Bliss, Texas for basic training. While at Ft. Bliss, Ovid applied for and was accepted into Officer

Candidate School. He then went to Ft. Lewis, Washington for advanced individual training.

As he finished AIT, the 4th Infantry Division was deploying to Vietnam and Ovid decided he wanted to go with them. He went in to see the 1st Sergeant to tell him about his decision.

The sergeant took him into his office and kicked him in the behind and said, "You want to do what?" Ovid repeated his request. The sergeant kicked him in the behind again and said, "You want to do what?"

Once again Ovid repeated his request and the sergeant kicked him in the behind and said, "Now tell me what you want to do." Ovid replied, "Go to OCS." "That's what I thought you said," replied the sergeant. And off to OCS he went.

Ovid was in the class of 96 at Ft. Benning and graduated as a 2nd Lt. in November 1967. Then it was on to airborne training. After five jumps and much physical training, he was assigned to the 82nd Air Borne Brave Company as the 1st platoon leader. His unit was sent from Ft. Benning to Ft. Bragg when the Pueblo was captured by the Koreans and placed on alert. For three days they sat on the tarmac waiting for word to go overseas and free the Pueblo. It never happened, but a few days later they were on alert again and this time the 3rd Brigade of the 82nd was sent to Vietnam.

In February, 1968 they landed in Chu Li and convoyed up to Hue. It was there that they established HQ for the 3rd Brigade (Camp Rodriquez).

New 2nd Lieutenants were usually transferred to brigade jobs to gain some experience. Ovid was assigned to S4 Supply. He ran convoys from Hue to Da Nang. After several months he became an exhibitor. He carried a brief case full of blank orders and flew all over Vietnam to get supplies that the brigade needed…any way he could.

Later in 1968 he was transferred to the 101st Airborne, as the Army did not want all the 2nd Lieutenants rotated out at the same time. He became the platoon leader of Alpha Co. 501st Infantry. They were in an area outside of Bostonge at the edge of the Asahau Valley. They conducted search and destroy missions and were involved in combat on a weekly basis.

About 15 to 25 men were involved in each operation. They received orders from the company commander, but when on an operation Ovid was responsible for, he directed his platoon.

To his credit he lost no men during his tour of duty in Vietnam although he had several wounded. That is quite a record for a young officer.

In February, 1969 Ovid returned to the states.

Ovid relayed an interesting story. While his platoon was on patrol in a valley, a dog kept following them and barking. Afraid the barking would give away their position, Ovid ordered one of his men to shoot the dog. The man refused. Ovid took a wild shot and missed (probably intentionally) and the dog ran away. Relieved that they didn't have to worry about the dog or destroy it, they moved on. Reaching the valley, the dog showed up and began barking again. This time dogs from the top of the valley on both sides returned the barking. This usually was the sign of large enemy units and was true this time as well. Ovid called in support, his unit responded and their mission was successful, because of the dog they couldn't bring themselves to destroy.

Ovid returned to Ft. Bragg in February 1969, attached to the 18th Airborne Corp and was promoted to 1st Lt. He was then transferred back to the 82nd, promoted to Captain and sent back to Vietnam in September, 1970.

He became an advisor to the South Vietnamese Army Infantry (23rd Infantry Division). He worked out of Song Mau. He and one American Sergeant spent time in the field and fought with the South Vietnamese Army.

Again Ovid experienced significant combat against the North Vietnamese. He had the same authority to call in air strikes, request support from Navy ships and support from Air Force jets as he did when he was a platoon leader with U.S. troops. He found the South Army to be very professional during his time with them.

After eight months, Ovid transferred to Ban Me Thout as an advisor to basic training units of the South Vietnamese Army. He finished his second tour of duty in this capacity.

In September 1971, Ovid was sent to Frankfort, Germany as a staff officer for V Corps. In 1973 he was transferred to Gelenhausen as a combat support commander, 2nd Battalion, 48th Infantry. In November there was a reduction in force and Ovid separated from the Army after seven honorable years.

Ovid moved to Oregon where he became a state police officer. Twenty two of his 24½ years were spent as a detective. In 1993 he bought a horse ranch. He began dating his lovely wife Billie in 1991 and they were married in 1994. They became tired of the cold weather and during one of their trips came through Mesquite. Love at first sight! They bought a home here in 2005. Ovid and Billie have four children from previous marriages, eight grandchildren and two great grandchildren.

Ovid received the following commendations during his honorable service to his country:

3 Bronze Stars (one with Valor)
2 Army Commendations (one with Valor)
Vietnam Gallantry Cross
Good Conduct National Defense
Vietnam Service Combat Infantry Body
Parachutist
Vietnam Training Medal

Ovid now enjoys shooting and is president of the Mesquite Pistol Club. He also enjoys hunting, fishing, ATVing and traveling.

Ovid, we thank you for your service to your country!

Larry Stump, US Army

Larry was born March 14, 1940 in New Ringgold, Pennsylvania. At the age of seven, his family moved to Hayward, California. Larry attended and graduated from Hayward Union HS in 1959. While attending school Larry was a member of the high school's ROTC program. He was also a member of the rifle team, which went to the state competition his senior year. Upon graduation, Larry enlisted in the US Army and went to basic training at Ft. Ord, California followed by a 33 week long signal school at Ft. Gordon, Georgia. Graduation from signal school brought an assignment to Korea with the 13th Signal Corp, 7th Cavalry, 1st Cavalry Division. He spent the next 13 months in this deployment. After Korea he was assigned to Ft. Huachuca, Arizona as part of the 232rd Signal Corp. This military installation was located on an Indian reservation.

In 1962, the 232nd was deployed to Saigon, Vietnam. The members of this unit were deployed all over the country to provide communications during the war. Upon completion of this tour of duty in Vietnam, Larry returned home and decided to get out of the active Army; however, there weren't many good jobs around and after looking for a while he decided to re-enlist. He was sent to Ft. Bragg, N.C., and assigned to the 4th Signal Command. Shortly after being assigned, his unit was sent to Karlsruh, Germany as part of the Theater Signal Group. Larry spent the next year on this assignment.

Now a sergeant E5, it was back to Vietnam in Quinion as part of the 1st Logistics Group. After 12 more months in country, Larry was sent back to Ft. Gordon for 33 weeks of additional signal school training. Ft. Hood, Texas was the next stop for Larry as part of the 2nd Armor Division, direct support. This took up another year of his enlistment.

In 1968, when the Koreans stole the USS Pueblo, Larry was with the Signal Corp Battalion, 1st Corp as the CESCOM operator. He was sent to Korea and was attached to HQ where 26 divisions were controlled. While part of the 8th Army in Seoul he made E6 and completed his 13-month tour. On his return to the states, he was sent to Ft. Carson, Colorado, as part of the commandant maintenance team for the 4th Army. Larry became the Battery Communications Chief for the 1st Brigade 12th Infantry Division. His battle support plans and communication skills were noticed and appreciated by a Lt. Colonel whom Larry reported to, thus his assignment. He was in this position from 1968 to 1973.

Larry was off to Germany again, this time to Funari Barracks in Manheim, as part of the Signal Corp General Support Unit, Electronics and Communication Equipment. From there he was sent on another assignment to the U.S. Combat Equipment Group in Europe. After significant time overseas, he returned to the USA via Ft. Knox and was assigned to the 1st Armor Brigade.

It was here that his life changed a bit. While stationed at Ft. Carson Larry met a lovely lady named Margaret, who was a waitress at a truck stop. She had some problems and Larry helped her out. He then went to visit his sister in Georgia and ran into Margaret who—unknown to him—was a friend of his sister's.

The next thing you know, Margaret goes to Ft. Knox with Larry and they get married so she can accompany him to his next assignment – Manheim, Germany.

Larry and Margaret went to Germany as Mr. and Mrs. Stump, where Larry was promoted to E7 and became Battalion Communications Chief of the 8th Infantry Division.

Margaret later returned to the USA prior to Larry as they had decided 21 years in the Army was enough. Larry headed to Ft. Dix, New Jersey in 1981 where he retired after 21 years of honorable service as an E7.

Next the Stump's were off to Reno where Larry's dad had left him some property—14 rental units. He and Margaret took over the units. Margaret managed them while Larry maintained them. After 20 years they sold the property and received a 27-foot motor home as part of the deal. As if Larry hadn't traveled enough, they spent the next five years traveling all over the USA.

They had been through most of Nevada, including Mesquite and loved it; so in 1995 they settled there. Larry went to work at the Virgin River, but after a year he quit. He and Margaret went on the road again for another year. They repeated this again before settling in permanently.

Margaret worked as a home care nurse and became close with the daughter of one her patients. When the patient passed away the daughter remained close to the Stumps. She became the manager of an RV Park that Margaret and Larry eventually moved into with their motor home. Mesquite Trailer Park has been their home ever since.

Unfortunately, Margaret passed away earlier this year, but will always be remembered as a wonderful caring woman. She and Larry were involved in a number of volunteer programs, especially involved with the Mesquite Veterans Center.

Larry is a member of the Vietnam Veterans of America Chapter 993.

Larry, we thank you for your service to your country!

James McCluskey, US Army

The following interview was done by my good friend Ed Fizer. Again, I thank him for his permission to include some of his interviews as he started this program. To only include mine would be a disservice to the veterans of Mesquite with whom he spoke.

I have known James (Mac) McCluskey for eight years. He was born January 23, 1930, at Ft. Smith, Arkansas (also the home of Judge Roy Bean). He soon moved to Lawton, Oklahoma, where he sold newspapers at Ft. Sill, and was active in school sports. He was four year letterman and captain of the basketball team.

After graduation from St. Mary's HS, Jim attended Cameron College for a year. He decided to apply to West Point Military Academy and was accepted and reported to Class G-2. He graduated four years later and was commissioned as 2nd Lt. in 1953.

Jim's first assignment was Ft. Bragg, North Carolina, where he attended parachute school with the first air borne class there since WWII. Modern day jump school is now located at Ft. Benning, GA.

Jim said he was so impressed with his first meeting with an old 82nd Airborne NCO that throughout his military career he allowed his non- commissioned officers to have input into his command decisions, and often placed his young Lieutenants alongside a seasoned NCO to help them become more skilled.

Jim was later sent to Germany with the 5th Infantry Division, Artillery Battalion. During that tour, Jim transferred from Artillery to the Ordinance Corps. After returning to the states, Jim earned his Master's Degree from Babson Institute and was selected to attend the Command and General Staff course. Next he returned to the 82nd Airborne at Ft. Bragg where he commanded the 782nd Maintenance Battalion until 1969.

Jim was sent to Vietnam and was assigned to the 173rd Airborne Brigade where he spent most of the time at a camp close to Quin Nhon, a large seaport on the South China Sea. Upon his return to the USA, Jim was assigned to the Pentagon for a few years. After his escape from the big house he went back to Ft. Bragg.

There he was the commander of the 269th Ordinance Group and he was able to earn his senior jump wings.

Next Jim was assigned to Detroit, where he was selected to be program director for the redesign of the Bradley fighting vehicle. His final assignment was as commander of Tooele Army Depot near Salt Lake City. There he oversaw the destruction of our country's older chemical and biological weapons.

Jim retired as a Colonel in 1979 and immediately took a position with Morton Thiokol Corporation where he served as the program director for the redesign of the solid rocket used by NASA. We all remember the Challenger Space shuttle accident. Jim was given the assignment of solving the problem. He and his crew built a $12-million static testing unit and essentially kept the space exploration program alive.

Jim met his lovely wife Ann at Ft. Dix, New Jersey and they have been married for 53 years. They have four children. They moved to Mesquite in 1999, after living in St, George, Utah for 10 years.

Jim we thank you for your military service and civilian service to our country. I salute you my friend.

Jim McCluskey was one of the first veterans I met when I came to Mesquite, and for whatever reason, we hit it off right away. We had wonderful conversations about everything you could think of. I'll never forget one day during a discussion at the veterans' center, Jim said, "You know, Jim, you are like the little brother I never had." Well, coming from a guy I had so much respect for, I almost broke down. I did reply, "Well, you know, Jim, being the oldest, I always wondered what it would be like to have an older brother, and now I do."

Jim and Ann and my wife Kathy and I became friends. We socialized some and kept in touch. Unfortunately, Jim came down with leukemia last year. Several vets, myself included, took turns taking Jim to St. George for treatments. I had the occasion to also take Ann and had some of the most wonderful discussions with both of them. My wife and I were traveling to visit family last year (we were driving), and I received a call that Jim was not doing well and was in the hospital. We were really upset. The next day, my very close friend and big brother passed away. The most difficult issue was that it was virtually impossible to get back for his funeral as we were in Pennsylvania. We still have occasional contact with Ann, and she is doing well; her children make certain of that. Jim was one of the greatest guys I ever met, and I miss him.

8

THE VETERANS OF THE US AIR FORCE

Hector "Moose" Munoz, US Air Force

Moose was born in Morenci, Arizona, January 1, 1942. He played football and the baritone saxophone while attending Morenci HS. After graduation in 1962 he moved to California with his father and attended Chaffey Junior College in Alta Loma, California. He was part of the second class of the newly formed school. He worked as a general laborer in construction to pay for school.

After a year of school, Moose visited a recruiting office where he planned to enlist in the Marine Corps. The recruiter wasn't there however, and although the Navy recruiter in a nearby office had his eye on Moose, the Air Force representative said, "Come here son. I think we have something for you." The Air Force apparently gave him an offer he couldn't refuse and Moose enlisted in April 1962.

Moose went to boot camp at Lackland Air Force Base in San Antonio, Texas and then to Rantoul, Illinois, for school as an Aircraft Electrician Repairman. As soon as he finished school Moose was assigned to a field maintenance squadron in Yokota, Japan where he spent the next two years.

After being promoted to E4, Moose was assigned to Dover Air Force Base in Delaware as an electrical repairman where he worked primarily on chartered aircraft.

In 1966 his unit was sent to Thailand where Moose worked on F-105's, a fighter/bomber used in Vietnam. The base was also used as basic training for the Thai military.

Then it was off to McConnell Air Force Base in Wichita, Kansas, where he worked on whatever aircraft flew in. After additional training on F-105's, Moose was sent to Vietnam where he worked on C-5 transports.

The C-5's flew to various locations and Moose would come out of the back of the C-5 to work on aircraft in the field in need of repair.

More than once, repairmen were the target of rocket attacks. Part of Moose's Vietnam tour was spent in Cam Rahn Bay also subject to enemy fire.

After a 12 month tour in Vietnam, Moose was sent to Nellis Air Force Base in Las Vegas where he spent the next five and a half years. Although he fell in love with Southern Nevada and would have loved to finish his career here, the Air Force had other ideas and sent him to Mountain Home, Idaho, a significant different climate.

Moose spent four years in Idaho and then retired honorably with twenty years of service.

He quickly got acquainted with civilian life and accepted a position with Lily Tulip Paper Co., where he worked as an electrician/electronics technician in the plastic foam injection mold division. Moose, who spent 16 years with Lily, was responsible for maintaining the equipment that included fiber optics and scanners with nuclear isotopes.

Moose decide he needed a change and became a pharmacy technician where he trained on the job with Save-on Pharmacy. After eight years, Moose retired for good and settled into the good life.

He was familiar with Mesquite because of his years at Nellis and he and his lovely wife Donna, who he married in 2000, moved here.

Moose loves to bowl and play golf. He and Donna have a combined family of three daughters and three sons.

Moose, we thank you for your service to your country!

Stephen Kilp, US Air Force

Steve was born on a farm in a small town near Miami, Missouri, April 16, 1939. His family moved to Marshall, Missouri, where he attended high school and played football, baseball and basketball. After graduating in 1956, Steve attended Missouri Valley College for two years before enlisting in the US Air Force in February 1959.

He spent 11 weeks in boot camp at Lackland Air Force Base in San Antonio, Texas and then trained the next seven months at Keesler Air Force Base in Biloxi, Mississippi, to be a ground radio repairman.

After training, Steve was transferred to Empire Air Force Station, Empire, Michigan, where he spent the rest of his enlistment as part of NORAD Air Defense Command.

His Air Force life was fairly calm until the October 1962 when the Cuban missile crisis erupted. Everyone in NORAD was on edge since they were the first line of defense in the continental U.S.

After his leaving the Air Force in December 1962, Steve returned to college at the University of Missouri and earned his Bachelor's Degree in Physics in 1964. Steve later earned a Master's in Engineering Management.

After college he went to work for Raytheon Co. in Burlington, MA, as a field service engineer. He spent a year at Aviano Air Force Base in Italy.

After a couple of more years at Raytheon, the aerospace industry started bottoming out. Engineers were being laid off at an alarming rate so Steve started looking for another job.

In September 1968 Steve accepted a position with the Department of Defense (DOD) as a Systems Test Engineer. His early assignments included Portsmouth

Naval Shipyard and Hanscom Air Force Base, Mass. In 1972 he moved to Edwards Air Force Base in California where he retired from the DOD in1995.

His notable test projects at Edwards, include KC-135, B-52G, C-5A, B1A, F-5E/F, F-16 C/D and finally the B2A Stealth Bomber. He spent three years at the NASA Test Center EAFB associated with the X-37 Program. His assignments included system Test Engineer, Project Engineer and Engineering Manager. He lived in Lancaster and Tehacchapi, California.

Steve had two children who were in college and to help them get through without college loans, Steve worked for several aerospace companies for another nine years, including Boeing, Dynacorp and SAIC. He retired for good in 2004

Steve met his lovely wife Debbie in 1975 at Edwards AFB and they were married in 1976. They bought a home in Mesquite in 2002 and moved into it in 2004. They picked Mesquite for its great outdoor opportunities and Nevada's lack of an income tax.

Steve is an avid hiker and explorer, who loves to play golf and fly fish.

He is a founding member of Mesquite Jeeps and More and has spent four years as a volunteer with the Arizona Bureau of Land Management and the Parashant National Monument for the National Park Service.

Some notable assignments included the spring survey where he participated in locating and inventorying springs in the Arizona Strip. He loves hiking and has explored Gold Butte, the Mormon Mountains and the Arizona Strip.

Steve has three children. A daughter in Boston who is a nurse; a daughter in Seattle who works for Homeland Security and is married to a career Air Force member; and a son in Long Beach who is a web site developer.

Steve and his wife Debbie are good friends with whom we share membership in Mesquite Jeeps and More. We have done a lot of off-roading with them and the group.

Steve, thank you for your service to your country!

Bill Wells, US Air Force

Born May 14, 1939 in Lexington, Nebraska, Bill Wells attended Gothenburg HS where he participated in football, basketball and track. Upon graduation in 1957, he entered the University of Nebraska as a Business major and became a member of the ROTC program. Bill graduated from Nebraska in 1961 with a Bachelor's Degree in Business and a commission as a 2nd Lt. in the U.S. Air Force. Bill attended pilot training at Vance AFB in Oklahoma in 1962 and remained there as an instructor in the T-33 and T-38 aircraft.

In March of 1967, Bill was assigned to Cam Rhan Bay, South Vietnam, where he flew the F4. On one particular mission during an extreme under cast day and occasional showers, Bill's squadron flew down a valley where an ARVIN Unit was pinned down and helped an Army chopper evacuate wounded. The mountain tops were hidden in the clouds. He dropped his ordinance where they wanted and strafed the area with 20mm cannon fire before flying home. Later the unit reported he destroyed a complete company of NVC and forced the other two to pull out saving the ARVIN Unit that surely would have been over run. Bill received the Distinguished Flying Cross and the Viet Cross for Gallantry for his actions.

After a year in Vietnam, Bill was assigned to Bitberg AB in Germany in the F-4D. His special duties included Flight Lead, Flight Commander and Standards Evaluation. Bill spent three years at Bitberg. Then it was off to MacDill Air Force Base in Florida where he performed duties as a Flight Instructor and Flight Commander. Bill attended Command and Staff College at Maxwell AFB in Montgomery, Alabama and rose to the rank of Captain.

During Bill's days at Cam Rahn Bay, he mentioned that they had a macadam runway, which was a metal surface with holes in it. It was extremely bumpy and with a heavy load was sometimes too bumpy. On one occasion during takeoff it was so bumpy that the glare shield fell into Bill's lap and he shouted to the weapons systems operator sitting behind him to "take over the controls." A bit of a surprise to the WSO! On another occasion, flying at night, he was ordered by the forward control operator to salvo his rockets. He was a bit bewildered as he had six pods with 35 rockets each. But orders are orders and fire he did. The brightness of the fired rockets was incredible and again you heard "WSO take control." Sometimes there are situations that are not so serious.

In 1974 and 75, Bill became the Operations Staff Officer at Udorn AFB, Thailand and followed with an assignment as a Staff Officer in the Plans and Programs Directorate at the Pentagon from 1975 to 1979. Bill was promoted to Lt. Colonel while serving at the Pentagon. While there he was responsible for 5000 F4's and where they were assigned. There had to be staff action if any of them were to be moved from one location to another. There were many modifications made to the F4's and a computer program had to be developed to segregate the capabilities of these planes. An Air Force attrition expert would flood planes into a program and predict how many would be lost and when you would need to replace the force.

After his stint at the Pentagon, Bill was assigned to Nellis AFB in Nevada as the Fighter Operations Officer from 1979 to 1981 flying the F-4D. From 1981 to 1982, he was assigned to Air Forces Iceland in Keflavik, Iceland as Vice-Commander flying the F-4E and was promoted to Colonel. In 1982, Bill was sent to HQ Tactical Air Command at Langley AFB, Virginia as the Director of Operations in the 325th Training Wing flying the F-15 and T-33.

In 1986 Bill retired from the US Air Force with 24 years of active service as a Colonel. Upon his retirement he was selected by McDonnell Douglas to be site manager at Luke AFB in Arizona and was responsible for the development of the F-15E aircrew courseware. After the completion of this contract he moved to Dayton, Ohio as a marketing rep for McDonnell Douglas Training Systems. In 1992 he was transferred to St. Louis to work on marketing programs for the Royal Saudi Air Force. In 1994, he transferred to Kamis Mushayt AB, Saudi Arabia as the site manager for the F-15 Formal Training Unit. From 1996 to 1999, he served as the Regional Director of Marketing in the Boeing Middle East Regional Office, Riyadh, Saudi Arabia. From September 1999 to January 2001 he was the Manager of Defense Programs for CDI Corp.

In 2001 familiar with Mesquite from his assignment at Nellis, Bill moved here. He served on the airport task force committee for four years and served as City Councilman from 2005 to 2009. Bill secured his Masters Degree in Systems Management from Southern California University in 1971 and an additional Masters Degree in Aviation Management from Embry Riddle in 1989. Bill is currently fully retired and enjoys playing golf.

While in Cam Rahn Bay, Bill Wells flew 312 combat missions, and while serving in the US Air Force received the following: Distinguished Flying Cross, Meritorious Service Medal with Two Oak Leaf Clusters, Air Force Commendation Medal with one Oak Leaf Cluster, Air Force Achievement Medal, Air Force Outstanding Unit Award with Valor, Combat Readiness Medal, National Defense Service Medal, Vietnam Service Medal with Two Devices, Air Force Overseas Short Tour Ribbon, Air Force Longevity Ribbon with Four Devices, Small Arms Expert Marksmanship Ribbon, Republic of Vietnam Gallantry Cross with Device and Republic of Vietnam Campaign Medal.

Bill, we thank you for your service to your country!

Tom Oliver, US Air Force

Tom was born November 28, 1939 in Brooklyn, New York. He started school in New Jersey but when he was eight years old began attending Greer School in New York. Greer was started, owned and operated by the Episcopal Church, primarily for kids from broken homes.

Except for a few weeks a year, the students lived there year round. The church had purchased an old monastery and operated a farm where the students grew vegetables and tended to the dairy farm. The operation produced pasteurized, bottled and solid milk; grew, prepared and canned (in tin cans) vegetables. They sold them as well. In addition, they planted trees to replace fully grown ones that were cut down and sold as pulp. What a learning experience about becoming self sufficient and developing workable skills. Talk about team work!

Tom participated in baseball and hunting during his high school years at Greer. After graduation, Tom went on the Rhodes School, which was a prep school. The teachers at Rhodes all had at least a Masters Degree and some a PhD. Here Tom received further instruction primarily in math and science.

From Rhodes, he enrolled at Brooklyn Polytechnical Institute which at the time was New York's MIT. During his second quarter in Flushing, New York, Tom saw an Air Force recruitment sign for pilots. He stopped in and asked if it was legit. He was told that it was, so he took the initial test. He passed and moved on to a battery of tests, which he also passed.

He then went on to Mitchell AFB for more tests, these to qualify for the Air Force Cadet Officers program. Tom passed and was now a U.S. Air Force Cadet Aviation Airman detached, went on to Lackland Air Force Base and then to San Antonio for pre flight training and then Moultrie, GA., for primary flight training.

The class was sent to Webb AFB in Texas for basic where many of the cadets washed out, including Tom. They were told, although not officially, that word had come down the instructors were to wash out a cadet for any error no matter how small because of a number of reasons. Although Tom and the other cadets could have been released from their commitment, Tom elected to stay the course and went to navigation training in Harlington, Texas. This was right on the border near Brownsville. After nine months of training Tom graduated in December 1961 as a 2nd Lt.

From here it was off to Mather AFB in Sacramento and Electronic Warfare School. This program was the art of using electronics to interfere with the enemy's radar and defense systems so they were unable to track our operations. It also played havoc with their communications.

Then it was off to Marsh AFB in Riverside, California, for B-52 ground school and then to Walker AFB in Roswell, New Mexico for B-52 flight school. At Amarillo Tom was assigned to his first flight crew in 1963. It is also where he met his lovely wife Vicki in 1964.

They were married in 1965 and in that same year his unit was deployed to Guam for six months where they made four 12 hour flights into Vietnam and back.

Tom and his unit made about 60 bombing runs during their time in Guam. Because there were already two wings in Guam when his unit was brought back, they were sent to U Tapao, Thailand. From there the mission was only a three hour trip. Amarillo was closed and the unit broken up in January 1968 after 11½ years. Tom was contacted by a colonel assigned as a cost reduction officer to come up with some ideas to reduce operating expenses.

Suddenly he was told to get ready to report to Takhli, Thailand, so it was off to Miami for sea survivor school and then EB66 School. The EB66 was a converted high wing jet bomber converted into an electronic warfare plane. Tom's family came to Sumpter, South Carolina and then went to Texas to stay while Tom went to Clark AFB in the Philippines and jungle warfare school.

Tom spent a year at Takhli and ran 100 missions flying cover for drones. The electronic warfare planes would fly over Cambodia and the South China Sea so the North Vietnamese could not find the drones. From here Tom requested and was granted an assignment to Hill AFB in Ogden, Utah to fly the EB57, a medium to light bomber converted to electronic warfare.

This plane was used to go jam S.S. radar and defense systems for training purposes. It was used to simulate the enemy attacking one sector at a time or the entire USA at once. This assignment lasted for a little over two years.

From here Tom was sent to Malmstrom AFB in Great Falls, Montana. Tom was now a captain and had been for quite a while, so after being at Malmstrom for eight months and being passed over for major, he decided to get out of the Air Force after more than 13 years. Tom enrolled at Oregon St. University as an Engineering Major. During his second semester a friend at the Burlington International Airport and the Air National Guard in Vermont contacted him. They were getting the EB57 and needed someone flight qualified.

Tom finished his semester of school and was off to Vermont. He became a member of the Air National Guard, was promoted to major and spent the next ten years training and converting the Air Defense Command. The Guard had to get rid of their B-57's as they were running out of engines and parts were hard to get. They converted to F4's.

In 1984, Tom retired after 24 years of service in the US Air Force. After the Air Force Tom became involved with computers and designed software that was used in support of housing for urban development. In addition, he worked for a company that landed an Air Force contract to convert Lear jets to electronic warfare planes.

After four years the company lost the contract and Tom went back to writing computer programs and actually ended up working for both companies on an as needed basis. In 1996 Tom and Vicki bought two homes in Mesquite after selling their property in Vermont. They then moved to Scranton, Pennsylvania where Tom managed a flight school for two years.

Not liking the winters, they built their home in Scenic, Arizona. Tom and Vicki are involved in a number of activities in the Mesquite area. Tom continues to fly out of the Mesquite airport and is a member of the Mesquite Pistol Club.

Tom, we thank you for your service to your country!

George Rolf, US Air Force

George was born in the Bronx, New York on May 11, 1946. He attended Christopher Columbus HS and participated in track and cross country. Upon graduation in 1964 George went to work in the yacht yards and received his draft notice while employed there. Not wanting to be drafted, George enlisted in the U.S. Air Force on November 23, 1965. Three days later his induction notice showed up.

It was off to Lackland AFB in Texas for basic training and then to Lowry AFB for Munitions and Weapons School for the next four and a half months. This training included maintenance of weapons involving everything from grenades to 20mm to 50 caliber weapons to 500/1000 pound bombs to sidewinder missiles. George was promoted to E2 right out of school.

He was off to Aviano AFB in Italy, where George was promoted to E3. A staff sergeant who had been in charge of the munitions storage area was being rotated back to the states when George arrived in Italy. He was the Sergeant responsible for storing the munitions and maintaining it.

The Air Force needed someone to take over this responsibility and since George was fresh out of school, he was given the job. This was quite a break for a new airman in his first overseas assignment. However, since the staff sergeant was rotating home, he didn't much care about training George.

So Airman 1st Class Rolf had to hit the books very hard to learn the job he was about to undertake. He learned quickly and well. George was soon promoted to E4. His area was noted as one of the finest in all of Europe. This was quite a distinction as the area also had nuclear capability.

In case of an alert, George was responsible for waking everyone, including the officers. The flight line would provide a list of what munitions were needed and George's crew would pull and deliver the goods to the flight line, including conventional and special munitions.

After the alert ended George's crew was required to return everything they pulled back into storage. They were the first ones there and the last ones to leave. Not an easy job as combat-loaded planes were always involved in the action.

George was promoted to E5 during his three tours at Aviano. He loved his assignment and did a great job, but it was now time to accept his discharge and move on with his life.

After the service George went to work for the New York Telephone Company as an installer/repairman. The neighborhood had changed quite a bit since George had joined the Air Force and after several close calls (one with a Doberman) he decided it was time to look for a change.

So after three years on the job he moved to Kingston, New York and took a job as an electrician. While working as an electrician, he started his own contracting business which he still owns today. George started it in 1974, a successful endeavor.

After working as an electrician for 10 years and the director of buildings and grounds of a rehabilitation agency, George went to work for the Culinary Institute of America as the Superintendent of Plant Operations. He worked there for the next eight years, then it was on to The National Historic Landmark Hotel, where George the manager and project planner.

After 14 years, George decided it was time to retire. He bought a place in Mesquite in 2011, and splits his time between New York and here. "It won't be long before I'm in Mesquite full time," George said. "I have a place on the water in upstate New York and I love to fish, however it may be time to give it up!"

George and his wife Sandy have two children and three grandchildren.

George, we thank you for your service to your country!

George has become a great friend. He is always willing to help out with any project; he just doesn't know how to say no. Many of us are looking forward to his move to become a full-time resident of Mesquite.

Vern Petry, US Air Force

Vern was born in Atchison, Kansas in January, 1941, the home of Amelia Earhart and the Atchison Topeka, Santa Fe Railroad. He grew up here and attended Atchison HS. He competed in intramurals and was on the varsity golf team.

Vern graduated in 1959 and went to work for a transportation division of Rockwell International. Vern had worked there during his senior year in high school on a work study program, where he attended classes half a day and worked half a day. After graduation he continued working full time for Rockwell. He did this until 1961, when he enlisted in the Air Force.

It was off to basic training at Lackland Air Force Base in San Antonio, Texas for the next seven weeks.

Basic wasn't quite completed when he was transferred to Lowry AFB in Denver to complete Basic and attend B52 Electronics School Bomb navigation). He attended school for half a day and completed basic training the other half of the day. This went on for nine weeks.

One day he was pulled out of class to clean floors and class rooms and had no idea why; however he did have a message to report to the commander!

He was ordered to Malmstrom AFB in Great Falls, Montana as an air traffic controller. The NCOIC (non commissioned officer in charge) did not want to accept Vern since he had not been through air traffic school. The NCIOC was informed by SAC (strategic air command) that Vern would in fact, would be in air traffic control and trained by existing operators.

Vern's roommate was in the same situation. After the two of them were trained on the job they were informed that they would be responsible for making up the test that on-the-job trained traffic controllers would have to take upon completing their training. They did as ordered and, and of course passed the test to become level 3 controllers. A short time later they took another test and became qualified to sit alone at a console and were designated level 5 operators.

Vern and his partner Bill were E3's at the time. E5 and E6's were pulled from listening posts and sent to Malstrom to be trained as air traffic controllers. They had to pass the test Vern and Bill had developed to become level 3 operators. After completing their testing they received orders to Clark AFB in the Philippines and Osaka AFB in Japan.

From 1962 to 1964 Vern was involved in air traffic control and training at Malstrom. He had the opportunity of interacting with Senator Mike Mansfield of Montana, who was the Majority Leader at that time. Sen. Mansfield flew in and out of Malstrom on many occasions and several times Vern was on duty. Sen. Mansfield and his wife often came to the tower to wait for incoming or outgoing flights. Vern said Sen. Mansfield was a true gentleman.

During his assignment, Vern was transferred to "chopper operations" where he worked with two E5's, three days on and three days off from 3 AM to 5 PM. The choppers which were Huey's made trips to and from missile sites in the mountains of Montana. They carried personnel and/or paperwork but once they left, they had to be back before dark as they could not fly at night. Vern's job was to keep track of them.

Here's one you enlisted guys will enjoy! The controllers were responsible for keeping the area clean and had to do so when they got off duty. The Lt.'s who mostly flew the choppers would come in before and after their flights and tended to mess up the four rooms that made up the area. One day a Lt. was eating peanuts and throwing the shells on the floor. The enlisted guys were cleaning up the mess when the operations colonel came in.

"What are you doing?" he asked. "Cleaning up sir," the airman replied. "Did you guys make this mess?" asked the colonel. "No sir," the men replied. To make a long story short, the colonel found out what took place and from that moment on the Lt.'s became responsible for sweeping and mopping the area, by order of the colonel.

There would be joint exercises with the local Air National Guard Units on a weekly basis using T-33's and F-89's. When Vern received his discharge in December 1965 he responded to an invitation to join the 120th Fighter Group Air National Guard Unit in Great Falls. Due to the high amount of activity in Vietnam there were no openings and it was suggested Vern use the GI Bill to go to school and then join the guard.

He did just that, enrolling at Dunwitty Technical College in Minneapolis. He majored in HVAC and worked for an electrical company while attending school. While doing this he noticed there were no wiring diagrams for the switches he installed; needless to say he developed them and they are still used to this day.

In 1974 Vern joined the National Guard as an E3 and retired with a total of 24 years service as an E7. During his working career he had to move several times and therefore had to transfer National Guard units, but all of the time counts. Vern worked hard at his military career as well as his civilian career. He took and completed a total of 63 courses while in the Air Force.

He was promoted every year for four consecutive years from E3 to E7 while in the National Guard. Quite an accomplishment!

While at Malstrom AFB, Vern was in town doing his laundry. As he was leaving, another airman was walking by and asked if he could hitch a ride to the base. Vern agreed, but as they were going through town the airman asked Vern to follow a car that he said his girlfriend was driving. Vern did and they stopped at a hamburger place. The airman and his girlfriend disappeared for a while and Vern ended up talking to another girl who was in the car. Her name was Linda. In July, 1963 they became Vern and Linda Petry. They have two sons.

Vern we thank you for your service to your country!

Herman Brooks, US Air Force

Herman was born March 7, 1932 in Valley City, Illinois. He attended Gregsville HS and participated in baseball and basketball. He graduated in June of 1950 and enlisted in the US Air Force in October of the same year. This certainly didn't surprise anyone as Brooks came from a military family. His father served in the latter stages of WWI. He had two older brothers, Wayne and Donald who served in WWII. Donald retired from the military after serving in the Navy, Army and Air Force with tours of duty in WWII, the Korean War and Vietnam. Herman also had a brother Richard who served with the US Marine Corps during the Korean War.

Herman was sent to Lackland AFB for basic training and then Air Police Training at Ft. Gordon, Georgia. Once training was complete, he was assigned to Barksdale AFB in Shreveport, La. He remained permanently assigned to Barksdale throughout his active duty career, although he traveled all over the world.

His unit was assigned to guarding C-124's regardless of where they might be located. They were part of Strategic Air Command (SAC) and delivered supplies throughout the world. Brooks spent time in England, North Africa and Guam in his assignments. His unit guarded the C-124's 24 hours a day, seven days a week while they were on the ground.

While at Anderson AFB in Guam, they were assigned to guard the planes with four men per plane. This was highly unusual, as normal procedure was one Air Policeman per plane. Although he can't prove it, Brooks and the men were certain that President Truman had given the indication that they were going to blow North Korea off the face of the earth, and that a major U.S. strike was inevitable. Therefore, the extra guards were on all of the planes.

It was back to Barksdale for the final time, as Herman's discharge time was near. Duty had been expanded to include a facility that belonged to the Atomic Energy Commission. This was located directly behind Barksdale AFB and the Air Police now were responsible for the security there as well.

He found out about an opportunity to receive an early discharge (two months early) and put in for it. He was granted his request.

Brooks made many great friends while in the Air Force and some were still at Barksdale, so the day he went to Shreveport to wait for the bus to take him home, he invited his beat buddies to tag along. They went to a local bar and he told the bartender that the drinks were on him until his bus came. An expensive day, but well worth it according to Brooks.

Back in Illinois, Brooks went to work for a cold storage company while getting his feet back on the ground. Shortly thereafter, he was hired by Caterpillar in Peoria, Illinois. He worked there for about four years, but became tired of the on again, off again lay-offs and decided to take a job as a fire fighter with the Peoria Fire Department. That turned out to be a great decision as he was fire chief when he retired from the fire department November 27, 1987.

During his working career, Brooks' sister introduced him to a lovely young lady named Shirley. Things must have worked out because they married 18 months later in 1955. They have six children and 10 grandchildren.

While accomplishing many things during his working life, he had remained a member of the Air Force Reserves. After several years in the reserves he transferred to the Air National Guard. With all of his responsibilities as fire chief, Herman still managed to retire from the Air Force with 26½ years of service which included active duty and reserve time. He retired as an E7.

Brooks and his wife Shirley had a condo in Las Vegas where he and a salesman would have coffee together several times a week. He asked the salesman if he knew of Mesquite—as someone had mentioned it to Shirley.

Of course, the salesman said, it was a nice community, and he offered to take them there if they wanted to see it. That was over twelve years ago and Herman and Shirley bought a home in Mesquite and have been residents ever since. They do go back to Peoria in the summer.

One issue Brooks asked me to bring up is the Korean War. He and some of his friends feel like it is the forgotten war. It never seems to get the notoriety it deserves, nor do those who fought there seem to get there just recognition.

Over 33,000 men lost their lives during the Korean War, a war that lasted a little less than three years. I can't speak with any authority about those concerns, but I can say that Brooks is truly a patriot who served his country honorably along with the rest of his family.

Herman, we thank you for your service to your country!

Leo McGinty Jr., US Air Force

Earlier in this book there was a story about two Air Force veterans who teamed up to help one of them recover their lost dog tags. The following two interviews are of those two airmen.

Leo was born in Chicago, September 17, 1937. He moved to Los Angeles when he was four years old as his father worked for the railroad and was subject to transfers. Leo was raised in El Serino, California, where he attended All Saints Elementary School and Cathedral High School in downtown Los Angeles. He graduated in June 1956 and enlisted in the Air Force in July. He was sent to Parks AFB for eight weeks of basic training. From there, it was off to Francis E. Warren AFB in Cheyenne, Wyoming, by troop train for communications school.

When they arrived Leo was kind of surprised by a sign on the second floor of the barracks which read, "Do not shoot buffalo from the 2nd floor of the barracks."

It was very cold in Wyoming in the winter and each airman had to pull coal duty. This meant keeping the coal furnace in the barracks going throughout the night. If you ran out of coal, you had to see what you could confiscate from another barracks. Every once in a while an airman would doze off while on duty. This would enable another enterprising young airman the opportunity to stock up on coal.

Communications consisted of teletype as well as other types of communication methods and was three months in duration. While Leo was there, Cheyenne was put off limits by the post commander. The airman were not treated particularly well in town so the commander decided to keep them on post.

After a couple of weeks the mayor of Cheyenne came to the post and wanted to know why no airmen were coming to town. The commander explained his people were not being treated well by the folks in town. The mayor said they were losing a lot of revenue without the airmen's business and that things would change.

After another week or so the commander lifted the ban and the airman returned to Cheyenne and found a much different place, one that treated the airmen much better.

After completing his training, Leo was attached to the 781st AC&W (Aircraft Control and Warning) group in Battle Creek, Michigan. One corner of the base was once a prison camp for Germans during WWII. There were markers for seven German prisoners all with the same day of death, but he never found out what happened.

Ft. Custer had a terrific baseball team on which Leo played shortstop. They went to Ft. McGill AFB in Florida to participate in a huge Air Force tournament which they won. This qualified them for the Air Force National Tournament, but they couldn't go because they couldn't get enough airmen to pull double duty to cover their jobs.

After two and a half years at Ft. Custer Leo was sent to Labrador where he was attached to the 1932nd AACS Aircraft Control Warning System. He was part of the radio section called MATS (Military Air Transportation Service). They tracked four engine planes that flew troops to Europe. They would scramble jets in case of an emergency.

This was part of the 54th Air Rescue at Goose Bay Air Force Base in Labrador and part of the Strategic Air Command. Teletype machines were used to track information from the transfer station.

They would occasionally pick up Russian bombers that would go to the Bering Strait and then turn around. This was the Cold War.

A Russian plane crashed near the tip of Iceland and the 54th Air rescue went to check on the situation. Before they could get there a Russian sub showed up and picked up things from the plane and took off.

In another incident some fishing boats were out in the ocean surrounding a Russian ship. A coaxial cable had been laid from New York to London and this cable was cut. During this investigation, those on the Russian ship said it was an accident. A different time, strange things were happening.

Leo and his fellow airman endured temperatures as low as -45 degrees. Believe it or not, they still played baseball in Labrador as there were two other Air Force Bases not too far away.

While still in Battle Creek, Leo hitched a ride with a pilot who was going from Battle Creek to Smokey Hill, Kansas. While in the air the plane's (C-45) radio quit. The pilot was confused and took the plane into a dive. "What the heck are you doing?" Leo asked. Since I can't use the radio and I'm not familiar with this area, I need to get low enough to read the road signs," said the pilot.

Sure enough, he found a sign with an arrow pointing the way to the base and landed safely. He told Leo he could hook him up with another ride, but Leo thanked him and hitched all the way to California.

Leo's enlistment was up March 17, 1960. He went to work for Southern Pacific Railroad as a switchman/brakeman.

In September of 1993 while working in a road switcher operation with the Mexican government, Leo was injured and had to have his hip replaced, which forced him to retire from the railroad.

Before his retirement, Leo had driven a cab during a period when he was laid off. He was taking a Marine to Camp Pendleton and as he went through the gate to the barracks, his fare jumped out of the cab and took off. Leo went into the barracks and no one would give up the guy.

A few weeks later, the Commander at Camp Pendleton heard what happened and sent Leo his fare plus $20. He explained the guys didn't want to give up a fellow Marine who was having some difficulties, but they felt they should take care of Leo.

Leo is actively involved in Special Olympics in Mesquite in both the bowling and basketball programs. He has also helped out at the Mesquite Boxing Club. He is also an active member of the Knights of Columbus. Leo was married and has five children, four grandchildren and two great grandchildren.

Leo we thank you for your service to your country!

I think we all take for granted the service the veterans provided during the Cold War era. I have had the opportunity to speak with several veterans who served during the Cold War, and some of the stories are very interesting and sometimes scary. Some of those stories are covered in the interviews of the veterans that served during that period in this book.

Ed Jaworski, US Air Force

This is the second airman involved in the dog tag story!

Born in Milwaukee, Wisconsin on May 6, 1936, Ed attended St. John's Cathedral High School. While attending St. John's Ed was quite a musician playing the trumpet, clarinet, oboe and was drum major in the marching band. To make a little spending money, Ed started a seven piece band that played at dances and weddings.

He joined the Air National Guard and was sent to Lackland AFB in San Antonio, Texas for basic training. Upon his return he attended Milwaukee School of Engineering for a semester, but decided that engineering was not for him.

As a member of the Air National Guard he was attached to the 128th Fighter Squadron in Milwaukee, which flew P51's. Ed enjoyed the Air Guard and in 1956 joined the regular Air Force. He was sent back to Lackland for a four week refresher course and then off to Keesler AFB in Boloxi, Mississippi for Radar Operators School. He was placed in Heavy Radar School which tracked long range objects 200 to 250 miles. Ed graduated first in his class and since he was already an airman third class, because of his time in Air National Guard, was awarded a yellow rope and put in charge of 300 to 400 men during this training. He was second in command of the entire squadron.

After the four month school, Ed was sent to the Osceola Air Force Station in Osceola, Wisconsin. This radar site had three bubbles, one long range and two height finders. The station could detect objects up to 100,000 feet and a range of 250 miles. This was significant technology at the time and played an important role in the Cold war. However, ballistic missiles made these types of radar systems obsolete as folks became less and less concerned about bombers. Ed remained at Osceola from March 1957 until July 1959.

In 1958, the Air Force began to phase out manual radar and replace it with SAGE (Semi Automatic Ground Environment). To operate these systems, the radar technical personnel had to go back to Keesler AFB for an additional four months of training.

To qualify, an airman had to have at least two years left on his enlistment. Since Ed had less than that he considered a transfer to Alaska where the older system was going to remain for a while longer. He would have had to extend for a year, but could not be guaranteed a promotion, so he decided not to go.

This was a critical decision as Ed was one of only a small group of operators that had high security clearance. This was mainly because the main mission of these operators was to scramble jets when unidentified aircraft was picked up. This happened several times a month. Jets out of Minneapolis were F89 Scorpions and F102 Delta Daggers out of Duluth. In many instances the issue was planes that failed to issue a flight plan. By the way, these jets scrambled hot, ready for whatever might take place.

Ed was transferred to Truax Field in Milwaukee where he served out his enlistment and was discharged in January of 1960.

After the Air Force, Ed sold encyclopedias for a while and had a crew of sales reps within a month. He didn't care for the tactics of this type of sales so he gave it up. He bought a truck and trailer and went on the road with Mayflower. This worked out very well and after a few years, Ed and a very close friend started their own trucking company.

After 35 years he got out of the business, but became bored with retirement. Ed again started another moving company, only this time the company made arrangements for international moves. His organization works with companies all over the world arranging moves for their employees. Ed's company was the first one to make moves into China. After 10 years of additional success, he is again ready to call it a career.

Ed bought a home in Mesquite and is enjoying this part of the country as a snowbird, but he doesn't think it will be too long before he will be a full time resident. He loves to off road and visit with friends and his nephew in Henderson. Ed is also an active member in USAF RSV WW (US Air Force Radar Site Veterans World Wide)

Ed, we thank you for your service to your country!

This is a special veteran! Ed's nephew in Henderson, Nevada, is our son-in-law, so we know Ed very well, and he is a great guy. It is hard to be objective when the person you are writing about is family! But it is what it is! And we care about Ed very much.

Jesse Marsh, US Air Force

Jesse Marsh is well known in Mesquite. He was born May 13, 1937, in the small town of West, Mississippi. A farm boy, he worked the cotton fields until he joined the Air Force in October, 1955. By then he had moved to Mobile, Alabama and joined under the buddy system.

After basic at Lackland AFB, Texas it was bye bye buddy; one went to Oregon and Jesse got sent to New York.

While Jesse was in basic training he got a draft notice, so he was that close to being in the Army not the Air Force.

While he was stationed at Mitchell Field on Long Island he met Dorothy, his wife of thirty six years. Jesse is one of the few guys I know who never attended a tech school. He learned microwave tower and radio relay repair on the job or as they say OJT. He was sent to France in 1960, where he served until 1963 when he returned to Griffiss AFB in Rome, New York.

This assignment ended Jesse's radio career. The nation had just gotten involved in Vietnam. Jesse was assigned to be in charge of 15 men who honored our Nation's fallen, to their final resting place. He handled almost 100 funerals while in that job.

Then it was Jesse's turn to take a tour of Southeast Asia. He got to see a lot of Vietnam, first working as a supply sergeant at Cam Rahn Bay then Bien Hoa and Na Trang. I want to say, all those nice vacation spots we knew and enjoyed, but then some of you know better.

Jesse was one of those guys we all loved. The supply sergeant not only kept us in beans and bullets, but he got us cold beer, hot sauce and many other creature comforts like poncho liners and yummy C-rations. Jesse takes pride in the fact, as he should, that he could get anything for the troops, but never profited from it as some others did.

Upon returning to the states, Jesse wound up at Lowry AFB in Colorado. Another unique thing Jesse mentioned was that every base he was assigned to, the Department of Defense has now closed.

He retired at Lowry in December 1975, but stayed in the area working on Buckley AFB for the Air National Guard as a security policeman.

In 1980 he moved to Las Vegas where he worked at the Dunes and later at Circus Circus as a slot supervisor. He also became a shift supervisor, responsible for lots of money and people.

He tired of the big city life and moved to Mesquite to work at the Oasis and then at Players Island, working in both slots and security. His last guard post before retiring in 2010 was at the Star Convention center.

He met his wife Marilyn here in 1993 and they married in 1995. She had managed the gift shop at the Eureka until taking over management of the La Mesa Motel with Jesse. Jesse has two daughters, four grandchildren and one great grandchild.

Jesse is an active member of the VFW, the American Legion and the Vietnam Veterans of America. I salute you my friend and am sure the community joins in thanking you for your service to our country and the community.

The above article was written by my predecessor, Ed Fizer.

Jesse has become a very good friend, and we have been in numerous projects together involving the Mesquite Veterans Center as well as the Mesquite community. As the article implies, he is a great guy who is always willing to get involved and lend a helping hand or lead if required to do so. He and Marilyn have been significant factors in Mesquite and the veterans' center for a long time. I thank you for all you do.

VETERANS OF THE US NAVY

Kevin Smith, US Navy

Kevin Smith has a very unique story. He was born March 31, 1943 in Flushing, New York. He attended Stamford Central High School where he participated in basketball and was a standout soccer player.

Upon graduation he enrolled in the State University of New York where he took a double major of Math and Electrical Engineering. In addition to being an outstanding soccer player and leading his team to the collegiate playoffs, he graduated with a 3.5 GPA.

He then enlisted in the US Navy and was accepted into flight training in Pensacola, Florida where he became an officer pilot.

At that time there were more than 4000 tactical airplanes being developed each year but not enough pilots to fly them. In June 1965 Kevin became a naval aviator and he entered a post- graduate program that took him into further formal training which included combat training school.

He trained in the F Crusader in Florida and ended up flying the F8 in various squadrons for 20 years. While stationed at Naval Air Station Miramar (Fighter Town USA) in San Diego (now called Marine Corps Station Miramar) he was assigned to the USS Constellation as squadron commander.

The ship was deployed to the Pacific during the Cold War and operational capabilities were continuing to increase. The Constellation was a "super carrier" staffed by 5000 men. It was the second super carrier—the Kitty Hawk was the first.

The Constellation had a large air wing and while in the Pacific, Kevin spent time in Hong Kong, Philippines, Japan, Singapore, Korea and Okinawa to name just a few locations.

He eventually became captain of the Pacific Fleet Fighter Wing and was awarded the Unit Citation and the Seventh Fleet Commendation. These were awarded for running the best air wing aboard the carrier. Kevin retired from the Navy in 1985 with 24 years of honorable service.

Kevin went to work for United Airlines as a pilot where he captained the Boeing 777 for more than 25,000 hours of flight time. He was the pilot in command of 15 different types of airplanes.

He is the only pilot currently licensed to captain Boeing 737's, 747's, 757's 767's and the 777. Although it's possible, but highly unlikely, that Northwest pilots (now Delta pilots) could theoretically have a pilot licensed to captain all of these aircraft. As of this article we know of no one other than Kevin.

During Kevin' military and civilian career he became involved with developmental ways of approaching problems and issues. He called it critical thinking.

Sounds simple, but it is much more involved than meets the eye and impossible to fully explain here. However, it is important enough to bring to the reader's attention.

Kevin became involved in the development of this program by being appointed chairman of the Federal Training Integration Task Force. The Federal Aviation Administration and a blue ribbon panel were responsible for appointing the members of this panel as well as its chairman.

Their job was to figure out how to develop a critical thinking program for airline pilots that included—what to do in an emergency, how to handle it, how to assign tasks and most importantly how to prevent a catastrophe. Although he was given assistance, Kevin developed the program used universally by pilots at United. He authored two books that are used in formal academic training courses in the military and civilian venues.

Kevin and Ronald Lofaro, Ph.D. co-authored a book, "Hostile to Reason," that is on its way to becoming very successful. Among other things it explains critical thinking and certainly gives one something to ponder.

In 1992 Smith and Lafaro were the first to propose the central role of the airline pilot, and especially the airline captain, as a risk manager. This primary role and function was in opposition to the then current paradigm that saw the captain as systems operator and monitor. To this end the authors created a body of knowledge called Operational Decision Theory to support the airline captain's most important role in risk management. The result was a comprehensive body of work written and presented to the aviation community in 14 papers and two recently published book chapters.

When Kevin was a young bachelor in his first squadron, his commander requested his presence in his office. "Do you have a date for the Crusader Ball?"(a formal black tie military affair), asked the commander. "No sir I do not." Kevin replied. "Well you do now" the commander said. "A friend of my wife's has a daughter who would like to go to the ball and she instructed me to take care of it. You will have a good time, I know the young lady and she is lovely." "Yes sir," said Kevin.

That is how Kevin met his lovely wife Sue. They started to date and were married. As Sue traveled with Kevin through his military career, she finished her education obtaining a degree in Math and Engineering.

They have three sons and four granddaughters. One son has his Doctorate in Electrical Engineering, another is superintendent of a construction company and the third a straight "A" student in school. They also have a granddaughter who is an ROTC student at the University of Wyoming.

Kevin we thank you for your service to your country!

This is not only a unique story, but also unique circumstances as to how Kevin and Sue and my wife Kathy and I became good friends. Sue is the president of a local Mesquite organization, and Kathy sits on the board. Kevin and I would go to some of the meetings and were introduced. I asked him if he would let me interview him. He agreed. As time went on, I gave a lot of thought to putting all these interviews into book form. Since Kevin is a published author, I ran the idea past him, and he was very positive about the idea. He assisted me in writing a letter of recommendation when I sent in a proposal. It all worked out. We continue to have in-depth discussions about many significant subjects. I thank Kevin for his help, assistance, and guidance in my new endeavor.

Paul Levan, US Navy

Born in Easterville, Iowa April 7, 1947 Paul's family moved to Omaha, Nebraska when he was in the second grade. Paul was active in his high school's musicals as a singer and was also a member of the choir. Paul was a member of the varsity golf team for four years until he graduated in 1965.

Before graduation, Paul enlisted in the U.S. Navy in the 120 day deferred enlistment program. In August, 1965 he left for Great Lakes in Illinois. He took some aptitude tests and was told he had a knack for communications and was enrolled in technical school at Pensacola, Florida.

There were no openings at the communications school when Paul graduated from boot camp so he was shipped off to Glencoe, Georgia to wait for an opening. He spent about 4½ months there and was able to attend the Masters Golf Tournament in Augusta. Quite a thrill for a guy who loves golf as much as Paul!

Finally, it was off to Pensacola for communications school where his instructor selected Paul to get involved in X-band training to listen for enemy aircraft. Paul completed schooling and went to U.S. Naval Base Subic Bay in the Philippines, where he was assigned to the USS Oxford. The Oxford was a freighter that patrolled just outside China and Vietnam waters 30 to 35 days at a time.

Paul did this assignment for a year and a half. While Paul was serving on the Oxford, its sister ship, the Pueblo was taken by the North Koreans.

The Oxford traveled as far as Adka (the next to the last island in the Aleutians) to Okinawa, to Da Nang, to the Philippines. Its stay was always thirty days plus one so the unit qualified for combat pay. The ship's job was critical. The sailors' job was critical. The sailors were responsible for listening for enemy aircraft, especially near the runways in Vietnam. Paul remembers their plane being fired upon when they left for the return trip to the U.S.

From the waters of China and Vietnam it was back to the states and an assignment to the National Security Agency at Ft. Meade, Maryland where Paul served from December 1968 to February 1969. Promoted to E4 he was scheduled to go to Horizon Radar School but had to enlist for an additional two years to get the training. He did and finished first in his class.

Then it was off to Japan where he was stationed at Atsugi Naval Air Station and assigned to VQ1 Recon Squadron. Just as Paul arrived in Japan, PR-21 was shot down by the Koreans, and all aboard were killed. Nothing was ever done about the incident.

Paul was assigned to crew 4 PR-27 and until 1971 his squadron flew recon missions against North Korea and Russia. There were 14 in the crew. One of the most interesting things to Paul was when his ship crossed the equator, the crew members became "shellbacks" instead of just "pollywogs," or men who hadn't crossed the equator. This was a big deal in the Navy.

Although he considered making the navy a career, Paul accepted his discharge in June 1971 as an E5. He arrived at Travis AFB in California and went to visit his parents who had moved to San Jose. He eventually headed to Denver, a place he had been to and liked, and enrolled at Metro State College. He graduated in June 1976 with a Bachelors Degree in Aviation Management and a Minor in Business Administration. During that time he met his lovely wife Susan and they were married in December 1972.

After graduating Paul had a hard time finding work because of the recession. Continental Airlines was looking for part time help, however, and he was hired.

One of the regular workers failed to return after the holidays so Paul was able to stay on a little longer. This continued to happen and Paul eventually spent nine years with Continental moving all the way up to assistant general manager.

Paul lost his job when Continental went bankrupt, but he was hired by United as kitchen supervisor and became zone controller after 18 months. During his 20 year career Paul worked as zone controller, gate controller and gate security coordinator. He stayed in Denver the entire time.

After retiring in June 2003, Paul stayed in Denver for two more years working for the Denver Broncos as an

Ambassador during games at the VIP suites and as a jack of all trades at a small casino in Central City.

In January 2005, Paul and Susan moved to Mesquite. It's the perfect spot since Paul is an avid golfer and he can play year around. Susan loves the weather and an occasional trip to the casino.

They have a son Brian who is doing very well and a daughter Shannon who is just a sweetheart. Paul is active in the Mesquite Men's Golf group, tournament golf, Special Olympics, The Mesquite Veterans Center and is coordinator of the Virgin Valley Honor Guard, a member of the Veterans Center board of directors and his HOA.

Paul, we thank you for your service to your country!

Paul is another one of the Mesquite veterans who has become a very good friend. As a member of the honor guard, we interact often, as we do on the board of directors. He is a great guy to work with on projects as he has significant experience from his business background.

Bill Lilienthal, US Navy

Bill is a retired Navy veteran who served his country well. He has always provided the rest of us with wonderful stories from his experience during his service, and the following is no exception.

Having fought battles in the North Pacific and North Atlantic, the US Navy learned it needed more cold water weather operational experience. As a result, in 1946, in an effort called Operation High Jump, the Navy began surveying coastal operations. Two US Coast Guard cutters were assigned to the task. A couple years later in an exploratory expedition called Operation Deepfreeze, I laid the groundwork for kick-off of the International Year (IGY) under the command of Rear Admiral George Dufec.

America and seven other nations were participating. The Americans provided the greatest number of men and portion of materials for the expedition, which was called Operation Deepfreeze II. The US Navy and Coast Guard were tasked with transporting personnel and supplies for the Antarctic expedition. Several hundred sailors and international scientists were assigned to the project.

The first goal was to enlarge or build six additional stations in Antarctica. They included South Pole Station, Ellsworth Station, Byrd Station, Hallet Station, McMurdo Sound Station and the Wilkes Station.

In 1955 I volunteered, while stationed aboard the USS Breckenridge, to a troop ship hauling men and supplies to and from Korea. I was transferred to the US Naval Station Quonset Point, Rhode Island. After a considerable number of physical and psychiatric tests and much physical labor—like 20 mile hikes—I was assigned to the Wilkes Station, Antarctica along with other members transported from Seattle, Washington to Christchurch, New Zealand aboard the ice breaker USCG Northwind.

Two large cargo ships, the USS Arneb and the SUNS Greenville Victory, joined them. From here they proceeded south to the ice.

First stop, McMurdo Sound Station to off load supplies and pick up their civilian counter parts. They then steamed ahead in a westerly direction about 600 miles to the Cape Hallet Coast.

Before construction started, about 500,000 Adelie penguins had to be relocated to clear a 10 acre site for the station. The task group spent two weeks off loading supplies and building the Hallet Station. Once the station was deemed self sustaining, the task group proceeded south and west about 2000 miles to Vincennes Bay on the Knox Coast of Antarctica.

It was not an uneventful journey. The ice was extremely thick and the Northwind often only advanced a few miles a day. Several routes were explored. On Christmas Day 1956 the Arned was trapped in the pack ice.

The Northwind was unable to reach those aboard.

As a result a passing iceberg ripped a 30 foot gash in the Arned's hull under the water line and the Northwind had a blade broken off one of its twin screws, which only compounded the problem. This is how we spent Christmas.

When the weather cleared, the Arned had to be tilted 20 degrees while the crew members welded steel plates over the gash. At long last we finally entered open water in Vincennes Bay.

Priority number 1, on February 2, was to blast a ramp from the water's surface to a reasonable level on the ice cap. Immediately after the last explosion, M boats bringing personnel started a 24 hour operation bringing personnel, equipment and supplies ashore. After two weeks of all hands effort (officers included) the station was ready for habitation.

The task group departed on February 23 after commissioning ceremonies and flag-raising by Capt. Charles Thomas and Capt. Gerald Ketchum along with the entire crew present.

Their motto became, "Many are cold but few are frozen."

Bill is a retired Navy veteran and active within the Mesquite Veterans Center. Bill wrote this article and was gracious enough to pass it on so you could enjoy it.

Bill, we thank you for your service to your country!

Craig Dickason, US Navy

Craig was born in Montabello, California on May 25, 1953. He was raised in nearby La Mirada and attended Neff HS where he played varsity baseball as starting outfielder. When he graduated in 1971, he and two friends enlisted in the US Navy on the buddy plan. Craig and one buddy stayed together their entire enlistment. The third had a severe bout with pneumonia during boot camp and was held back.

Craig went to an eight week basic training at the Naval Training Center in San Diego. After boot camp he was assigned to the USS Blue Ridge LCC-19 (land communication command), which was part of the major combat amphibious engagement of the Vietnam War. He was a machinist mate assigned to work on air conditioning units and filter systems.

Craig had two weeks leave then left on the Blue Ridge for White Beach, Okinawa. The ship conducted maneuvers off the coast of the Philippines.

A month later the ship sailed to US Naval Base Subic Bay in the Philippines from which it patrolled the coast of Vietnam.

The ship approached the mainland through a canal and proceeded to Tiger Island where it received enemy fire. Naval "big guns" leveled the island.

Aboard the Blue Ridge there were 30 logistic Marines responsible for a Marine Corps amphibious assault force. The USS Blue Ridge was a flag ship that had an US Navy Admiral and a Marine Corps general on board who controlled the amphibious attachment. During the ship's eight month deployment in Okinawa, 3½ weeks were spent in Vietnam patrolling and giving orders for the amphibious operations.

After eight months it was back to San Diego where everything on the ship was torn down, redone and repaired. The entire crew participated in the Blue Ridge overhaul.

The ship and crew spent nine months in San Diego. Then it was back to White Beach, Subic Bay and war games that included helicopters and the Marine Corps. During these operations Craig was responsible for maintaining the diesel motor that operated the air conditioning system.

Saigon fell during the Blue Ridge's tour and the ship was forced to spend some 2½ months in Vietnam.

The crew could only stand and watch as seven US helicopters were destroyed because the ship could only accommodate two and there was nowhere to put the others. A South Vietnamese pilot would fly the chopper out over the water, push the stick one way and jump out the high side. A boat would retrieve the pilot after each chopper went down.

The Blue Ridge returned to San Diego after nine months.

Craig and the friend who enlisted with him on the buddy plan took an early out. They had both enrolled at Fullerton Jr. College in Fullerton, California, and since classes started in September they were allowed to leave the Navy then instead of October. After 3½ years of honorable service it was time to get on with life.

College didn't work out for Craig. While attending truck driving school he drove a school bus. Driving a truck worked out great for Craig who's spent 37 years behind the wheel. During his career he drove for Saturn in Tennessee for 14 years and currently is employed by Mesquite's own Primix. Craig has been with the company for almost six years and loves working for the organization. "It is a wonderful company to work for," Craig said.

Craig was recently married to a lovely lady, Cheryl and they reside in Mesquite, where Craig came to live six years ago.

Craig is the current president of the Mesquite Vietnam Veterans of America Chapter 993.

Craig, Thank you for your service to your country!

Tom Dart, US Navy

Born September 1, 1947 in Kansas City, Kansas Tom was raised in the Kansas City area and attended Turner High School. Tom participated in cross country and track and field as well as playing the trumpet in the school band while attending school. Tom graduated in 1965 and received his draft notice shortly thereafter. He immediately visited the Navy recruiter and enlisted for four years.

It was off to basic training in San Diego where Tom became a member of the unit's Drum and Bugle Corps. He was good enough to be offered an audition with one of the Navy bands but decided not to pursue it.

After boot camp Tom was assigned to the USS Navasota (AO106) a "replenishment oiler" responsible for refueling carriers, destroyers and every other ship except submarines. The ship even provided fuel for some jet fighters.

Tom was assigned to quartermaster, steering and navigation based out of Long Beach, California and he spent his entire enlistment on the Navasota.

The ship eventually sailed to Vietnam and US Naval Base Subic Bay in the Philippines where it refueled all the other ships. It was a delivery ship and spent two weeks out of port and then three of four days back in Subic Bay reloading.

After nine months at Subic Bay the Navasota returned to Long Brach for three months then back to Subic Bay for nine more months. Tom did this for his entire four year enlistment. It was Tom's job to steer the ship when it was refueling or pulling up to refuel other ships. It was a difficult especially in rough waters.

When the USS Pueblo was captured by the North Koreans, the Navasota left Long Beach for its normal trip back to Subic Bay but the crew noticed the course had been altered a bit. Not until the captain explained they were headed to Korea did the men realize what was going on.

The Pueblo incident was resolved before the Navasota arrived in Korea, however and so it was back to Subic Bay. Tom was discharged in 1969 as an E5.

Back in Kansas City, Tom went to work for Coca Cola, where he worked on the docks loading trucks. While in Long Beach he had met a young lady from Montana, who was attending college and they had dated. In 1969 they married just before Tom's discharge.

After a couple of years the couple traveled to Montana to attend the 25th anniversary of Tom's in-laws. He and his wife decided to move there and for the next 28 years Tom worked as a driver/sales rep for Hostess.

Tom had friends in Henderson, Nevada and visited them. He discovered Mesquite and settled here in 2002 after taking an early retirement. Tom has one son who teaches history in Montana and three grandchildren.

Tom loves to play golf and works part time at Wolf Creek Golf Course. He is also involved with Mesquite Jeeps and More, an off-road travel group.

Tom, we thank you for your service to your country!

My wife and I have become great friends with Tom through the Jeep travel group. He is a terrific individual who is very active in the group and often leads in some of our adventures.

Geno Withelder, US Navy

Geno was born May 17, 1939 in Pottsville, Pennsylvania. He attended Tremont High School, where he played basketball and baseball. He was also a member of the marching band and sang in the choir. Additionally he was a four year spelling bee champion and was the class statistician. Only one member of his class did not complete school, opting for a job in the coal mines before graduation. Geno attended his 30 year reunion and all classmates were still going strong.

Upon graduating in May 1956, Geno enlisted in the US Navy and left for boot camp at Bainbridge, Maryland, July 10. After boot camp Geno went to Norman, Oklahoma, for Aviation Administration school.(ANP) The school was during Bud Wilkinson's glory days as coach of the Oklahoma Sooners and Geno got to see some of the Oklahoma games.

After school Geno was assigned to Moffett Field in Mountain View, California as part of the UF53 Fighter Squadron where he served until August 1957. He was then assigned to the USS Kearsarge CVA33 an aircraft carrier for a nine month tour of the Far East. The ship had stops in Hawaii, Guam, Philippines, Japan and Okinawa. After the tour, it was back to Moffett Field where he was assigned to DA125 Training Squadron where pilots were trained on the new A4-D plane. This aircraft was an attack bomber.

Geno was discharged in May 1960 and he returned to Pennsylvania.

After spending two and a half years in Tremont, Geno decided to go back to Mountain View. He had grown to like warm California weather. He became involved in the restaurant business and later in real estate.

Working both industries kept him pretty busy. Geno met his lovely wife Barbara in 1970 at a competitor's restaurant where he occasionally lunched. He eventually convinced Barbara to come to work for him and on December 7, 1979 they were married in San Jose.

Their son and daughter-in-law who live in Park City, Utah told them they ought to consider retiring in St. George. After being in business for 29 years in California, that sounded like a good idea. To get to St. George, however you have to go through Mesquite and Geno loved Mesquite.

He and Barbara settled in Mesquite in 2002 and have been here ever since. Much to Geno's credit he has been involved in many Mesquite activities.

He is an active member of the Veterans Center, he heads up six to eight charity golf tournaments every year, he is a member of the Mesquite City Council and is running for re-election, he is on the board of Virgin Valley Artists Association, on the board of the Salvation Army, president of the Falcon Ridge Golf Club, on the board of Virgin Valley Little League, VP of the Southern Nevada Golf Assoc. and very involved with the Elks.

He and Barbara find some time to play golf. They have four children and six grandchildren with one on the way.

Geno, thank you for your service to your country!

Steve Francis, US Navy

Born in October, 1945 in Seattle, Washington, Steve graduated from Ballard High School in 1963 and attended the University of Washington for a year. Steve then accepted a job with Standard Oil and worked there for four years. He became assistant manager of a company owned station.

While working at Standard, Steve received his notice to take his physical for the draft. His older brother had spent three years in the Navy and was still a member of the Naval Reserves and suggested that Steve visit a Navy recruiting station. He took Steve under his wing, and steered him to NASA in Sand Point.

While talking with the recruiter, a nearby radio had an announcement by President Lyndon Johnson that our ships had been fired upon in the Gulf of Tonkin. Steve agreed to enlist in the Navy Reserves.

However, he had an interest in electronics, but there were no openings for that school for quite a while. So he agreed to accept an opening slot for Electricians school that would be available within 120 days of his enlistment. He took his physical for the Army and received his draft notice two days after enlisting in the Navy.

It was off to Memphis, Tennessee, for four weeks of basic training and then to Jacksonville, Florida for Electrician's school. This school lasted for six months and much to his credit, Steve was the Honor Graduate, first in his class.

For the next 5½ years, it was weekend training and Steve was part of an 11 man crew aboard a Neptune Bomber that was land based. The crew included four officers and seven enlisted. During his enlistment the base where he attended drills was closed and there was a rule that if you had to drive more than 50 miles to a drill you were exempt.

Steve still had a year and a half to go when this happened. However it was determined that it was 50 air miles and those who thought they were done with drills had to start attending again. Steve could not get reassigned to his previous crew and was attached to a crew of four.

This included two officers and two enlisted men. They were attached to a S2F, a four seat plane that was carrier based. Steve enjoyed the Navy and agreed to re-enlist if they would guarantee his re-assignment to his original crew. They could not promise that, so in October 1971 Steve accepted his discharge.

Steve's working career included four years with Household Finance where he became the credit manager. From here an opportunity arose with Levitt Furniture, which Steve accepted. He eventually became operations manager. They wanted Steve to re-locate to accept a branch manager's position but he wanted to stay in the Seattle area. So after six years, he moved on. He went to work for Fremont Electric, a company that started as a recharge station for cars in 1910.

When Steve joined them they rebuilt starters, alternators and generators. After a year he went on to Onan Generator which partnered with Fremont. After a period of time and many business moves, Cummings Engine purchased Onan and Steve became an employee of Cummings where he worked for 30 years.

He was a mechanic in the generator business as well as a licensed electrician. The mechanics had to pass the electricians test in order to get their license and certification to continue their work on very large generators.

Steve seemed to have a knack for doing well on multiple choice tests. He took the test, passed and developed a training program that all the mechanics could use. They all passed the test.

Steve became a trainer for Cummings his last two years there and taught himself how to develop a web page that mechanics could use to prepare for the electricians test. He became a certified network instructor for Cummings and one of the top networkers in the country. He was also promoted to foreman.

Steve and his lovely wife Bonnie have four children and have been in Mesquite since 2006. They are involved with Mesquite Jeeps and More, are huge NASCAR fans and Steve plays softball in the Mesquite Geezer Softball League.

Steve, we thank you for your service to your country!

Steve and Bonnie have become terrific friends of ours. We met them through the Jeep off-road travel group. Steve got me off my fanny and on the softball field to play after not playing for thirteen years. Like most of the guys that play, we all played for a lot of years once upon a time but gave it up. Now we're back doing things we did when we were much younger.

"Spike" Lowry, US Navy

Spike was born in New Rockford, North Dakota, October 5, 1940. He attended Fessenden High School where he participated in football, basketball and track and graduated in 1959.

Spike enlisted in the US Navy six weeks before graduation from high school and departed for the Great Lakes Naval Station right after graduation. He was following in his father's footsteps as his father served with the 8th Cavalry in the Philippines directly after the Spanish American War. From Great Lakes it was off to Bainbridge, Maryland for radio school which lasted six months and then an additional six weeks at Bainbridge for Submarine School.

Spike was assigned to the USS Wahoo (SS565) an electro diesel sub based out of Pearl Harbor. They were part of West-Pac, which included trips to Spain, Korea and the Philippines. The boat spent six months deployed and two to three weeks in port to do repairs transfer people, etc. In addition to doing local operations, Spike made two complete West-Pac tours.

After four years and the completion of his second West-PAC tour, he accepted his discharge and was transferred to Treasure Island, California. He was able to qualify for an early nine month release from the navy and left as an E5.

Spike met his lovely wife at a dance in Wilmington, Delaware while he was in school and she was attending Business College. After his release from the Navy, he went to work for his father- in-law as a laborer. He decided that wasn't what he wanted to do so he re-enlisted in the Navy as an E5 radioman although he lost time and grade.

He spent the next two years as a station keeper (instructor) at a reserve training center in Binghamton, New York where he became an E6. From here he was off to advanced radio school and back to Bainbridge for nine months. After finishing this program, Spike was assigned to the USS Lafayette (SSBM616) in Charleston, South Carolina, but his sub was ported in Rota, Spain. There were two crews, blue and gold and they worked in three month cycles. Spike spent four months aboard the Lafayette.

Spike was promoted to E7 during this assignment and was transferred to the Nathan Hale (SSBM623), based in Pearl Harbor and ported in Guam, from where it operated. This boat also operated on three month cycles. Spike was only on board for one year but was promoted to E8. He was responsible for operations and maintenance.

After this assignment Spike went to shore duty and attended Florida Junior College of Jacksonville, where he received an Associate's Degree in Business management. He spent two years on shore duty at White Oaks Communications Center as a teletype equipment operator. Then it was back to sea aboard the Lewis and Clark (SSBM644) based out of Charleston. Here again there were two crews that worked three month cycles and Spike was the chief petty officer. He was the senior enlisted man on board and Chief of the Boat (COB)! He spent three years aboard the Lewis and Clark.

Again it was shore duty for Spike. He was promoted to E9 and was the command master chief at Naval Base Charleston. His boss was the commandant of the Sixth Naval District. He and Spike were the host to 100 other commands. Spike's next assignment would have been back to sea and he decided had had enough sea duty so retired after 23 years of active service.

Spike had obtained his real estate license, but at the time, with 15% interest rates, houses were not selling, so Spike moved to Seattle. He worked with a friend of his and developed training materials for the Trident submarine.

While doing this he obtained his Bachelor's Degree in Business Administration from Southern Illinois University through an external degree program. After three years Spike moved on to the Civil Service Administration and taught at the Trident Development Center. He trained the instructors from the Trident subs. After 15 years Spike retired.

Spike had visited Mesquite a while back and liked it. He moved here in 2011. Spike has two sons. One graduated from Clemson University and went on to a 20 year career in the Air Force. The other graduated from Washington State and won the Big Twelve high jump in track.

Spike we thank you for your service to your country!

John Berard Jr., US Navy

John was born November 21, 1948 in Mobile, Alabama. His family moved to Norfolk, Virginia, Charleston, South Carolina and Treasure Island, California before he was old enough to attend high school. Why all the moves?

John's dad, John Sr. was a career Navy man and you went where they sent you.

John attended Mt. Diablo High School where he participated in football and graduated in 1967. He received the Senior Industrial Arts Award for his proficiency in class. Soon after graduating, John enlisted in the Navy and left for basic training in San Diego in August 1967.

Because Vietnam was so hot at the time there was no "A" school for John and many other boot camp basic graduates.

It was off to Travis AFB to catch a flight to the Philippines to meet the USS Ranger. This was the aircraft carrier to which he and seven other recruits had been assigned. They landed at Clark AFB and took a bus ride to Subic Bay where the Ranger was in port.

A junior officer had the eight lined up and began asking questions. "What do you want to do here." He asked the first sailor. "Be a boiler attendant," the sailor replied. "Good report to boiler number one," responded the officer. As he went down the line asking each sailor the same question, the sailors would reply with their desire. He responded to every one of them with "You're not smart enough to do that."

He finished and asked everyone, "Anyone familiar with an evaporator?" John replied, "What's an evaporator?" "Oh, so you're interested," "Report to auxiliary number one."

So John Berard became a member of the team that produced fresh water from salt water on auxiliary number one.

The USS Ranger left the Philippines and ended up in the Gulf of Tonkin. There were two carriers. As well as other ships there including destroyers and others. Planes flew missions off one carrier during the day and off the other at night.

The crew worked six days straight, had one off and then they switched. Those that had the day missions went to night and vice versa. This went on for 30 days at a time.

The USS Ranger then proceeding on the remainder of its cruise.

The cruise usually consisted of starting in Alameda, California to Hawaii to the Philippines and back to Hawaii to Alameda. This was a nine month trip.

John wanted very much to become an electrician. He gathered the necessary books and information needed to study and took the test. Self taught, he passed and became an electrician. He became an E3 with an electrical patch, just as if he would have gone through "A" school. He took the test a second time and became an E4. He was reassigned to A&E (aviation and electrical) and was put in charge of all the gas stations on the flight deck.

After each nine month cruise, the crew spent three months in home port. Occasionally the ship went into dry dock for repairs.

John did four complete tours of duty with the USS Ranger and each tour spent time in the Gulf of Tonkin. John was a Vietnam veteran who visited the country on four different occasions.

As mentioned earlier in this article, John's dad was a career Navy man and before John Jr. third cruise, he and his father put in a request to serve on the same ship and it was granted.

John Jr. and John Sr. spent an entire nine-month cruise together on the USS Ranger. Although located on different parts of the ship due to duty requirements, they were able to get together for chow and some off duty hours. What a great experience that must have been!

John Sr. retired from the Navy after returning from that cruise. By the way John SR. is a Korean War veteran. John Sr. and his wife had five children and they all graduated from Mt. Diablo HS, quite unusual for a career military man.

After four years, John accepted his discharge and moved on with his life. He attended Diablo Valley Jr. College and majored in administration of justice.

Following that he became a police officer for a year in Pleasant Hill, California. After getting his education and becoming an officer, John decided he didn't care for that line of work and went to work for a termite company where he spent two years as a journeyman and the following eight as a state licensed inspector.

The owner retired and John didn't want to continue working under new ownership so he departed as well.

In 1982, John went to work for Tosco Oil Co., as an oil refinery operator and spent the next 29 years there before retiring.

John and his lovely wife Carol have friends who live in Mesquite and they came to visit them. They had been looking around for a place to retire so they thought a visit here would be great. It worked out well as they purchased a home in Sun City in 2010 and are very pleased with Mesquite.

John is involved with the VFW, VVA the Mesquite Food Bank and the Mesquite Rotary Club. Carol is involved with the VVA as well and active as a volunteer in her church.

They have two children.

While on active duty John received the following: Armed Forces Expeditionary Medal—Korea, Navy Unit Commendation Ribbon, Meritorious Unit Commendation Ribbon, and the Armed Forces Gallantry Cross.

John we thank you for your service to your country!

Steve Tragale, US Navy

Born December 13, 1961 in Brooklyn, New York Steve moved to Arizona at a young age. Steve's father was a longshoreman and an on-the-job accident caused a severe injury to his spinal cord and forced him to take a disability retirement.

The next move was to Bullhead City where Steve's dad opened a sweet shop and shed business. When Steve was

16, his father fully retired and the family moved to Las Vegas.

Steve worked at the El Cortez, in the restaurant at night and attended high school during the day. This eventually became too difficult so Steve was able to enroll in a program where he could attend his high school classes from 3 PM to 10 PM and then go to work at 11 PM. The only activity Steve participated in during high school was weight lifting.

Steve graduated high school in 1979 and enlisted in the US Navy in December of the same year as soon as he turned 18. He wanted to get out on his own.

It was off to San Diego for basic training and when that was completed Steve went onto specialized training in many areas. He elected not to discuss this part of his military training.

During his enlistment he spent time in the Indian Ocean assigned to the USS Samuel Gompers AD37, an auxiliary destroyer. Steve's active duty time in the Navy coincided with the conflict with Iran from 1980 to 1982.

Steve was discharged in May 1982 and it was back to Las Vegas and Steve began looking for a job. The economy was not booming and it took a little time before Steve hooked up with Bonnie Springs Ranch, an Old West Resort.

Bonnie Springs had a restaurant, petting zoo, gun fights, etc. Steve worked in the Old West area as a dish washer and had to live on site. After spending some time on this job, Steve moved on to others including fast-food restaurants, construction and driving semis. Things were not easy as Steve was working with a disability from the military that occurred during active duty.

While working in Connecticut on a construction job Steve met Carrie. They became friends and after several years of friendship they decided to marry in 2005 in West Haven, Connecticut. Due to health reasons Steve, Carrie and their daughter Kimmie moved to Mesquite. In 2007, after years of health issues, Steve received a full disability pension from the Navy.

Steve is active in the Mesquite Veterans Center and was one of the original veterans involved in the beginning. He has served on the board of directors and he and Carrie were responsible for maintaining the center's cleanliness. They are involved in many activities as volunteers.

Steve we thank you for your service to your country!

Cliff Anderson, US Navy

Cliff was born November 8, 1932 in Lancaster, Minnesota, just nine miles from the Canadian border. He attended Lancaster High School and participated in baseball, football and track and also played the drums in the band. He received the American Legion Award and was also an all state honorable mention in football. He graduated in 1951.

On November 11, 1951 Cliff enlisted in the US Navy and was sent to Great Lakes Naval Station in Illinois for basic training. Because of his ability to play the drums, Cliff was made a member of the Drum and Bugle Corps at Great Lakes, which got him out of duty during basic.

Upon completion of basic training, Cliff was shipped out to San Diego where he attended radioman school for 12 weeks. After completing this school he was assigned to the USS Taussig DD746, a Navy destroyer. The ship had just returned to the states, so the next six months were spent here doing maneuvers.

The USS Taussig left San Diego on Christmas day, 1952 on its West-Pac tour. This consisted of a trip to North Korea where it covered the coast for 30 days and returned to a port in Japan for three days. That was the normal rotation.

The ship experienced shore bombardments and had to avoid depth charges as it intercepted the San Pans that had Korean prisoners on board.

While patrolling the North Korean coast the ship came close to a submarine base in Russia and picked up many blips of submarines on sonar equipment.

One day the sailors received a message that a patrol boat was suffering damage from a shore bombardment, so they proceeded to the location. When they arrived the patrol boat had already managed to leave the area. They commenced with a bombardment of their own, but they must have been a little too close to the coast as the North Koreans returned fire. General quarters were sounded and Cliff's duty station was at secondary control, located on the torpedo deck.

The station has compasses surrounded by a half-wall. He was in communication with the bridge and after steering. The purpose of this was if the bridge was knocked out, the captain would come back to the secondary control and the ship could be controlled from after steering.

Shells were dropping all around them, and suddenly a man at after steering shouted over the intercom, "We've been hit." "Is anyone injured?" Cliff replied. The man said, "Yeah, me, you dumb SOB."

The ship managed to vacate the area and get into Japan for repairs. Several sailors were taken to the hospital. Once in awhile North Koreans would return fire and then the next time would pull their cannons back into the caves and do nothing. But if a ship got a little too close look out!

Some of the ports Cliff and the Taussig visited were Okinawa, Formosa, the Philippines and Hong Kong while patrolling the China Sea.

While coming and going via West-Pac, the ship always escorted an aircraft carrier. The biggest reason was in case a pilot had to ditch his plane the Taussig was responsible for rescuing the pilot.

On the way back to the states escorting the USS Oriskany, the Taussig received a message from the captain of the aircraft carrier. "Due to the moderate to severe rolls in the sea exercises will be cancelled for today."

Cliff's captain told him to radio to the other captain, "What in the hell does he think we are experiencing in this little destroyer?" Cliff thought the better idea was NOT to send the response.

The Taussig arrived in San Diego, July 20, 1953 and on July 27, the truce was signed with North Korea. Cliff did two more West-Pac tours as somebody forgot to tell the North Koreans there was now a truce and there was still plenty of action.

Cliff's enlistment was up before the ship was scheduled to return to the USA, so Cliff flew back to Formosa, Philippines, Hawaii and Treasure Island, California where he was discharged.

Cliff's next step in life was an easy one! Since Korea was a police action, Cliff decided to become a police officer and spent the next 43 years in law enforcement. His first job was with the railroad as a detective in Chicago. Then 23 years with the Minneapolis police department as a lieutenant, followed by 12 years as a background investigator with the Tampa Police Department.

Finally, Cliff spent three years with the state of Florida as an investigator with the Health Department. During this time Cliff's wife developed cancer and needed full time care. It was time to retire.

Cliff and his present wife Lucille split their time between Tampa and Mesquite. Lucille retired from Golden One Credit Union where she worked as a fraud investigator.

Cliff has been a member of the American Legion for 38 years and is currently a member in Tampa Post 152.

Cliff we thank you for your service to your country!

Don Clark, US Navy

Don was born on Christmas Day, 1959 in Torrington, Connecticut. When he was five years old, his family moved to Stockton, California. He attended Tokay High School and graduated in June, 1978. It didn't take Don long to decide what he wanted to do. He enlisted in the US Navy and left for basic training in September that same year.

He completed basic in San Diego and then a five week school in basic electronics. This was followed by an eight week "A" school in interior communications.

Don stayed in San Diego until his assignment to nuclear power school came through and then it was off to Orlando, Florida. At the time the Navy had a few cruisers that were nuclear powered, five or six carriers and many submarines.

Prior to nuclear power school, Don was extensively interviewed to determine what he was best suited. He wanted submarine duty because there was extra pay for nuke and sub duty. After all the interviews he was granted his wish.

Nuclear power school was all theory. There was 40 hours of classes each week, followed by 3 hours of nightly homework. Weekends brought an additional 15 to 20 hours of homework. The program was like taking a two year college degree program in six months. After successfully completing the theory portion, it was off to nuclear prototype school for an additional six months. This was in Idaho Falls. And was part of the Department of Energy Nuclear Test Facility.

The school involved a 1½ hour bus ride one way to the facility every day. Security was extremely tight as one would expect of a nuclear facility.

Training was intense. Don was on a schedule of seven days on, five days off; seven days on, three days off; seven days on, one day off.

Students also spent three to four weeks in additional classroom training and 12 hour shifts in the plant. This did not include the three hour travel time to and from the facility. Don said this actually became a stress test, because students could not make a mistake, there was no room for error.

As an operator/electrician, 1/3 of the day is spent making sure the reactor is operating properly. The training qualified these men as nuclear power plant operators. This was serious business and $250,000 was spent to train each one of them.

After completing all this training, Don was stationed in Gorton, Connecticut. His assigned sub was home ported in Holy Lock, Scotland. The sailors would fly from the U.S. to Scotland and then take a one hour ferry ride to the submarine which was a ballistic missile sub.

They would change crews and spend three weeks going over the sub to cover all the maintenance items. Then the 140 enlisted men and 15 officers would go out to sea for 70 days, underwater! The sub was 33 feet in diameter and had three levels.

You pretty much had to know everyone's job on the sub in order to survive in case of an emergency. This cycle was 105 days on and 90 days off.

The submarine was scheduled for nuclear refueling overhaul and went to the Naval Shipyard in Portsmouth, New Hampshire. This involved pulling out all the spent rods and installing new ones. Don spent six years with this sub, but when refueling came he was rotated to shore duty until refueling was complete.

Shore duty was spent in Naval Recruiting School for five weeks in Orlando and then an assignment as a recruiter in New Haven, Connecticut. After spending three years as a recruiter, Don was excited to get back to another ballistic missile submarine. During his stint as a recruiter Don was married and had two sons.

Now stationed again in Scotland, Don was part of two more patrols during the Cold War. Then sailors received the news their sub was being decommissioned.

The Trident submarine had been developed and for every one that was put into the water 1½ Polaris or Poseidon subs were taken out. So Don's sub was brought back to Groton and the crews were reduced 2 to 1.

It was later to be home ported at the Banger Naval Sub Base in Washington state. It had to be stripped and have all missiles off-loaded along the way.

It passed through the Panama Canal and docked in San Diego and was converted into a slow attack sub. It was used as a test platform for the Pacific Fleet. This went on for about a year. Then the sub was pulled into dry dock and taken apart until there was nothing left. However, everyone involved received a small piece of the hull.

Next came shore duty for Don as a nuclear planner. This involved a seven week school in Charleston, South Carolina, where he learned all things nuclear. This was quite an assignment as all those attending this program were E7's or E8's except Don who was an E6. Don spent the next 2½ years at the Banger Naval Sub Base as a Planner. A situation arose where Don could obtain retirement with less than 20 years service so he decided to take advantage of the opportunity and retired from the Navy in October 1995.

After the Navy, Don spent some time as a senior technical writer for a marine engineering and architectural firm. He then decided to move back east where he worked various jobs.

His mom lived in St. George, Utah so Don decided to come west again with his two sons. When his sons decided they liked the East Coast better it was back to Boston. Don worked for a waterproofing company as an estimator and planner for a number of years. However, he missed the west and after his sons were grown he came to Mesquite. Don is active in Mesquite Jeeps and more.

During his Navy career, Don received the Navy Achievement Medal, Meritorious Unit Commendation, the Sea Service Deployment and Secretary of the Navy Letter of Commendation.

Don, we thank you for your service to your country!

Bob Loya, US Navy

Born in Elizabeth, New Jersey March 14, 1944, Bob attended Linden High School but was not particularly happy with the way things were going and attempted to join the Army at age 16.

The recruiter noticed a discrepancy in Bob's paperwork and suggested he come back in a year. A year later Bob did just that except he enlisted in the US Navy in 1961, and it was off to the Great Lakes Naval Base in Illinois for basic.

Upon completion Bob was sent to the Naval Hospital in Philadelphia for training as a hospital corpsman. Bob became a Neuropsychiatric Technician assigned to the psychiatric ward of the hospital.

While there he was assigned the unpleasant task of escorting an individual who had shot and killed four people to Holmesburg Prison in Philadelphia. Bob did have FBI support.

In 1964 Bob put in for sea duty and left the hospital for assignment to the Intrepid CV5-11 as a corpsman. The ship was based out of Norfolk and from there went on to Guantanamo Bay and Jamaica.

While preparing to launch the ship from Guantanamo Bay, armed Cuban soldiers aboard boats watched every move.

After a visit to the Virgin Islands it was back to Norfolk and then off on a Mediterranean Cruise. The job was two-fold, retrieve space capsules and anti-sub warfare.

The ship tracked a Russian sub tender for 31 days during this Med Cruise. While there Bob had the opportunity to visit Palma, Majorca, Naples, Cannes and Valencia, Spain. He even had a chance to swim in the Riviera.

He loved being aboard ship and wanted to re-enlist. Then in 1962 he met a lovely lady named Patricia at a dance at the Philadelphia YMCA and they were married in 1963.

When Bob called her and said he wanted to re-enlist she mentioned he would come home to an empty house if he did. Needless to say Bob decided to get out of the Navy.

Prior to his discharge, Bob continued to enjoy his time aboard ship and became very observant of many things in the countries they visited. In Spain, for example he noticed that soldiers armed with rifles were very noticeable during festivals.

On the way back to Norfolk his ship picked up two space capsules. The astronauts would get out and be greeted by the crew. After 10 months and 27 days of sea duty Bob accepted his discharge.

Less than a month after receiving his discharge, Bob was hired by the Philadelphia Police Force in 1965.

As a beat cop he worked high crime areas where some 400 to 500 homicides occurred each year. In 1983, Bob was promoted to sergeant working the same district, but now was responsible for 20–22 other officers. In 1989, Bob was again promoted, this time to Lieutenant and had responsibility for 43 officers, three Sergeants and one Corporal.

In 1991 Bob became involved in a tussle with a convicted felon and tore the ligaments in his knee. After two surgeries, his superiors would not let him go back on the street so Bob accepted retirement after 29 years of service.

Later in 1991 Bob went to work for Wyeth Pharmaceutical as security manager responsible for three different sites. He retired from Wyeth in 2002.

In 2002, Bob passed through Mesquite on the way to Zion National Park after visiting his son who lived in Las Vegas. He liked Mesquite and he and his wife purchased a home.

An interesting fact about Bob is that he earned his GED in the Navy because he left high school before graduating.

While a member of the Philadelphia Police Force, he put in for and was accepted into a program for an Associates' Degree which he completed. Again not satisfied, he applied to another program that paid for his college tuition and in 1979 Bob received his Bachelors Degree in Administration from Penn State University.

Bob and his wife Patricia spent 48 wonderful years together. They had one son who is also a graduate of Penn State.

Bob, we thank you for your service to your country!

A short time prior to interviewing Bob, his wife Patricia passed away. Bob had a very difficult time coping with this situation, but as time passed, he got better. I am pleased to say that Bob met another terrific lady who also lost her spouse about the same time as Bob. They were married in the Mesquite Veterans Center just recently. We all wish them the very best!

Duane Johnston, US Navy

This is a very special bio, primarily because it's about a very dear friend of all, and particularly a small group of veterans who got together once or twice a week to play cards. A little background is in order.

Several years ago, shortly after the Veterans center opened its doors, John Nettle and I asked veterans if they would be interested in getting together to play cards for a couple of hours each week. The response was pretty good and so we began.

One of our initial Players was Duane Johnston. Duane was a great guy who always brought along a funny story or two and thoroughly enjoyed himself. All of those who played also enjoyed Duane's company. Our group decided to donate a little money every time we met to be used for local charities once we accumulated enough to make the donation worthwhile.

When the time came we would ask for suggestions to which charity we would like to have our donation forwarded. The group then voted on the suggestions.

What was interesting was that Duane always came up with a suggestion of a somewhat lesser known charity. One that didn't get the attention that many others received and our group seemed to admire that. You see as you got to know Duane, you realized how concerned he was about folks who needed assistance and was always willing to pitch in and help.

It was easy to become a close friend of Duane and we did. I used to ask Duane if he would let me interview him for the newspaper article that I did every week and his answer was always the same. "I didn't do much. Get the other veterans first and then we'll talk about it."

Well, unfortunately Duane passed away unexpectedly on June 26, 2012. So his friends and I took the opportunity posthumously to honor our friend and fellow veteran.

Duane was born September 17, 1929 in Neosho, Mississippi and graduated from Lincoln County High School in Panaca, Nevada. Sometime after graduation, he enlisted in the US Navy and served honorably until 1954.

He married Mary Ahlstrom in 1956. Duane spent the majority of his working career as a civil engineer for the Union Pacific Railroad. His career took him from Nevada to Utah where he and his wife raised a family until his retirement.

After retirement, Duane and Mary moved to Star Valley, Wyoming. They were active in many social and community events. Duane was particularly fond of playing cards and golf with his friends in Star Valley. Unfortunately, in 1995 Mary passed away.

In 2002, Duane re-connected with his long time friend, Jaqueline Cook. They spent the last few years traveling, playing bingo and slots and being constant companions to one another. They split their time between Star Valley and Mesquite.

Duane was an avid collector of railroad memorabilia particularly railroad china. He enjoyed selling and trading and attending railroad memorabilia shows. He loved E-bay. He also loved a deal and there wasn't a garage sale he didn't like. You could always find Duane early at our Veterans Center garage sales! He also had a love for music and was an accomplished banjo player. He played in a band in Star Valley. He played in Star Valley just a week before he passed away.

Duane and Mary had three children, Craig, Lee and Maureen (Andrews). They also have three grandchildren, Alex Andrews, Michael Johnston and Katherine Johnston. Duane's grandchildren were his pride and joy and he was so proud of their accomplishments. One of his favorite things was spending time with his extended family.

Duane was a member of the Golden Spike Masonic Lodge in Ogden, Utah, the VFW in Mesquite and the Mesquite Veterans Center. Duane is missed by all the veterans at the center and those of us who enjoyed his friendship and camaraderie at our card games.

When this article was printed in the local paper (Desert Valley Times) I sent several copies to Mary and to each member of his extended family. Jesse Marsh, friend and fellow veteran was able to dig up all the information for me to complete this task and I was sincerely grateful to him for doing that. Mary called me after receiving the article and was touched by the article and the feelings of our group and cried when we talked. Later I discovered the family had a copy of the article weather-proofed and put on Duane's grave marker. Now it was my turn to cry!

Duane, we thank you for your service to your country!

Bill Perkins, US Coast Guard

I would have loved to have had enough veterans from the Coast Guard to devote an entire chapter to, but in just didn't happen. It is certainly as fine a military organization as the others, but I just didn't have access to many of their fine veterans.

Bill was born October 16, 1947 in Indianapolis, Indiana. When he was only five years old his family moved to the San Fernando Valley in California. He attended Sylmar High School and graduated in 1965. Upon graduation he enlisted in the US Coast Guard, but they had a waiting list of about a year so Bill went to work for an engineering firm while he waited.

In August 1966 he received that call and it was off to Alameda, California for basic training. From basic Bill went to Radioman School in Groton, Connecticut, just across the river from the Coast Guard Academy.

After completing his six month school, Bill was assigned to a 311 foot Coast Guard cutter based out of Hawaii. The ship was manned with 5-inch mortars as well as 50 caliber and 30 caliber machine guns.

Two weeks after his initial assignment, the ship received orders for Vietnam attached to the Navy 1st Fleet. His job was to patrol the coast of Vietnam, stop and do searches of junks, and supply fire support when requested by the Army, Marines, etc. Bill spent a year on this assignment.

The cutter was assigned a patrol that included traveling half way between Hawaii and Japan at approximately a 10 mile radius. After six months they would continue on to Japan for R&R. Then it was back to their patrol area for six more months and then on to Hawaii for R&R.

The ship also responded to calls from ships with emergencies, especially medical emergencies. They would often EVAC medical patients to hospitals. Bill spent two years on this cutter.

In 1969 back at the Coast Guard Base in San Pedro, California, Bill ran into a friend who was assigned to another cutter. He was married with a young child and recently received orders for Vietnam.

Based on his family situation he didn't want to go to Vietnam, so Bill said he would take his place if they could work it out. Both Bill and his buddy were the same rank and had the same duty station, so they contacted their respective commanding officers and explained the situation. Both were E5's and had been in the service for awhile so their CO's agreed. Bill's new ship was the same except it was a bit smaller at 255 feet.

This time Bill was more involved with medivacs off the beaches. In addition, they kept spare crews and supplies on their ship for River Boat Patrol Boats and spent a fair amount of time being involved with crew replacement.

After another year in Vietnam it was back to doing posting patrols only this time it was between Long Beach, California and Hawaii.

A new opportunity came up and Bill accepted an invitation to school for advanced communications in San Diego. This took up the next six months of his career. After school it was back to the posting patrols. Then Bill was assigned to the Alaska Patrols which included the Aleutian Islands and did this for two years.

From here Bill was assigned to the Coast Guard Rescue in Honolulu. Now his recent schooling came into play as they were responsible for coordinating Coast Guard ships, harbor ships, rescues, enforcement etc.

Bill worked the communications end of the operations as helicopters played an important role in many situations. If a search for a missing vessel came in, everyone got involved including civilian help. Bill did this until he was discharged in 1977. Bill had every intention of making the Coast Guard a career, but as with many others, family issues prevented that from taking place.

Bill met his lovely wife Cheryl through a shipmate. She was his buddy's sister. They were married in 1974 and have three children and nine grandchildren.

After leaving the Coast Guard, Bill went into electronics and worked for Ratheon and Honeywell for awhile. He repaired radar and communications equipment with Ratheon and installed and serviced industrial instrumentation for Honeywell.

From here Bill worked as an electrician out of the Long Beach local and then went into business for himself. Bill is semi-retired as he likes to stay busy.

Bill, we thank you for your service to your country!

10

BRINGING IT ALL FULL CIRCLE

When I decided to undertake the assignment of writing the "Veterans' Corner" articles, I had no idea what it would become or be like to interview veterans. I hadn't written anything since I was in high school, with the exception of reports that were work related. Little did I know that this would become one of the most exhilarating experiences of my life.

After interviewing twenty-five or so individuals, I thought, *Wow these accounts of the veterans' lives are amazing. Not only is their military experience interesting, but what they accomplished afterward in civilian life is also significant.* It was at this point I had wondered if a book containing veteran interviews would be a possibility. As time passed and the interviews continued, I became more and more intrigued with the idea of writing a book.

During the course of interviewing, I met and interviewed a veteran who not only had a significant military and civilian background, but was also a published author. I ran my idea past him, and he thought it was a great idea, and so the dream continued. He provided some welcomed ideas and advice for which I will be forever grateful. Another interview produced another veteran who was also a published author. He too had an amazing story and provided additional thoughts and ideas that were welcomed and helpful. Therefore, I not only continued interviewing, but also thinking about how I was going to accomplish my goal.

However, I digress; the most important thing is the veterans I interviewed. I can't tell you how honored I was and continue to be that these men and women were willing to share their stories with me. There is one hard and fast rule, and that is I only print what the individual allows me to print. No exceptions! I will say this, however, there have been instances where a veteran has told me things I know he has never told anyone else, and words can't express how honored I am that someone would express that kind of confidence in me. What that means is now only two of us know something that no one else will know, unless that veteran tells them.

During some of the interviews, I have literally shed tears with a veteran as they relayed a story. You just can't help it when you get so involved. These folks become like family. It is hard to express the kind of camaraderie that exists. There were also times when we laughed until tears rolled down our cheeks. Stories are stories, some funny, some sad, but all wonderful when coming from the hearts of those willing to share them.

As I listened to the words from the veterans, I always watched their expressions. Sometimes I could almost predict what they were going to say based on their facial expressions. There was one common trait that I noticed universally with every individual I spoke with, and that was when they discussed their service, regardless of what it was, their eyes lit up. There was a pride that beamed like an automobile headlight. It didn't matter whether the person had been drafted, enlisted, was in for a single enlistment, or in for the long haul—the look of pride was the same. There was one other trait that I found prevalent during the course of many, many interviews that being that three things remained important to them: family, God, and country. The order is not important as every individual has their own priorities, and that is a personal thing, but it did come up many times during interviews.

This has been such an overwhelmingly positive experience that I plan to continue to interview veterans. It is a most rewarding and interesting endeavor, and Mesquite is a wonderful place to do it. I find it amazing that a city of about seventeen thousand residents has an estimated two thousand veterans. Maybe that isn't particularly unusual due to the fact that 60%–65% of Mesquite residents are retirees, putting them in an age group where many served their country. To Mesquite's credit, it is a wonderful community that is very supportive of its organizations and its veterans. The business community is especially supportive of the veterans and community projects. The people are terrific, and it is a nice place to live as there is much to do. Something for everyone's tastes!

This has been and continues to be a wonderful experience, and I don't know if it would have happened anywhere other than Mesquite. The situation was just right. The veterans' center was being developed, help was needed, I became involved, things just happened, and I am thankful they did. It has been a wonderful ride!

I would like to offer this poem written by WWII veteran Cal Price as a fitting end to this project. He has given his permission to let me include this.

Freedom Is Never Free
Caprice, 2010

Freedom isn't free
From Quonset Point on Old Rhode Island
To San Diego by the sea,
From the wide beaches of Miami
To Washington, DC
Freedom isn't free

James Carrick

I've roamed wild deserts in Wyoming
Seen those blue ice floes on Lake Erie

Watched a sunrise on New York Harbor
From the crown of Our Lady Liberty.
But freedom isn't free.

I've touched the memory of a friend, Orie Evans,
Engraved in white marble
In Pearl Harbor's Memorial

Fingered the names of Vietnam's fallen heroes
In DC on that black granite wall.
Freedom is never free.

I love windy Teton Mountain meadows
And digging clams on quiet Pismo Beach
There is nothing better on this earth
Than the taste of a tree ripe Georgia peach.
I've sailed beneath our Golden Gate,
I've crossed her wide speeding decks
White seagulls floating far below,
Darting, fleeting specks,
I've watched our coastlines fade from view
From forty thousand feet above,
Flying "a world away" to Old Beijing,
Then returning to this land I love

Proud in my uniform of service,
With my brothers standing tall,
I've felt the roar of cannons,
I've watched my comrades fall
Freedom isn't free.

They Raised Their Hand

From old Manila to Okinawa,
From Pearl Harbor to Mie Lei,
I've seen the flowing tears of loving mothers,
When they sent their sons to die,
Freedom isn't free!
From the staffs atop those Twin Towers
Standing tall in the New York sky,
The stars and stripes of our Old Glory
Proudly waving there on high.

They can tumble our tall buildings,
Scatter death throughout our streets,
They can wound and maim our brave soldiers,
But never, never will we retreat.
Freedom is never free!

Brave men spill their guts in battle
Then when the cannons cease
They watch vile politicians
Selling out our peace

Freedom is never free.